The Deborah Club

D. W. Pierce

"Women should remain silent in the churches. They are not allowed to speak, but must be in submission, as the law says. If they want to inquire about something, they should ask their own husbands at home; for it is disgraceful for a woman to speak in the church."

1 Corinthians 14:34–35 (NIV)

"A woman should learn in quietness and full submission. I do not permit a woman to teach or to assume authority over a man; she must be quiet."

1 Timothy 2:11–12 (NIV)

"So in Christ Jesus you are all children of God through faith, for all of you who were baptized into Christ have clothed yourselves with Christ. There is neither Jew nor Gentile, neither slave nor free, nor is there male and female, for you are all one in Christ Jesus."

Galatians 3:26–28 (NIV)

"When elephants fight, it is the grass that suffers."

—African Proverb

Chapter I

CRAIG DIDN'T REGRET writing the manifesto.

It was a compelling idea bubbling up from deep within, more from his heart than his head. After letting the pressure build for several weeks, he had to get it out of his mind and on his computer screen.

He did, however, regret being so proud of his manifesto that he couldn't wait to show it off to his wife immediately after writing it. He also regretted that when his wife's parents named her, they picked what turned out to be one of the most popular names of her generation--a name she shared with two other women in his congregation.

He regretted being so eager for his wife's affirmation that he didn't pay attention to whose email address his email client automatically inserted when he typed her first name and hit enter. More than anything, he regretted pasting the paragraphs he'd just written into the body of the email and sending it to a woman who was not his wife.

He didn't realize his mistake until he texted his wife a few minutes later.

Craig: Did you get my email?

Wife: What email?

Craig: The one with the thing I just wrote.

Wife: Let me check.

Wife: Nope.

Wife: Don't see it.

Wife: What was it about?

Craig: Let me make sure it went out.

Craig: Oh No!

Wife: What's wrong?

Craig: Check your email, and you'll see. Just sent it to you.

Craig: I also sent it to Amy Brandt. On accident.

Wife: How?

Craig: Typed in the wrong address I guess. Not good.

Wife: Why not?

Craig: Read it. You'll see.

While his wife was reading his manifesto, Craig googled instructions for retrieving an email sent to the wrong address. He knew there was no such mechanism, but he searched anyway. No dice. *Stupid idiot!*

Craig's phone beeped. It was his wife.

"Yeah," he said.

"I can't believe you sent that to Amy. Can you call it back?"

"I wish, but there are no do-overs with email."

"Can you call her and tell her to delete it without reading it?"

"Good idea," Craig said. "Maybe so. I'll try."

"Better hurry!"

"Okay. But first, what did you think?"

"About what?"

"What I wrote."

"Oh," she said. "Honestly, I think it is one of the best things you've ever written."

He grinned. "Thanks."

"And I think it was a big mistake to send it to Amy Brandt."

His smile faded. "Gotta go," he said and hung up.

Stupid idiot!

Chapter 2

"Hi Amy, this is Craig from church. I have a favor to ask of you."

"Well aren't you the busy bee this morning!" Amy Brandt said. "You light up my Inbox with that little email of yours, and now you're calling and asking for a favor."

Craig winced. "So you've read it?"

"Just a few minutes ago. I loved it. Thanks for sending it to me. I went ahead and forwarded it on to a few other ladies who I think will love it too. Hey, can I call you back later today? I'm about to step into a meeting."

"Hold on," Craig said. "Whom exactly did you send it to?" He braced himself as though he were about to receive bad news from his doctor.

"Carla, Joan, and Helen."

Craig swore to himself. "I wish you hadn't done that," he said. "That email could get me into a lot of trouble."

"Oh Craig, I'm so sorry. I thought you wanted other women to read it. I was just trying to get the ball rolling."

Craig had a vision of his head, rather than a ball, rolling across the floor. "Are you sure you only sent it to those three?"

"Just those three," she said. "I'm certain."

"Can you tell them not to send it on to anyone else? As soon as possible."

"Sure," Amy said. "I'm meeting with them later today. I really need to go."

"They need to know *right now*," Craig spoke slowly and reinforced the phrase "right now" as if giving a command.

"Easy there, Craig. I'm sorry, but I can't do it right now. If it's that big a deal to you, maybe you should call them yourself. Otherwise, I'll swear them to secrecy over coffee."

"Okay, I'll take care of it myself. Just promise me you won't send it to anyone else."

"Done," Amy said. "Sorry for the trouble. Bye."

Craig propped his elbows on his desk and ran his fingers through his thinning hair.

Get the ball rolling.

Meeting with them later today.

Had she really taken his manifesto seriously? It was a grossly impractical and outlandish thought experiment. Something fun to talk about with friends over a bottle of wine, but it was so out-of-the-box that no one at the table would ever have the guts to actually try it. Except for Amy Brandt, apparently.

Good Lord.

He opened his desk drawer and pulled out the telephone directory for the South Barkley Bible Church. Flipping through the pages and seeing all the church members' names reminded him of a Jewish folktale about a Rabbi who was trying to help members of his synagogue see the destructive nature of gossip. The Rabbi cut open a feather pillow and let the feathers scatter into the wind. With feathers blowing in all directions, he said, "It is easier to gather every scattered feather than it is to repair the damage you do when you gossip about another person."

The manifesto had nothing to do with gossip, but he felt like he had just cut open a pillow in a wind tunnel. If he wanted to save his job, he needed to make three simultaneous phone calls. Maybe he'd get lucky and none of the ladies would have checked their email yet, but he could already see the feathers flying everywhere.

His inner voice, the one that supplied running commentary-- mostly critical and usually sarcastic--on everything he did throughout the day, piped up.

Why are you wasting time thinking when you need to be talking, begging, pleading, and bribing. Lots and lots of bribing.

He found Helen's number, punched it into his cell phone, and got her voicemail.

"Hey Helen, it's Craig over at the church. Please do me a favor, and don't check your email until you call me back. I need to visit with you about a very sensitive email that has mistakenly found its way to your Inbox this morning. Call me back. Thanks."

Desperate much? You might as well have begged Helen to check her email before calling you back.

He called Joan and got her voicemail as well.

"Hey Joan, this is Craig over at the church. I'm pretty sure Amy sent you an email this morning. Please call me as soon as you get this message, and please don't read or forward the email to anyone else. Talk to you soon. Thanks."

Only two "pleases" in one sentence. Getting better.

He placed the third call. He was caught off guard when Carla answered her phone.

Of the four women who had his manifesto in their Inboxes, Craig was the least comfortable with Carla, who was the most attractive woman in the church. It wasn't even a contest. Carla never paid him any attention, but he couldn't help but do a double-take whenever she walked through the church foyer.

She reminded him of Tiffany, the prettiest girl in his high school, with whom he had shared a lab table for a few weeks during his junior year. She was the head cheerleader and homecoming queen. She was also a "mean girl," the kind who had no time or sympathy for an average guy like Craig. If he said something foolish or awkward, Tiffany would use it to ridicule him in front of the jocks after class. Whenever she was around, he kept his head down and his words to a minimum.

Although he had no reason to think Carla was as mean as Tiffany, Craig had taken the same approach with her. He was too intimidated to chat her up like he did the other ladies in the church. He would say "Hi," and she would say "Hi," and that was the extent of their conversations.

"Uh, hi Carla, this is Craig from church. How are you today?"

"I'm fine. Funny thing you're calling right now. We were just talking about you. You have perfect timing."

His stomach flipped. "Who's we?" he asked.

"I'm with Joan and Helen. We're talking about the email you sent to Amy."

"So you've read it?"

"Yep, we read it right here in the middle of Starbucks. The barista gave you a standing ovation."

"What?"

"I'm just kidding. I read it to them, and we're talking about what to do next."

What to do next? Stupid idiot!

He looked at the clock on his laptop screen. "How much longer will you all be there?"

"For awhile. We're waiting for Amy to join us after she finishes up with a meeting."

"Are you at the Starbucks by the mall?" Craig asked.

"That's the one."

"Okay. I'll be there in ten minutes. In the meantime, please don't send that email to anyone else."

"No worries. See you in a few."

He stuffed his phone in his pocket and rushed out of his office. He and Carla had just had their longest conversation ever, and he was too upset to congratulate himself.

⋯⊨ ⊨⋯

Craig walked into Starbucks and saw Carla, Joan, and Helen sitting around a square table. For the first time since discovering he had sent an unfortunate email to the wrong woman, he let himself believe it might be possible to round up all the feathers. He sat down in the empty fourth chair, no doubt reserved for Amy, and tried to take control of the conversation.

"Hi ladies. Thanks for letting me crash your meeting."

"No problem," Carla said. "We have quite a few questions for you."

"Before we get to your questions, I have one of my own. Have you sent my email to anyone else?"

They all shook their heads. Carla said, "No, but I can think of a few others who need to read it before we get started."

Craig laughed nervously. "That's a joke, right?"

"I'm serious," Carla said. "It's brilliant, and I think it will work."

"I'm sorry," Craig said. "I need to come clean on this. That email was meant for my wife. It's a rough draft of a crazy idea that was bouncing around in my head. I wrote it down so I would stop thinking about it. It was never intended for public consumption. I would really appreciate it if you all forgot you ever saw it and please don't share it with anyone else."

"So that's what this is about," Helen said. "I wondered why you sounded so anxious in the voicemail you left me."

"Don't worry," Carla said. "You're not in trouble with us." She gave him a big smile. "We think you're right."

Craig tried to maintain eye contact with Carla, but he couldn't do it without feeling like he was flirting with her. He focused on Helen instead. "It doesn't matter whether I'm right or wrong. What matters is that if the wrong people read my email, it will cause nothing but trouble for the church. And for me. That email is what the elders would call 'being divisive.'" He punctuated the last phrase with air quotes. "I can't afford that kind of trouble." He paused and scanned their unsympathetic expressions. "Do you understand what I'm saying?"

"We understand perfectly," Helen said. "The last thing I want to do is get you in trouble."

"Me neither," Carla said. "But there is one thing I do want to know. Do you believe what you wrote?"

He sat back in his chair and considered the question as he stared at the abstract painting on the wall above Helen's head. None of the women touched their coffee. They just sat there, watching him think, their eyes like bright spotlights trying to sweat an answer out of a handcuffed suspect. It felt like a cosmic moment of truth when the universe holds its breath, and the angels in heaven stop what they're doing to watch a man finally reveal what kind of person he really is.

He nodded his head slightly, working up the courage to speak. "Yes, I believe what I wrote."

They all gave him warm, satisfied smiles.

Well look at that. You're their hero.

"But I don't think anyone should take what I wrote seriously," Craig said. "At least, not at our church."

"Don't worry, Craig. We won't share your email with anyone else," Helen said.

Craig looked at the others. "Promise?"

"Scout's honor," Carla said, holding up her hand as if taking an oath. Helen and Joan held up their hands as well.

"Thanks for understanding. Have a great day." He got up to leave.

"Don't you want to stay and talk about what you wrote?" Carla asked.

Craig looked into Carla's brown eyes and savored the invitation. There was nothing he wanted more than to sit back down and visit with these women, especially Carla, about his brilliant idea, but he knew better. He shook his head. "Not a chance. I never intended for it to see the light of day."

He ran into Amy in the parking lot on the way to his car. He explained his mistake once again and asked her to make the same promise he'd extracted from the other ladies.

"Don't worry, Craig. Your secret is safe with me."

Chapter 3

AMY WALKED INTO Starbucks and saw the other ladies sitting at a corner table. She waved hello and ordered a fancy blended coffee beverage at the counter. She had promised herself she'd only drink plain coffee today. She was trying to lose twenty pounds and didn't need the empty calories, but this mini-drama with Craig and his mistaken email had stirred her emotions just enough to weaken her resolve. The barista offered to bring it over to her when it was ready. Amy eased herself into the empty chair at the table--she was sore from a workout the previous day--and waited for her sugar-laden, six-dollar drink to arrive.

Amy skipped the pleasantries and said, "I just saw Craig in the parking lot. He has really worked himself into a tizzy over that email. I thought he was going to make me swear on a Bible that I wouldn't forward it to anyone else."

"Same here," Carla said. "We had to give him Scout's honor."

"You all haven't sent it to anyone else, have you?" Amy asked.

They all shook their heads.

"I didn't even read it that closely," Joan said. "Just skimmed it on my phone."

"It really is a fascinating idea," Amy said. "Do you think it would work?"

"I think it would be fun to try," Carla said.

"Me too," Amy said. "I'm tired of waiting."

"Let's try it and see what happens," Carla said.

The barista delivered Amy's drink and she took a long pull from the straw.

"What about Scout's honor?" Helen asked.

Carla giggled. "I was never a Scout."

Amy nearly spit out her drink on Joan. "Me neither," she said and wiped her mouth with a brown napkin. "But I do love their cookies. I'm afraid Craig's idea is too good to set aside and pretend we never read it."

"It demands action," Carla said.

Helen frowned. "Didn't we just promise him we wouldn't get him in trouble?"

"Actually," Amy said, "I promised him I wouldn't send his email to anyone else."

Carla's eyes brightened. "That's all we promised too."

"Think about it. What is Craig most afraid of?" Amy asked.

"He's afraid the elders will find out about his email," Helen said.

"That's right," Amy said. "He doesn't want them to know that he doesn't agree with the way they're handling things. That's what will get him in trouble."

"It certainly will," Helen said. "If the elders ever read it, they'll run him out of town."

"You think so?" Joan asked. "That seems a bit extreme to me."

"Go back and read what he wrote more closely," Helen said. "It's pretty radical."

Amy took another drink from the straw and licked her lips, while she organized her thoughts. "According to Craig, we're the only four people who know he wrote it, right?"

They all nodded.

"What if we do what he suggests in his email but not tell anyone where the idea came from?"

"I like the way you're thinking," Carla said. "Besides, just like Craig said in his email, this needs to be something done by women. We shouldn't need a man's help to pull it off--that would negate the whole point of the exercise."

"I guess so," Helen said. She gave Joan a quick look. "But don't we need to make sure he's okay with us using his idea, even if we don't tell anyone it's his?"

"Maybe," Amy said. "But I'm not sure. Just because he was the one who wrote it down doesn't necessarily give him the right to tell us what to do. In fact, one could argue that forbidding us to take action would contradict what he wrote."

Helen cocked her head to the side. "Hmmm. That's a good point. I hadn't thought about it that way."

"It's a really good point," Carla said. "He gave up the right to control what we do with his idea as soon as he sent it to us, or rather, to Amy, accident or not."

"What about you, Joan?" Amy asked. "You're being awfully quiet over there."

"Like I said, I didn't read it that carefully, but it sounds like the kind of ploy that could hurt a lot of people. Sure, it might work, but it could also backfire and split our church. That's a pretty big risk to take, especially with Craig already telling us he thinks it will cause trouble."

"Joan, I appreciate that you're thinking about the worst case scenario," Amy said. "I'm sure it will upset a few of the good ole boys, but I doubt it will destroy anything, except maybe their fragile egos. Think about it. If the men dig in their heels and start a fight that destroys the church, then they won't have anything to be in charge of, will they?"

"I still like the way you're thinking," Carla said. She rubbed her hands together as though she couldn't wait to get started. "Let's do it."

"And Carla," Amy said, "I appreciate your enthusiasm, but let's not rush anything. This may be the opportunity we've been waiting for, and I think we'll regret it for the rest of our lives if we don't do something with it. But taking into account Joan's concern, let's take a few days and pray about it. That will also give us time to go back and re-read Craig's email to make sure we understand exactly what we're signing up for."

"*If* we decide to sign up for anything at all," Joan said.

"Right," Amy said. "We may wake up tomorrow thinking this is the dumbest idea we've ever heard."

"I doubt it," Carla said.

"I do too," Amy said. "But let's give God the chance to talk us out of it anyway. Deal?"

Carla and Helen agreed, but Joan said nothing.

Amy continued, "In the meantime, no matter what we decide, we have to make a solemn vow to protect Craig. We can never let anyone else know where this idea came from. Everyone agree?"

Carla raised her hand. "Scout's honor."

They all laughed, but Amy said, "Not funny. Let's try it again."

This time, everyone, including Joan, nodded in agreement.

"So what's the next step?" Helen asked. "After we spend some time in prayer?"

Amy said, "Let's meet next week as usual and see where we're at."

"But not here," Helen said. "We need to be able to speak freely and not worry about being overheard."

Carla said, "We can meet at my house if you want."

"Sounds good to me," Amy said.

"Me too," Helen said. "Joan?"

Joan looked up from her phone and said, "Sure. Fine with me."

"Okay," Amy said. "Next Friday. Coffee at Carla's house."

⇀═ ═⇀

Craig pulled into the church parking lot and texted his wife before getting out of the car.

> Craig: I talked with Amy about my manifesto. I think I'm okay.
> Wife: Good. You coming home for lunch?
> Craig: No. I have to get some work done.
> Wife: Okay. See you tonight.

Craig walked into his office with the same sense of relief he felt when he had talked his way out of a speeding ticket a few weeks before.

You are one lucky stupid idiot.

Chapter 4

Amy had read Craig's email at least once a day, every day, for the past seven days, and she kept waiting for a nudge from God telling her it was a bad idea. She had heard one of the more respectable preachers on TV explain how, in his experience, the Holy Spirit rarely yelled or screamed or jumped up and down trying to get our attention. He said the Holy Spirit usually sounds more like someone subtlety clearing her throat--Ahem, Ahem, Ahem--and only those who are really listening are going to hear it.

Amy believed she had been carefully listening, and as far as she could tell, neither Craig's idea, nor her intention to implement it, had produced even a trace of phlegm in God's throat.

She decided to read it through one more time before meeting with the other ladies later that morning.

"Okay God," she prayed. "This is your last chance. If you want to change my mind, clear your throat or elbow me in the ribs or strike me blind."

> *I just finished writing this "manifesto." What do you think?*
> *Craig*

I keep hearing stories from other pastors about how more and more churches are deciding to bite the bullet and tackle the issue of the role of women in public worship gatherings and congregational leadership.

While this may sound like a progressive wave of freedom is about to wash over these churches and clear out oppressive, patriarchal traditions, in actuality it means nothing of the sort. Instead, it means a group of men will get together and study what the Bible has to say about women, then read a few scholarly books, written by men, about how to interpret what the Bible says about women, then re-read for themselves what the Bible has to say, and then have a series of mind-numbingly legalistic discussions about what they believe the Bible says women can do at church on Sunday mornings without getting the male leaders of the church in trouble with God.

After these men are dragged--some kicking and screaming--to the conclusion that the New Testament is far more inclusive of women in church leadership roles than they originally assumed, they will announce their intention to incrementally "allow" women to do more than they have been "permitted" to do in the past.

Some will decide, in spite of their more progressive theological conclusions, to make no changes at all because doing so would put the unity of the church at risk.

Several months ago, I was sitting in a circle with a group of male preachers--please excuse the redundant language--who were talking about the injustice of how women are treated in our churches, and I realized how weary I am of the whole conversation.

I'm tired of hearing a bunch of open-minded guys sitting around trying to figure out how to empower women. I cringe when we use words like "let," "permit," and "allow." As in, "At our church, we let women pray out loud. We permit them to serve communion. Heck, we even allow them to make a few announcements." All we lack is a box of Cuban cigars and a bottle of Cognac to properly congratulate ourselves for striking the proper balance between prudence and progressive theology.

While the "good ole boys club" culture in our churches is an easy target, I do not believe the responsibility for our lack of progress rests solely on the shoulders of the male gatekeepers. Not when women are willingly participating in their own subjugation.

What I do not understand--likely because I am a white male of European descent--is why so many strong, gifted women have abdicated their power to a group of men who, when given the choice, will choose peace over justice. Every. Single. Time.

Why are women waiting for men to give them permission to lead, speak, and pray when the gospel has already set them free to do so?

If gender equality really is a justice issue, and not just an issue of preference (like worship style), then what are women waiting for? If their subjugation can be placed on the same plane as racial discrimination, then the oppressed cannot merely wait for those in power to start "allowing" them to use their gifts. As long as they are willing to wait, good ole boys will continue to drag their cowardly heels under the guise of "discernment."

Years will pass. Daughters will be born and raised. Many will move on to other churches where they're free to be themselves. All while their mothers, aunts, and maybe a few cousins will stay put, grinding their teeth at the injustice of being made to wait for a group of self-serving, peace-loving men to set them free.

Perhaps it is time for a different approach. One inspired by Jesus when he overturned the tables in the temple courts and in the tradition of the peaceful protests of the civil rights movement.

How about some good old-fashioned civil disobedience?

Everyone knows that churches run on the energy of women who serve behind-the-scenes in countless ways. They prepare communion, teach children's classes, change diapers in the nursery, prepare bulletins, make coffee, and keep the refreshment table stocked with doughy goodies. They maintain prayer lists, organize VBS, and coordinate receptions for weddings and funerals. Each one of these activities is essential. Church would be a very different experience for men if dedicated women weren't making sure these things happened.

What if the women decided to show the men just how different that experience would be?

Rather than waiting for men to set them free, let the women of so-called progressive churches unite and stand together as one and use their immense power as servants to claim their freedom. This must be a movement organized and orchestrated by women. Let those with natural leadership gifts lead the charge and articulate a preferred future. Let them build consensus among the women of the church and courageously proceed. Let them develop their own ground rules for how to stand firm in a Christ-honoring way. Some of the most gifted leaders in our churches are sitting quietly in the pews or serving anonymously in the children's hall. Now is their time to step forward and lead the charge.

Imagine what church would be like if every woman refused to serve in her usual capacity until all woman are free to serve in all capacities, just like men. Let the gears of local churches grind to a halt when women reclaim their power and altogether say, "No more waiting!"

Of course, the good ole boys are betting the gentle women in their churches would never have the guts to do such a thing, because it would be considered un-Christian. But what is the more Christian thing for women to do: Sit around and wait for Pharaoh to set them free out of the goodness of his heart? Or use their God-given power to show their taskmaster that the time for change arrived yesterday?

The only way to get the attention of the male gatekeepers is to knock a hole in the wall.

Ladies, the time has come.

No more waiting.

Knock down this wall!

Amy closed her eyes and sat still for what seemed like an eternity, but in truth, it was only fifty-seven seconds. She heard nothing.

"Okay," she said to God and to herself. "I'm done waiting. The time has come."

Chapter 5

"WHERE'S JOAN?" CARLA asked as she set a cup of steeping tea down on the kitchen table in front of Helen.

"She texted and said something came up at work, and she can't make it," Amy said.

Helen dipped the teabag in and out of the hot water in her cup. "Do you believe her?"

Amy shrugged. "Why wouldn't I?"

"I don't know," Helen said. "It's not like her to miss our get-togethers, and I picked up a strange vibe from her last week as we were leaving. She just didn't seem like herself."

"You don't think she has a problem with Craig's idea, do you?" Carla asked.

"It's not Craig's idea," Amy corrected. "At least not anymore. From now on, it's our idea. The sooner we get used to saying it, the less likely we will be to slip up and mention Craig when it matters."

"You don't think she has a problem with OUR idea, do you?" Carla said, conveying her irritation with dull, unimpressed eyes.

Amy ignored Carla's petulance and said, "I seriously doubt it. I've known her for twenty years, and trust me, she's just as excited about this idea as we are, or at least, as I still am. She's just busy."

"It sounds like you want to do something with Craig's, I mean, our idea," Helen said.

"I do," Amy said. "Every time I read what he wrote I'm struck by how much sense it makes. To tell you the truth, I'm kind of ashamed it took a man to think of it."

Carla smirked and said, "Oh, but Craig didn't think of it. We did." She lifted her hands as though she were receiving a blessing from heaven.

"That's another good reason not to let anyone know where this idea came from," Amy said, refusing to let Carla draw attention to herself. "If the other ladies find out this is a man's idea, it might kill our movement before it ever gets started."

"So we're a movement now?" Carla asked.

"I don't know," Amy said. "Are we? I'm in."

"Me too," Carla said.

They both looked at Helen, who had wrapped her tea bag around the handle of her spoon and was wringing it out like a wet towel at a car wash.

She looked up at them. "I don't know. I'd like to do something, but I don't want to cause trouble for the church."

"What church?" Amy asked.

"Our church, of course," Helen said.

"Do you mean the building or the people?"

Helen rolled her eyes. "The people. I grew up going to Sunday School too. I know the difference between the church and a building."

"Then which people do you not want to cause any trouble for?" Amy asked.

"All of them," Helen said.

"Are you sure?" Amy asked. "Because as it stands right now, over half the people in the church are being silenced by a few powerful men. Seems to me there's already trouble in our church, and they're the ones causing it."

"That's a bit extreme, don't you think?" Helen said. "Not every woman wants to speak in church or be an elder. You might be surprised how many women are fine with the status quo."

"Are you?" Carla asked.

"Of course not," Helen said. "But I also don't think every man in our church is part of a conspiracy to keep women silent either. It's not fair to say they are."

"Who said anything about a vast male conspiracy? I said a few men are silencing us, and by a few, I mean the elders." Amy looked from Helen to Carla and back to Helen. "I'll go ahead and say it: I don't mind causing the elders some trouble. They had their chance to solve this problem on their own. Now it's our turn."

Helen shook her head. "I just don't know. This is not some revolution against a third world dictator. We've known these men and their families for years."

"I know," Amy said. "And that's what makes the way they've tried to *handle* us so much more unacceptable. You handle horses, not people. And certainly not women."

"You're not messing around, are you?" Carla said.

"No, I'm not. The more I talk about it, the angrier it makes me. Helen, which would you prefer, to cause a little bit of trouble for a few men right now or to continue having to go to the trouble of explaining to our daughters why they're treated like second-class citizens in our church?"

"Do I really have a choice?" Helen said, looking down at her cooling tea.

"Yes, you do," Amy said. "You don't have to be a part of this if you don't feel right about it." She looked at Carla. "But Carla and I are going to move forward, with or without you."

Carla nodded.

"Okay, I'm in," Helen said. "But promise me we'll give the elders a chance to change before we do anything to embarrass them."

"I promise," Amy said. "If we do this right, no one but the elders will ever have to know what we have planned."

"And what exactly is our plan?" Carla asked.

Amy gave a sheepish smile. "I'm not sure. Craig's email sketches out a basic idea, but it doesn't really give us a plan to follow."

"And the devil is always in the details," Helen said.

"Some things never change," Carla said. "Men talk, and women do."

"That's right," Amy said. "It's easy to come up with an idea that you have no intention of implementing. So let's figure it out. Other than the threat of all the women in the church going on strike." She looked at Helen. "Which we hope will never happen. Let's forget everything else Craig wrote. We'll just start at the beginning and go from there."

Carla and Helen waited for Amy to say more. But she didn't. The pregnant pause became an awkward silence, the only sound being the ticking of an old fashioned cuckoo clock hanging on Carla's kitchen wall.

Finally, Carla said, "How about we start by listing all the women we need to talk to?"

"That's pretty easy to figure out, isn't it?" Amy said. "We eventually need to talk to every woman in the church. This won't work unless they're all on board."

Helen nodded as if everything was settled. "Let's call a meeting of all the women in the church. We can tell them Craig's, I mean, our idea and get their input."

"On second thought," Amy said, "Maybe that's not such a good idea. Too many cooks in the kitchen. We need a smaller group--a steering team that can formulate a plan of action. Then we can take the plan to the others, and there will be no doubt about what we're asking them to do.

"Or not do, as the case may be," Carla said.

Amy tapped her nose with her right index finger as if they were playing charades.

"So who should be on the steering team?" Helen asked.

"Well, the three of us for sure," Carla said.

"And Joan," Helen said.

"Yes, of course," Amy said. "Joan is part of this too. We can't move forward without her."

"She should be here then," Carla said.

"It's okay. I'll bring her up to speed," Amy said.

Helen wrote something on the notepad in front of her. "Who else?"

"What if we keep the team small while we're formulating our plan and then add more women as we go along?" Amy asked.

"I like it," Carla said. "You're thinking just the three of us for now?"

"And Joan," Amy said. "But yes, that should be enough."

"So what's the next step?" Helen asked, ready to take more notes.

"What if we write out some rules of engagement?" Amy said. "We need to clarify how we will conduct ourselves as we take our stand. We want to make sure things don't get out of hand."

"I like that idea," Helen said.

"First rule," Carla said. "Wives must not tell their husbands what they're doing until it is too late for the men to do anything about it."

"Easy for you to say," Amy teased.

"Am I wrong?" Carla said.

Amy gave a nod in Helen's direction. "Write it down."

They were off and running.

Chapter 6

EXACTLY TWO WEEKS after the unfortunate, and almost disastrous, incident of the accidental email, Craig sat at his desk, pecking away at his laptop and putting the finishing touches on his sermon. He was in the zone, and the words were flowing. Unlike the other four days of the week, distractions weren't a temptation on Friday mornings. He and his wife had a long-standing agreement. If he could finish his work by lunch, Friday afternoon was his to do with as he pleased, as long as he spent Saturdays with the family. There was to be no sneaking away to work on his sermon if he didn't get it done on Friday morning. At his current pace, he'd have no trouble making it to the 1:30 showing of the latest superhero movie. His two boys would be mad at him for going without them, but if it was as good as the critics were saying, he wouldn't mind seeing it twice.

He took a break from his sermon at 11 a.m. and checked his email. He knew he was risking getting sucked into a church member's drama and ruining his afternoon off, but he couldn't help himself. Nestled between the multiple marketing emails from online retailers and newsletters from non-profits was an email from Amy Brandt.

Subject: The Deborah Club
Craig squinted and clicked on it.

Hi Craig--Hope you're having a good day. Just wanted you to know that a few of us are fleshing out what we think is an excellent idea. We're excited about it, but it's not going to be easy for some of the men at our church to accept. You can read more about it below.

As you read, please keep in mind that we're doing this for the long-term good of our church. We know this is going to cause some short-term pain for everyone involved, but we believe this is an idea whose time has come. I'm sharing this plan with you as a courtesy. We want you to know what's coming. Please don't share this with anyone else, including the elders. We believe it is our job to present this to them. I welcome your feedback on our plan of attack and rules of engagement.

Thanks,
Amy, Carla, Helen, and Joan
The Deborah Club

He swore to himself. He didn't have to read the attachments. He knew what this was about. They weren't going to leave it alone.

I guess you're not so lucky after all. Stupid idiot!

He re-read the last line of the email. The phrase "plan of attack" made him shudder. They are gearing up for war. Wars create winners and losers.

You will be the biggest loser of all. Instead of a cash prize, you'll get a one-way trip to the unemployment line.

29

And why were they calling themselves "The Deborah Club"? He felt a headache coming on. Although he really didn't want to, he clicked on the first attachment at the bottom of the email entitled "Letter to the Elders."

> To the ALL MALE Leadership of the South Barkley Bible Church:
>
> What was once considered to be hopeful rhetoric from the elders about including more women in leadership roles at South Barkley has become a source of frustration. We have waited patiently for our male leaders to "study," "discuss," and "discern" the best path for setting the women of our church free to use our spiritual gifts and natural talents in the service of our Lord.
>
> After years of "discussions" and "seasons of study" and "exercises in discernment" nothing has really changed. Nor do we expect it to, so long as the decision for initiating change rests in the hands of men who believe their primary responsibility as spiritual leaders is to keep the peace at all costs.
>
> We have, therefore, sadly concluded there will be no meaningful change in this area until we, the women of South Barkley, take the initiative upon ourselves to make change happen. This is exactly what we are prepared to do.
>
> On Sunday morning, November 6th, the women of South Barkley will no longer serve in our customary roles. We will attend the worship gathering, sing, share communion, and listen to the sermon, but this will be the extent of our participation. We will not teach children's classes, serve in the nursery, make coffee, prepare communion, or attend to any other behind-the-scenes details.

We are going on strike from these activities in protest of the way our leaders have "handled" this "conversation." And by handled, we mean postponed and ignored. While there has been plenty of lip service given to the intention of bringing about change, there has been no visible action taken as a result of the many clandestine meetings you all have supposedly had to discuss this matter.

Frankly, we are tired of waiting for a group of men to decide when to give us the freedom Jesus secured for us two thousand years ago. We confess our guilt in abdicating our responsibility for our spiritual well-being to others and then complaining about the way they are managing our growth as Christians. We apologize for our immaturity. From this moment forward, we are declaring our intention to change the conversation by changing our behavior.

This means we will no longer wait for someone else to set us free.

It is not our desire to cause unnecessary trouble for South Barkley or to derail the smooth operation of our Sunday morning programming. We do believe, however, the best way to catalyze real action is to demonstrate what life at South Barkley would be like if every woman in our church refuses to serve in her usual capacities. We are committed to non-action until all women at South Barkley are free to serve in whatever ways God has gifted and called them. We hope we will never find out what church would be like without the participation of women. The only way to avoid this outcome is for our church's all male leadership to stop postponing and start doing what you already know to be the right thing.

It would be tempting to view this declaration as selfish and un-Christian. We believe we are being un-Christian only to the degree that Christ was being un-Christian when he turned over the tables in the temple courts in protest of what the temple had become.

While we cannot say our efforts are completely devoid of selfish motives, we can say with certainty that we are not doing this solely for ourselves. We're doing this for our daughters, those already born and still to come. We have decided they will not be raised in a church where limits are placed on their involvement in leadership and public worship simply because they were born without a penis.

We are also doing this for our sons, who desperately need to grow up in church hearing women's voices and understanding how in the Kingdom of God, giftedness is more important than external plumbing.

And we're doing it for our mothers and grandmothers, who spent their whole lives quietly serving behind-the-scenes. Some served in this way because it was what they were gifted to do, but others were raised to believe this was their lot in life, their curse for being born a woman.

And yes, when it comes down to it, we are doing this for ourselves, because we've come to realize just how unacceptable it is to sit and wait for someone else to do it for us.

There is much to discuss before November 6th. We look forward to the conversation.

Sincerely,
The Deborah Club

Craig closed the document and grimaced. He massaged his right temple with his first two fingers. It felt like someone was jabbing an icepick into his temple. He didn't bother opening the other document labeled "Rules of Engagement." He grabbed his phone and called Amy Brandt instead. He stood and walked a lap around his office furniture while waiting for her to answer.

Chapter 7

As they had the week before, Amy, Carla, and Helen--Joan was tied up at work again--moved their weekly coffee meeting to a more private setting: Amy's house this time. They were sitting in the living room and editing the letter to the elders.

Amy thought it was a really good start. She had written most of it, with input from Carla and Helen. She had sent a copy to Joan, who hadn't responded with any suggestions. Carla loved it and was ready to send it to the elders straightaway. Helen was worried the tone was too harsh and combative.

"Do we really need to use the word penis?" she asked. "It seems too crass for a formal letter."

"I like the word penis," Carla said while managing to keep a straight face. "It has shock value."

Amy's phone beeped, and she looked to see who was calling. "Hold that thought. It's Craig. I bet he's calling about the email I sent him this morning."

She slid her thumb across her phone screen and hit the speaker button. "Hi Craig, I'm here with Carla and Helen. I have you on speaker phone."

"Good," Craig said. "Because I want all of you to hear what I have to say. I just read your letter to the elders. Please tell me you haven't sent it to them yet."

Amy spoke for the group. "Of course not, Craig. That's just the first draft. We wanted to get your input before we get too far down the road."

"My input? You've got to be kidding me," Craig said, his voice crackling through the little speaker on Amy's phone. "How many other women are part of this club you've started?"

"No one new, not yet anyway," Amy said. "We're thinking a series of mixers, like they do in multi-level marketing, is the way to go. We'd keep the groups small. No more than ten ladies at each one. That way we can--"

"How can you talk about this like it's just another committee you're chairing?" Craig asked. "You promised me you wouldn't do anything with my manifesto. You all gave me your word. Every single one of you."

"No, Craig," Carla said. "If I remember correctly, we promised you we wouldn't tell anyone it was your idea." She flashed her eyebrows at Amy, a quick apology for stealing her argument. "And we will keep our promise. No one will ever know."

For a moment, Craig said nothing. Amy gave Carla a thumbs up.

"Please don't go through with this," he said. "It's a horrible idea."

"Is that why you were so eager to show it off to your wife?" Carla said. "Because it was so horrible?"

"It's one of the dumbest ideas I have ever had. I'm sorry I ever wrote it down." He sounded deflated.

"You shouldn't be," Amy said, trying to sound sympathetic. "It's going to make a huge difference."

"No, it's not," Craig said, with fresh resolve in his voice. "Listen, dumb idea or not, it's still mine, and I forbid you to use it. This ends right here, right now. Understood?"

Amy's tone hardened. "No, Craig. We don't understand. And apparently, despite what you wrote, neither do you. We've waited long enough. This is the first time in years I've had any hope of real change. We're not backing down."

"Ladies, I'm telling you, no I'm promising you, if you go through with this, it will split our church. South Barkley is not healthy enough to survive this kind of conflict. No church is."

"Well maybe our church shouldn't survive," Amy said. "Maybe it's better off dead, with every family scattered into the wind and attending churches that don't discriminate against women."

"You have no clue what you're getting into," Craig said. "It's more complicated than you can possibly imagine. There is a reason the elders have been so slow to move on this."

"Sorry Craig, no more waiting," Amy said.

"I'll go to the elders and tell them what you're planning," Craig said.

"You will do no such thing," Amy said. "Because if you do, we'll show them your email and tell them you were the mastermind behind this scheme. Then you can explain to them why you should keep your job. How does that sound?" She looked to the others for approval of her strong-arm tactics. Carla was nodding. Helen was frowning.

Craig said nothing.

Amy softened her tone. "You can't give us an idea and then tell us we can't act on it, Craig."

"Yes, I can," Craig whined. "It's my idea. You can't use it."

"Craig, will you listen to yourself?" Carla said. "You sound like a two year old who doesn't want anyone else playing with his toys."

"And stop worrying about splitting the church," Amy said. "The elders will never let it get that far. They'll do whatever it takes to keep the peace. They always do."

"Not this time," Craig said. "You have no idea. No idea."

"We promised to keep you out it," Carla said, trying to pacify Craig.

"And that's what we'll do as long as you don't try to stop us," Amy said.

"Then keep me out of it completely," Craig said. "No more emails. No more asking what I think about your plans. I'm not your silent partner. I'm not your ally. I want nothing to do with this."

"Suit yourself," Amy said. "But when it works, don't go trying to take credit for it."

"Fair enough. Goodbye."

"Wow," Amy said, trying to catch her breath. "That escalated quickly. It didn't go at all the way I expected."

"You know what's funny?" Carla asked.

"Not that conversation," Helen said. "That was horrible. I feel terrible."

"You didn't even say anything!" Carla said.

"Still, that was awful," Helen said.

"Better get used to it," Amy said. "This isn't going to be easy."

"What's funny," Carla said, "is that he's a card carrying member of the good ole boys club he says he despises, and he doesn't even realize it."

"You think so?" Amy asked.

"I do," Carla said. "I'm not sure if he even meant what he wrote. He may have just been trying to impress his wife so she'd give him some."

Amy chuckled. "I hope she did. He deserves at least a little love for the effort."

"Speaking of the other Amy," Helen said. "Do you think she will want to be a part of this?"

"I don't think we should invite her," Carla said.

"Do you not think she'll like our plan?" Helen asked.

"Oh, she'll love it," Amy said. "Remember, Craig was writing to impress her."

"So she's already one of us then," Helen said.

"No, she's the pastor's wife," Carla said. "She'll never be one of us."

Helen flinched at Carla's remark.

"Come to think of it," Amy said, her lips curling into a devious smile. "I think we should include her as soon as possible. Maybe even right now."

"Why would we want to do that?" Carla asked.

"Because she'll love our plan, and she's the pastor's wife," Amy said.

Carla tapped her fingernail on the rim of her coffee cup while she considered Amy's suggestion. "You're right," she finally said. "We need her."

"I have no idea what you two are talking about," Helen said.

"I don't have time to explain," Amy said. "We need to call her before it's too late."

Chapter 8

CRAIG'S MIND SEEMED to be following the pattern of his movement around his office. Or were his feet tracing his thoughts? Either way, he was going in circles. He'd walk a few laps in one direction, then turn around and walk a few in the other. No matter which direction he let his mind wander, he kept arriving at the same conclusion.

You are so screwed.

Part of him loved knowing his manifesto had stirred Amy Brandt to action. When he had written it, he let his passion and imagination run wild. It had felt good to fantasize about being a catalyst. In another life, he could have been a bold leader, the kind both men and women willingly follow into battles against social injustice and systemic evil. In another life, he could have written a best-selling book and earned enough royalties to quit his job as a pastor, move to Hollywood, and run a hit TV show. In another life, women like Carla would take him seriously instead of talking down to him. But in this life, he felt destined to preach safe, boring sermons to a church too stuck in its own traditions to ever look beyond itself for a better future. He was trapped, and there was nothing he could do about it, except channel his frustration into writing something dangerous. What he hadn't expected, what took him by devastating surprise, was how much he enjoyed getting his revolutionary rocks off by writing down his true thoughts in such an aggressive voice. But when he went back and read what he had written, he felt an emptiness, not unlike the twinge of longing he experienced the split second after climaxing with his wife. What had been furiously building within him had exhausted itself without delivering anything more than a fleeting moment of pleasure. What a waste of a great idea, but good Lord, it had felt good to write.

How could you have been so stupid?

His wife was always asking him what it would take to break the logjam and get some movement on the "women's issue"—she hated the term, but no one could ever come up with a better name for it-- at South Barkley. He kept telling her to be patient. These things take time. The wheel of progress turns slowly in a conservative church, and sometimes it takes a few funerals to get it spinning. While she never said it out loud, he sensed her disappointment with him in these discussions, like she expected him to do more than wait for the right people to die, or worse, that she judged his weakness as a leader to be part of the problem. Thank God she never said any of this to him. He could handle having his leadership questioned by others. As a pastor, such criticism was part of the job. He was the first to admit he was no Alexander the Great, but if his wife ever voiced this opinion of him, it would be a cut too cruel for him to bear. He wanted her to see what he was capable of and to know what kind of leader he could be, under different circumstances and in another life. So he had sent her the manifesto.

How could you have been so stupid?

He needed someone with whom he could think out loud, but he dare not let anyone else know that The Deborah Club existed. He considered reaching out to one of his pastor buddies, but he was too ashamed to explain how and why he created this mess for himself.

He usually avoided involving his wife in church politics and the conflicts it produced, but she already knew about the accidental email, and she would want to know about this latest development. With no other options coming to mind, he called her. He was disappointed when her phone went straight to voicemail. Instead of leaving a message, he texted her.

> Craig: Can you talk?
> Wife: On the phone.
> Craig: Call me when ur done.
> Wife: OK

Craig piddled around the office for the next thirty minutes, looking busy but accomplishing nothing. He had a sermon to write, but he couldn't focus his mind on anything other than figuring out how to derail The Deborah Club without Amy and Carla finding out he was the saboteur. If they believed their plan failed on its own, they wouldn't tattle on him to the elders. The embryo of a plan was forming in the back of his mind, but he needed to bounce it off someone. He texted his wife again.

> Craig: Gonna call soon?
> Wife: Still on the phone.

Craig: Please call soon. It's important.

Wife: So is the call I'm on right now! :-)

Her smiley face puzzled Craig. She loved to use emojis in her texts, most of which Craig didn't know how to interpret. She said they helped clarify her meaning, and he should use them too. He didn't think real men should use emojis. What did the smiley face mean? Was the call she was on causing her to smile? Was she getting good news? Or was it a sassy smiley face, meant to show him he wasn't the only one who talked about important matters on the phone? So much for clarity.

His phone beeped. It was his wife. Finally.

"That took long enough," Craig said.

"You can be in a bad mood all you want. There's nothing you can do to bring me down." She was talking fast.

"Maybe you can cheer me up then," he said. "I need some good news."

"Well, here you go," she said. Her voice rose with excitement. "I was just talking with Amy Brandt. She was with Carla and Helen. They told me their plans."

"I hope you told them how stupid they're being."

"Absolutely not. I told them they could count me in. I'm ready to help any way I can."

"Are you crazy?" Craig asked. "Don't you remember saying that what I wrote was a terrible idea?"

"I never said it was a terrible idea. I said it was one of the best things you have ever written."

"Yes, and you told me sending it to Amy Brandt was a mistake."

"I changed my mind."

"No, I think you've lost your mind," he said.

"I was initially afraid you would get in trouble for making trouble. But Amy said they had already talked it through with you, and you were fine with what they were doing, as long as they didn't tell anyone it was your idea."

"That's a very loose paraphrase of my last conversation with them," Craig said.

"They said you were worried it would split the church and everyone would blame you, but they think you're overreacting. And now that I've had some time to think about it, so do I."

"You cannot join The Deborah Club," Craig said. "I won't allow it. It will get us fired."

"It's not going to get us fired," she said. "And you can't tell me what to do. Not about this. Have your forgotten what you wrote? I don't need your permission to be free."

"I didn't mean what I wrote," Craig said. "I was blowing off steam and seeing what it would feel like to say something like that."

"You meant it, Craig. You and I both know you did. Don't be ashamed of what you believe."

"Please don't do this, honey. I'm begging you. Stay out of it."

"I'm already in it, Craig. I have been since the day I was born a woman. This is the right thing to do. And it's time."

"Let's see if you still feel that way when I'm looking for a new job."

"Do you really want to work at a church where a group of men tell your wife what she can and can't do?"

"Somebody needs to, because my wife sure as hell doesn't listen to me."

"Oh, I listen, Craig. I hear you talk about how things ought to be and how you would change things if you could. I've been listening to you talk for years. But I've never seen you actually do anything with any of your great ideas. Well, now you have. Call it an accident if you want, but I'm glad it happened. We both know you're not a leader, but God made sure your email ended up in the hands of someone who is. I'm going to follow her."

You're not a leader.

Craig almost hung up, but he didn't want her to know she'd scored a direct hit to his heart. His silence said enough.

"I didn't mean it that way," she said. "I know you're not in a position to lead the charge on this one. Our boys need to eat. You're doing the best you can."

"Stop it," he said. "I know how you meant it and all the back peddling in the world isn't going to change what you said."

"I'm sorry," she said.

"Sorry enough to stay away from The Deborah Club?"

"That's not fair, Craig."

"No, what's not fair is you putting my job in jeopardy for your own selfish agenda." *I'll teach you to question my leadership.*

"How dare you! This is every bit as important to you as it is to me. We've talked about it a thousand times."

"It was all just talk," he said. "Apparently my talk isn't worth much."

"You don't mean any of this, Craig. You're just mad. I'm going to hang up, and you're going to call me back in five minutes and apologize."

"You want an apology? Here you go. I'm sorry I'm not a better leader. If I was, I'd be able to keep my wife from getting me fired just so she can speak into a microphone."

"You're a bastard."

"It's not my fault you can't pee standing up."

"I hate you right now," she said and hung up.

I hate me right now too.

She had been wrong about him calling her five minutes later. He texted her instead.

Craig: I'm sorry.

Wife: I know.

Craig: I guess there's no way I can talk you out of this now.

Wife: There never was a way. I'm in.

Craig: I can't help you.

Wife: We don't need you're help. You've done enough.

Craig: What did they ask you to do?

Wife: Nothing. That's the beauty of your plan. I don't have to do anything except stop doing my usual stuff.

Wife: They don't even want me to be part of the organizational meetings. To protect you.

Craig: It's not my plan, and there is nothing beautiful about what's coming.

Wife: Stop being so negative.

Wife: And send me some flowers you jackass.

Chapter 9

THE DEBORAH CLUB'S steering team was strategic about whom they invited to their first luncheon. It hadn't been hard to brainstorm a list of fifteen women who would be ready to claim their freedom. They were the epitome of what Craig had originally described as gifted leaders waiting for permission to be themselves. Ten of the first fifteen women they invited were able to attend.

Amy read a trimmed down version of Craig's email as if it were her own, laid out the plan for going on strike, and walked the women through the rules of engagement. A few ladies had questions about some of the details, but there were no objections to the overall strategy. They all agreed it was time to act. Amy wrapped up the meeting by reading the latest draft of the letter to the elders.

The consensus among the early adopters was that The Deborah Club shouldn't send the letter to the elders until enough women were on board to give their movement critical mass. After some quick math at the end of the first meeting, they decided the magic number to trigger their next step would be sixty-five.

The second and third meetings went like the first with unanimous buy-in. The hardest part was finding a good time for so many busy women to meet. Between work, kids' school activities, and weekend sporting events, it took multiple tries. They abandoned their luncheon strategy and scheduled meetings whenever they could. This slowed the progress toward critical mass considerably.

Amy was the spokesperson for the group. She presented the plan at each meeting and answered the majority of questions. She and Carla spent a lot of time on the phone talking and texting each other about ideas and next steps. Helen coordinated the details, mostly tracking RSVP's and making sure at least ten women were coming to each meeting. Joan was always too busy to meet with them it seemed, but they kept her apprised through email and text.

They didn't encounter any significant resistance until the fourth meeting. It was a coffee and dessert gathering at Helen's house on a Sunday afternoon in September. Helen's husband was out of town, and the other husbands were so pre-occupied with watching football they barely noticed their wives leaving for a meeting.

Amy had anticipated a few early objections from peacekeepers concerned about causing trouble, but breezing through the first three meetings left her both overconfident in her persuasive abilities and unprepared for an attack from an unlikely source. She had just finished laying out the plan to go on strike and was about to read the letter to the elders when Jane Gilmore interrupted her. Jane was a straight-talker in her late sixties.

"This is a joke, right?"

"Yeah right," Amy said, thinking Jane was joking about it being a joke. She read the first line of the letter, and Jane interrupted her again.

"You're not serious about this, are you?"

"Yes, Jane. We're serious. Why wouldn't we be?" Amy asked. She shot Carla a puzzled look.

"Because it's the silliest thing I've ever heard."

"We may not have thought through every detail or possible outcome, but it's hardly silly," Amy said, sounding more defensive than she intended.

"I can't believe you think something like this will work," Jane said.

"Why won't it work?" Amy asked.

"Because your plan depends on every woman in our church going along with it," Jane said.

"Not every woman, necessarily. We expect a few won't have the stomach for it, but if the most influential and respected women stick together, then the elders will have no choice but to listen to us."

"I'm not going along with it," Jane said. "There's nothing you can say to talk me into it. Don't even try."

Jane was one of the oldest women invited to the first few meetings. She was known for her blunt remarks in Bible class discussions. She wasn't afraid to let whatever man happened to be teaching the class know when she thought he was in over his head. This gave others the impression Jane believed she could do a better job teaching than most of the men who were allowed to do it. This is also why the leaders of The Deborah club believed she should be one of the first fifty women to join the movement. When they added her to the list, Amy never envisioned being on the receiving end of one of Jane's lacerating declarations.

Amy tried to regain control of the exchange. "Jane, I'm surprised to hear you say that. Do you mind me asking why you don't want to support this effort?"

"Because I like things fine just the way they are," Jane said. "I don't need to hear a woman pray out loud in order to feel closer to God."

"But what about the women who are asked to pray?" Amy asked. "What if praying out loud helps them feel closer to God?" Amy saw Carla wrinkle her nose and wondered what mistake she had just made.

Jane didn't let her stay in the dark for long. "I certainly don't want to hear a prayer from a woman who wants to be heard by others just so she can feel closer to God. Is she praying to God or to us?"

"She's praying to God, of course," Amy said. "But why should the church only hear male voices praying?"

"If it were up to me, we wouldn't hear anyone praying out loud," Jane said. "I get so tired of hearing men pray the same things over and over. I say just give us all a few seconds of silence to speak our peace to God and then move on."

Amy looked around the room at the other women. She saw crossed arms and tapping toes. One young mother was staring at the ceiling slack-jawed as if she had fallen asleep with her eyes open.

"That's a fine idea, Jane," Amy said. "However, I don't see our church moving in that direction. We're always going to have someone praying out loud. We think it would be beneficial for the church to hear a woman's voice express her heart to God. Who knows? Maybe women would pray differently than men, and you wouldn't keep hearing the same old tired clichés."

"No, after the first few months, we'd just hear a different set of clichés prayed over and over," Jane said. "And just who is 'we'?"

Amy was confused. "We?"

"Yes, you said, 'We think.' Who is this genius 'we' that's been doing all this thinking?" Jane asked.

"Well, initially it was Carla, Helen, Joan, and myself who put all of this together. Then we expanded it, and now we have somewhere around twenty other women who have joined The Deborah Club."

"Joan and I, not Joan and myself," Jane corrected. "It drives me crazy when people make that mistake, especially those who want to stand up and talk to a group." Jane looked around the room. "Speaking of Joan, where is she?"

"She couldn't be here today," Amy said. "But she loves what we're doing." Amy had no idea why she added the last bit about Joan loving it when the truth was she hadn't talked to Joan in almost three weeks. They'd both been so busy lately their only communication had been through texts and one sentence emails.

Jane stood up and addressed the group, "What do the rest of you think about this?"

Amy could feel her heart pounding. She had lost control of the meeting. She said, "Um, first, before you answer I'd really like to finish reading this letter."

Kara Jensen, a young mother who missed the first luncheon because her toddler was sick, chimed in, "It doesn't matter what the letter says. Count me in."

Several other women nodded in agreement.

Jane shook her head and said, "If you all want to stir a pot that's simmering just fine on its own, be my guest. But count me out."

"So if it comes down to it, you're still going to do what you normally do on Sunday mornings. You won't strike with us?" Amy asked.

"No, I won't *strike* with you," Jane mocked. On her lips, the idea sounded ridiculous.

Amy said, "Well, would you consider--"

Carla cut her off. "Jane, what are you currently doing on Sunday mornings?"

Jane thought about it for a moment. "I sit there and sing when I'm supposed to sing and listen when I'm supposed to listen and I keep my mouth shut, just like I wish more people would do."

"If the rest of us refuse to serve on Sundays, would you take up the slack and serve in our place if the elders asked you to?" Carla asked.

"You mean like teach a children's Bible class or work in the nursery?" Jane said.

"Yes, or maybe help prepare communion," Carla said.

"Oh no," Jane said. "I've already served my time in the back with the kids. When mine grew up and moved out I retired from children's duty. And I'm not going to spend my Sunday morning in the church kitchen pouring grape juice into little bitty cups either. I spend enough time in the kitchen at home. I don't come to church to do more work. I come to get an hour of rest."

Everyone smiled, except Amy.

"Well, Jane," Carla said, "I really wish you would reconsider supporting us, but I also respect your decision to stay out of it. Amy, do you have anything else?"

"I guess not." Amy looked at Jane. "You're not going to tell anyone about our plan are you?"

"No, I'll keep my mouth shut," Jane said. "I don't agree with you, but I'm no tattle-tale. Just don't go burning your bras. Been there, done that, and bounced around in a T-shirt to prove it."

Everyone giggled, except Amy.

"We appreciate that, Jane," Carla said. "Amy, why don't you leave the letter to the elders on the counter so those who want to read it can look at it before they leave."

"Right. Good idea," Amy said. "I'll put it over on the bar, by the coffee."

Carla closed the meeting with a quick prayer asking God to bless their efforts. Most of the ladies lingered to ask a few more questions and to add their names to The Deborah Club membership roll. Jane left immediately after everyone said "Amen."

Amy watched her leave and fought the urge to chase Jane to her car and take one more shot at winning her over.

Chapter 10

Twenty minutes later, Carla and Helen were rinsing dishes in the sink and transferring them to the dishwasher, while Amy leaned against the counter and stared down at the shiny wooden floor in Helen's kitchen. With nine new names on the roster, the meeting had been another smashing success. Jane's interruption hadn't deterred any of the other women from signing on, and Jane had promised not to tell anyone what they were up to. There was no reason for Amy to be pouting, but she couldn't help herself. She was furious, though not with Jane.

Carla and her husband, Nick, had moved to town seven years earlier because of his work. When they joined the church, their oldest was three, and Carla was five months pregnant. Amy volunteered to throw her a baby shower. Carla reminded Amy of a younger version of herself. She was an ambitious woman who refused to let motherhood be the only defining characteristic in her life.

Before her first child, Carla was building a nice career at a public relations firm. When the baby was born, she took a few months off and then worked part time. Not because they needed the money, but because she didn't want to completely give up on her career.

Hiring a sitter so she could work a few hours during the week and going into the office on Saturdays when Nick could watch the baby kept her foot in the door. She was looking forward to enrolling her son in preschool and increasing her hours at work when Nick was offered a promotion that required the move. It was a great opportunity for Nick, and he convinced Carla the timing was right to get pregnant again, so that's what they did.

Carla and Amy hit it off while coordinating the details of her shower. Amy liked Carla's energy. Carla saw Amy as an older sister in whom she could confide. One day, when Amy was dropping off a few gifts from the women who couldn't attend the shower, Carla invited Amy to stay for a few minutes and visit. As they talked about the move, the shower, the plan for the baby's room, and Nick's new job, Amy sensed that Carla was struggling with the transition more than she was letting on.

When she asked Carla how she felt about leaving her job behind, Carla wept and apologized for her pregnancy hormones. She then confessed her bitterness to Amy. She regretted putting her career on hold for her son. She also resented having to leave the firm for her husband's job. It wasn't fair. She realized how blessed she was to have a husband with a great job and a healthy son. She said she was trying to be a good Christian wife, but she was also afraid her family was slowly erasing her identity as a woman. She knew she sounded selfish and that it was wrong to blame her husband for his promotion or her son for being born. She was afraid getting pregnant again was a mistake. It was going to make starting her career from scratch in a new city even more difficult. All of this came pouring out in run-on sentences, punctuated with heaving sobs.

Amy knew from experience how Carla felt. She also knew there was nothing she could say to make her feel better in that moment. There would be time for talk later but not while the tears flowed and the hormones wreaked havoc on Carla's emotions. Instead of saying something meaningless, Amy scooted across the couch next to Carla. Carla collapsed into Amy's arms, and they sat there rocking back and forth until Carla's tears were spent, and Amy's arms were tired.

After Amy left her house, Carla was mortified she had revealed so much of herself to someone she hardly knew. Yet, Amy proved to be a faithful friend and never shared the details of Carla's struggle with anyone else.

Several years later when Nick divorced Carla, Amy was Carla's lifeline during the legal proceedings and negotiations for joint custody of the boys. When Nick remarried a few weeks after the divorce was final, Carla came to stay with Amy and her family the first three nights the boys were with Nick and his new wife. Amy worried that Carla was on the verge of a breakdown, but after the third night, Carla came out of her funk and said she was ready to get on with her life.

To help her recover from the shock of the divorce, Amy encouraged Carla to start getting more involved at South Barkley. Carla took her advice and channeled her pain into an almost obsessive level of volunteerism, often doing the work of an entire committee by herself. Amy believed Carla could accomplish anything she set her mind to, but she also saw how the combination of Carla's good looks and aggressive personality could intimidate weaker, less attractive women. Carla loved getting things done more than she loved being part of a team, and she wasn't afraid to run over anyone who got in her way. Amy coached Carla to dial back her assertiveness so she wouldn't alienate every other woman at South Barkley, without much success. When Carla finally grew bored with church work and got her real estate license, she redirected her energy into getting deals done, and everyone, including Amy, was relieved.

In all their time together, Carla had never before challenged Amy's leadership. Though Amy always defended Carla and asked others to give her the benefit of the doubt, she could hardly blame the many women at South Barkley who didn't like working with her. From the beginning, Amy had realized that if Carla exercised too much public leadership of The Deborah Club, it would keep more women from joining. She had been careful not to give Carla too much airtime at the meetings. She never dreamed Carla would hijack one.

Amy heard Carla say something and snapped to attention. "What was that?" she asked.

Carla continued to wipe the counter with a damp cloth and repeated, "That Jane is a character, isn't she?"

"She sure is," Helen said. She tied the plastic drawstrings on a trash bag into a perfect knot. "I thought we were in big trouble for a few minutes. Carla, I'm sure glad you jumped in when you did. Amy, how do you think it went?"

"Huh?" Amy said, still not fully dialed into the conversation.

"How do you think the meeting went?"

"Okay, I guess. I was a little disappointed with Jane," Amy said.

"Jane's harmless," Carla said. "She just likes to talk, which is funny considering how she doesn't want anyone else to."

"Isn't that the truth," Helen said.

"I don't know," Amy said. "I'm worried she might cause trouble for us later on."

"She's fine. Don't worry about her," Carla said.

Amy frowned and shook her head. "I wish I had pushed her a little harder for a commitment. She could be a powerful ally. We need older women to join us." Amy looked up from the floor and directly at Carla. "I think I could have won her over if you hadn't interrupted me."

"Were you not paying attention?" Carla asked. "She's going to sit there on Sunday mornings and do nothing, just like the rest of us. We don't need her endorsement. She's not that influential. Most people think she's a grumpy old lady."

"I wish you had let me finish the meeting," Amy said. She didn't like sounding so whiny. She slowed down and lowered her tone. "I just don't think we ended on a high note like we have at the other meetings."

"What more do you want, Amy?" Carla asked. "Everyone except Jane signed their name. It's all good."

"You're right," Amy said. "I guess I just thought I was in charge of the discussion part of the meeting, and I didn't get to wrap it up the way I had planned."

Carla stopped her cleaning and put her hands on her hips. "I'm sorry if you feel like I messed up your meeting. I was trying to rescue you from an endless back and forth with Jane. You were so obsessed with debating her that you didn't realize the other ladies were getting restless."

"I noticed, and I didn't need to be rescued," Amy said. "I was going to get Jane on board and then move on."

"Well, it wasn't working," Carla said. "And it looked to me like you needed some help. That's why I jumped in."

Amy crossed her arms and said, "Well, I didn't need your help. Next time, please trust that I know how to run a meeting."

Carla grabbed the washcloth from the counter and threw it in the sink. "Next time, please don't force the group to sit through a one-on-one conversation between you and someone who doesn't even matter."

"Okay, that does it for the dishes," Helen said. She timed her interruption perfectly, before Amy could speak again. "Do you two want another cup of coffee?"

"No thanks," Amy said. "I need to get going."

"Me too," Carla said.

"We have another meeting at Carla's house next Saturday," Helen said. "Do we need to get together before then?"

"I don't think so," Amy said.

"Me either," Carla said. "I'll see you all on Saturday."

Amy disappeared into the bathroom, and Carla gathered her things and left. A few minutes later, Helen walked Amy to her car.

"That was awkward," Amy said. "I can't believe Carla did that."

Helen said, "Amy, you may not be able to see it right now, but trust me, Carla did you a favor. You were about to let Jane ruin that meeting."

"I don't know," Amy said. "I'm disappointed in the way I handled the whole thing."

Helen gently placed her hand on Amy's back and said, "Don't take it out on Carla."

"I'll talk to her."

"Don't talk. Text. That's the best way to say you're sorry these days."

"You're right," Amy said. "That's how Tom apologizes to me."

On the way home, Amy texted Carla.

Amy: I'm sorry about today.

Carla: It's okay. Jane is a piece of work.

Amy: I don't mean Jane. I mean what happened in the kitchen.

Carla: No worries. I was just trying to help.

Amy: The next meeting will be better. I'll be better. I promise.

Carla: I'll hold you to that! :-)

I bet you will, Amy thought. I have to be better. If I'm not, you'll take The Deborah Club away from me.

Chapter 11

AFTER ONLY FOUR meetings, The Deborah Club membership roll boasted thirty-nine names. Jane would have made it a perfect forty. The next day, sitting in her office and getting nothing done, part of Amy still felt like she had let one get away. Another part of her was still trying to come to terms with Carla's intervention. Yes, Amy had apologized, and yes, Carla had accepted. But why hadn't Carla offered an apology in return? She wasn't without fault, especially in the way she responded when Amy confronted her after the meeting. While Carla may have done the right thing and kept Amy from wasting everyone's precious time, she hadn't necessarily done it in the right way, and who knew what Carla had been thinking while she was doing it. Maybe Helen was right, and Carla was just trying to be helpful. But maybe Carla had intentionally undermined her leadership. Amy couldn't be sure, and it was ruining her day. She wasn't paying attention during meetings, and she couldn't make herself do anything productive at her desk.

She was always reminding her daughter that giving others the benefit of the doubt was the Christian thing to do. Now she was reminding herself not to let her Christian virtue be the first casualty in their revolution.

Easier said than done, especially if you want to win, Amy thought. She knew Carla was every bit as competitive as she was.

But Carla wasn't her opponent. She was a teammate--a strong teammate who obviously wasn't going to put up with any signs of weakness from her leader.

Don't forget who the real enemy is or you'll lose, she told herself.

To put her mind at ease, she needed to make sure they were still on the same team. She sent Carla another text.

Amy: Thanks again for your leadership in the meeting yesterday.

Carla: Ur welcome.

Amy: I definitely couldn't have handled Jane without you.

Carla: We make a good team.

Amy: Sorry I wasn't more appreciative yesterday.

Carla: It's all good.

Amy: And I'm sorry for getting snippy.

Carla: No worries! Let's get back to work.

Feeling a little better, Amy used the rest of the morning to clear her Inbox and check off a few low-priority items on her to-do list that she'd been putting off since launching The Deborah Club. Instead of going out for lunch, Amy closed her office door and revised the letter to the elders one last time.

After nearly forty women had read the letter and offered feedback, the language had been toned down in a few places and most of the sarcastic quotation marks had been deleted, but the basic demands and the deadline remained untouched.

Reading back over it again, Amy didn't see the need to wait for twenty-five more women to join The Deborah Club before sending it. It was ready to go now. They were going to hit their target of sixty-five women with no problem, and she was so tired of waiting. She was anxious to confront the elders and see how they would respond. While she didn't expect them to roll over as soon as they read the letter, she also didn't expect the catastrophic results Craig, the prophet of doom and gloom, had predicted. She envisioned a tense, but productive, conversation leading to meaningful change. Finally.

The more she thought about it, the more sense it made to go ahead and send the letter on to the elders. That way she would already be in the process of setting up a meeting with them when they achieved critical mass. She considered running it by Carla and Helen first but talked herself out of it. She didn't need their approval. Sometimes leaders have to take a risk based on a gut feeling. Her gut was telling her to send the letter. So she did.

Rather than send it to all of the elders, whose email addresses she did not feel like tracking down, she sent it only to Ellis Monroe, chair of the elder board. She wasn't sure what his job as chair included, but today it afforded him the distinct honor of being the first elder to read her letter.

Subject: A Letter From The Deborah Club
Dear Ellis:
I have attached a letter from a group of concerned women at South Barkley. I think it will speak for itself. I look forward to your response.
In Christ,
Amy Brandt (For The Deborah Club)

An hour later, Ellis replied to her email.

Dear Amy:
I have read your letter several times. I would really like to talk with you about it before I show it to the other elders. Can I call you later today, perhaps around four?
In Christ,
Ellis

Amy didn't give her response to Ellis's email much thought. She let her gut lead the way.

Dear Ellis,
I appreciate your desire to visit with me about the letter, but I have a meeting then and can't do a phone call. I'm also not sure a conversation is necessary. I'm guessing your intention is to talk me out of sending it to the other elders. While I respect your desire to keep the peace, I am unwilling to reconsider our position in the letter. If you are

not willing to send the letter to the other elders as is, I will be more than
happy to send it on to them directly.
    Thank You,
    Amy

Ellis wrote back a few minutes later.

    Amy,
    I forwarded your letter to the other elders. I will let you know
when we have an official response. It will take several days, I'm sure.
    Regretfully,
    Ellis

Amy wrote a quick email to Carla and Helen explaining why she decided to send the letter on to Ellis. While she apologized for not consulting with them first, she also emphasized how the timing seemed right to her. Momentum was on their side, and she was simply expediting the inevitable showdown with the elders. Remembering the old adage about how it is easier to get forgiveness than permission, she closed her email by offering a second apology for not including them in the decision.

She took a moment to read aloud what she had written and didn't like the tone. She came off sounding weak, almost afraid. She had apologized enough in the last twenty-four hours, maybe too much. She deleted the email. She'd reveal her plans when she had more information to share. It felt good to be in the driver's seat again, taking action and making things happen, just like good leaders are supposed to do.

Chapter 12

Amy kept her promise to Carla to do a better job at their next meeting, a Saturday brunch at Carla's house. Helen got commitments from nine women, and they had plenty of questions. As they worked their way down the list from the most obvious leaders to the more reticent, the concentration of peacekeepers in each meeting was increasing. Several expressed serious reservations about the proposed strategy. Amy was at the top of her game. Carla nodded as Amy answered each question with patience and insight. All nine agreed to participate.

As everyone else was leaving, one of the women, Mary Tasker, circled back around to Amy and said, "I didn't want to mention it during the meeting, but I heard you say Joan is on the steering team or whatever you called it."

"That's right," Amy said.

"Okay, good. There's probably nothing to it then if she's on board," Mary said.

"Nothing to what?" Amy asked. She hoped what came next wasn't about to ruin her post-meeting high.

"My sister attends the big community church over by the High School, and she told me she saw Joan and her family there on Sunday. She said she went over to say hi, and Joan said they were just visiting. I was afraid they were changing churches, but that doesn't make sense if she's helping with this."

"No, it doesn't make sense," Amy said. "It was probably for a special event."

"I hadn't seen them at church for a couple of weeks, so I was just wondering," Mary said.

Amy faked a smile. "Thanks, Mary. I know Joan will be glad to hear she was missed." She walked Mary to the door and then came back to Carla and Helen with the scuttlebutt.

"Call her right now," Carla said.

Amy called and left a message.

"We should go see her," Helen said.

"Let's not overreact," Amy said. "I'm sure there's a good reason why they were there."

"Maybe," Carla said. "But is there a good reason why she's too busy to ever be here?"

"I'm not worried," Amy lied. "I'll text her right now."

Amy: I heard you all were at Oak Grove Community Church on Sunday.

It took a few minutes longer than usual, but Joan finally replied.

Joan: Yes, we were there.
Amy: Special event?

Joan: Not really. Just visiting.

Amy: Why?

Joan: Because it's not far from our house, and we've always wanted to check it out.

Amy: Now? We're in the middle of something.

Joan: You're in the middle of something.

Amy: Give me a call. We obviously need to talk.

Joan: I don't want to get into it over the phone. I'll send you an email later.

Amy: Email? Later? Let's talk now. Want me to come over?

Joan: No. Busy.

Joan: Email. Later.

Joan: Sorry.

Carla handed Amy's phone back to her after reading the texts. "I knew she was avoiding us."

"Do you think it's because of The Deborah Club?" Helen asked.

"What else could it be?" Carla said. "She's afraid to take a stand."

"No way," Amy said. "She's not afraid. Let's wait to hear what she has to say instead of speculating about her motives. She deserves the benefit of the doubt."

"When do you expect her email?" Helen asked.

"It doesn't matter," Carla said. "She's out."

"I'm not sure she was ever in," Helen said.

"Of course she was," Amy said. "She's one of us."

⊷═◉ ◉═⊷

Amy stopped by the grocery store on her way home. She sat the bags on the kitchen counter and walked into the living room to turn on the TV. She wanted to catch up on the news while she put the groceries away. On her way back to the kitchen, she saw her laptop sitting on the coffee table. She couldn't resist the urge. When she saw Joan's email in her Inbox, she decided the groceries could wait.

Amy--I know you're going to hate me for doing this over email. But right now I'm not up for a face-to-face meeting. So please forgive me.

We're going to leave South Barkley. We're not sure where we're going yet, but it will probably be the Oak Grove Community Church. This has been a long time in coming. Blake has been struggling at South Barkley for a while now. He doesn't want to come on Sunday mornings, and he's not engaged when he's there. He says it's boring, and he'd rather be anywhere else. Mike has felt the same way for years, but he's kept coming for the boys and me. With Wilson out of the house and Blake wavering, Mike is having a hard time forcing Blake to go to a church he doesn't like either. Wilson has already told us he wants to go to a different church when he comes back from college in the summer.

It breaks my heart when I think about how the three most important men in my life don't want to come with me to the church I love. I wish I could change the way they feel, but I can't. So I've decided to see if a change of scenery will do them some good.

Mike and Blake seem to really like Oak Grove. They say it's exciting. I don't get it. The auditorium is too dark, the music is too loud, and the pastor's sermons are a mix of stand-up comedy and Dr. Phil-like advice. He talks a lot about how to "man up and lead your *family." I can't stand it, but my men love it. At this point in their lives, they need to love their church more than I do. I want my boys to see their dad going to church. Their dad needs encouragement to be a spiritual example for his sons. There is only so much I can do for them. We only have a few years left with Blake. I hope it's not too late for Wilson. I'm going to "take one for the team," as Mike likes to say, and go with them to Oak Grove. I'll miss you and Helen. Feel free to share this email with them.*

Love you,

Joan

Amy hit the "reply" button and started typing.

Joan--Is this really why you all are leaving? You've never mentioned Mike's dissatisfaction with the church before. I had no idea Blake was struggling at South Barkley. Wilson always seemed happy here. I sense there is something else you're not telling me. Let's get together and talk. I promise I won't try to talk you out of leaving. I just want to get the whole story. Can I come over to the house later today?

Amy

She finished putting away the groceries and did a few household chores. After completing each one, she stopped to check her email.

Amy and Joan had been friends for twenty years. They met in the young professionals class at South Barkley when they were both fresh out of college. Amy was an account manager at the bank by the mall, and Joan was just starting as a nurse at the hospital downtown. Before South Barkley stopped having evening services, they would go out to dinner after church on Sunday nights. Sometimes they celebrated being single. Sometimes they wondered if they would ever meet a guy they could see themselves marrying.

They went on several double dates with their future husbands, but the men never hit it off. Once they settled into married life, Amy and Joan's friendship was curtailed to seeing each other at church and getting together for lunch several times a year. This would have been the extent of their interaction had they not gotten pregnant within a few months of each other.

The shared experience of pregnancy connected them like an umbilical cord for the next eighteen years. Shopping for maternity clothes, decorating the babies' rooms, breastfeeding their newborns in the nursing mothers' room--they did it all together. Amy had a girl and Joan a boy. They joked about how fun it would be if their kids grew up and fell in love with each other.

Amy's daughter, Amanda, and Joan's son, Wilson, played together when they were toddlers. But Wilson eventually figured out Amanda wasn't a boy and didn't like to play with guns, and Amanda couldn't understand why Wilson no longer wanted to play dress up with her. So the weekly play date, which was nothing more than an excuse for Amy and Joan to see each other, fell off the calendar.

Joan had a second son, Blake, three years later, but Amy was done after one. Helen had her first daughter a few months after Blake was born, and another friendship was formed in the nursing mothers' room. Amy and Joan remained good friends, talking on the phone several times a week. Amy and Helen got to know each other through Joan. When their children were little, their primary place of interaction was at church where they all volunteered in children's ministry, teaching classes and helping with special events like Vacation Bible School.

Amy's husband, Tom, dubbed them the "Three Amigos." When Amy corrected him and said it should be "amigas," he said it didn't sound right and continued to call them amigos. The name stuck, and that was how their little group was known around the South Barkley Bible Church.

When Helen's youngest daughter entered kindergarten, they met for lunch once a week, except in the summer. Over the years, they moved their meetings around to different days, times, and restaurants to accommodate their increasingly chaotic work and family schedules. At Joan's request, they had recently shifted to a mid-morning coffee on Fridays, which sometimes bled into an early lunch. It was not a convenient time for Amy--she always had a stack of paperwork to finish by the end of the week--but she made it work. She would never give up meeting with her amigos.

Joan finally replied almost two hours later.

> *Amy--Please don't make this harder for me than it already is. Once things settle down a bit, maybe we can get together and talk. For now, please let me move on in peace.*
> *Joan*

"No freaking way," Amy said to her empty living room. She stabbed at her keyboard with angry fingers.

The lines of friendship drawn between the amigos varied in weight. Amy and Joan were closest, as they had known each other the longest. Helen felt more connected to Joan, but if Joan couldn't make a meeting, Helen and Amy got along just fine. Amy liked Helen. Everyone liked Helen. She was reliable. If she said she was going be somewhere at a certain time or if she said she was going to take care of a key detail on a project, you didn't have to worry about her following through.

After her divorce, Amy invited Carla to join the group whenever they got together. Helen and Joan weren't crazy about adding another person to the group, but they went along with it as more of a favor to Amy than out of sympathy for Carla. Though she was included in everything they did, Carla would never achieve "amigo" status in their eyes. No matter how much time Amy spent mentoring Carla-- though Carla would never describe their relationship this way--Joan would always be Amy's best friend. They knew each other's secrets.

Amy had walked alongside Joan through her bouts of depression. Joan had been there to console Amy when she found out she couldn't have any more children. Amy had talked Joan out of having an affair with a doctor she worked with at the hospital. Joan knew about Amy's wild stage during college.

Amy thought of Joan as more of a sister than a friend. She was sure Joan felt the same way. Sisters didn't have to sit together at every potluck or agree with each other on how to parent or how to vote. The bond between them wasn't the result of mathematical calculation: time spent together divided by secrets known. They had moved beyond math and science, inputs and outputs. They loved each other. They couldn't stop being friends any more than siblings could stop being family. That Joan would even consider leaving South Barkley while The Deborah Club was building steam left Amy dumbfounded. It felt like a violation of their sisterhood.

Joan could send all the vague emails she wanted, but they weren't going to be enough. Amy wouldn't settle for anything less than sitting down with Joan over a cup of coffee and getting to the bottom of what was really going on. Once they talked it out, everything would be fine. Just like always.

> *No way Joan. This is unacceptable. We've been friends for too long and have been through too much together for you to leave like this. WHAT IS GOING ON?*
> *Amy*

She fired off her email without taking the time to go back and read what she'd written. If she had, she might have softened her tone some, but not much. Amy had never worried about offending Joan in the past. No need to hold back now.

Joan responded to Amy's email in the worst way imaginable. She didn't. Amy checked her email obsessively throughout the rest of the evening. Just before midnight, she checked one more time before going to bed. It was a mistake she would regret for the rest of her sleepless night.

> *Amy--I can see you're not going to let this go, so I'm going to tell you the truth. I guess you deserve it. While Mike has never "loved" South Barkley the way I have, he has never expressed a desire to leave until I told him about The Deborah Club and what you all were planning to do with Craig's idea. His exact words were, "That's just what we need, another church taken over by women. You can tell your friends they can count us out." I knew this is how Mike would react*

when I first heard the idea. That's why I wasn't thrilled with it at Starbucks and why I dodged all the meetings when you all were getting organized.

Don't worry, I didn't tell him it was Craig's idea. Not that Mike cares. He's never been Craig's biggest fan, but he wouldn't go after Craig's job. He'd rather leave than cause trouble. I guess I would too.

Amy, as bad as you think the status quo at South Barkley is, have you considered how this boycott or strike or whatever you're calling it may end up only making things worse? Isn't this why Craig came to meet us at Starbucks that day? He knows the damage this idea can cause. I honestly can't believe you're going to ignore his wishes and go through with this. Have you really thought through where this might lead? I know you've been holding luncheons and drumming up support from women who are ready to stick it to the men in our church. Do any of them see the big picture? Do you? What if other families leave? What if it destroys the church? Are you willing to tear our church apart just to see your will be done?

Amy, is The Deborah Club really about setting women free, or is it about you being in charge of something? Are you sure this is something God wants you to do? I'm asking you as your friend and as your sister in Christ. Have you been praying about this? What is God saying to you? I've been praying, Amy. I've been praying for you and for the church, and I've been asking God for clarity. As I pray and listen, I hear God saying The Deborah Club is a terrible idea. Even if you win and the women at South Barkley are free to pray and preach and do whatever else men get to do, there will be nothing to celebrate because of the way you're choosing to fight the battle. I'm sorry, Amy, but I can't be part of it. So, since you asked, this is why we're leaving.

Now please stop asking me to meet with you. Perhaps your time would be better spent meeting with God in prayer.
In Christ,
Joan

Amy closed her laptop and cried. Hard. She cried tears of pain first, then tears of disappointment, and finally tears of anger. Joan's words hurt her as much as anything anyone had ever said to her. She couldn't believe Joan hadn't shared her misgivings at the beginning. More than that, her best friend was abandoning her in the middle of a fight. Carla was right. Joan was a coward and couldn't be counted on. She wasn't cut out to be a founding member of The Deborah Club. They would be better off without her.

Amy kept telling herself this throughout the night. But no matter how much she rationalized why it was good for Joan and her family to leave, she kept coming back to the stinging realization that Joan wasn't rejecting Craig's idea, or the other members of The Deborah club, or even the men leading the church. Joan was rejecting her. Joan didn't trust her enough to follow her. As much as Amy tried to make Joan's email about Joan, she knew it was really about her. This haunted her throughout the night and into the early hours of Sunday morning when she finally fell asleep just after 5 a.m.

Amy was still angry with Joan when she awoke three hours later, but she was also mad at herself. How could she have been so blind? Joan had been avoiding her for weeks. On some level, Amy had known something wasn't right, but she kept denying it and using their busyness as an excuse.

She needed to get out of bed and start getting ready for church, but church was the last place she wanted to be. She wondered what the ladies who had already put their trust in her would think about her leadership skills when they learned of Joan's departure. She couldn't stand the thought of seeing them this morning. She wouldn't be able to look them in the eye. How could she possibly keep recruiting other women to join The Deborah Club when she couldn't even keep her best friend on board? Who did she think she was, trying to lead others to freedom?

She heard Tom rattling pans in the kitchen. She called out to him. He appeared in their bedroom door a moment later.

"Yeah, hon. You almost ready for breakfast?"

"I don't have much of an appetite. Sorry."

"You tossed and turned all night. Something bothering you?"

"No. I'm just not feeling well."

"Are you sick?"

"I think so." She wasn't lying.

"No church today?"

"You can go if you want." She hoped he would. She needed to be alone.

"I'll stay here and take care of you."

There's nothing you or anyone else can do for me right now, she thought. "I'll be okay," she said. "I need to sleep it off."

Chapter 13

AMY SLEPT THROUGH lunch and finally forced herself out of bed at 1:16 p.m. She couldn't remember the last time she had slept into the afternoon. She turned on her phone, and it dinged repeatedly as texts Carla and Helen had sent throughout the morning were delivered.

> Carla: Where are you?
> Helen: Didn't see you at church today. Everything okay?
> Helen: BTW did you hear back from Joan?
> Carla: Call me when you can.
> Carla: Hello?
> Carla: You better respond soon, or I'm coming over.

Amy wasn't ready for a conversation, either by phone or face-to-face. She hoped to buy herself some time with a group text.

> Amy: I wasn't feeling well this morning. Skipped church. How was it?

Carla: We were all looking for you. Let us know next time, will ya?

Helen: Sorry you're not feeling well. Did you hear back from Joan? I didn't see them there today.

Amy: I did. I'll forward you her email.

Carla: What's the deal?

Amy: Check your email in a few minutes.

Amy had no intention of sending them Joan's final email. She didn't want them to see Joan's assessment of her leadership. She forwarded them Joan's first email instead--the one in which she blamed their decision to leave South Barkley on the men in her family--and hoped it satisfied their curiosity.

To further distract them, she confessed to sending the letter to the elders without first consulting them. In between two apologies, she sandwiched how confident she was that the elders would be ready to make a deal when they learned almost fifty women had already joined The Deborah Club. She encouraged them to keep their heads up and not let Joan's email get them down. They were too close to their goal to give up. She was overselling, and she knew it, but it was more for her benefit than theirs.

After eating a bacon and egg sandwich for lunch, Amy checked her email and found Carla and Helen discussing Joan's email. They were going back and forth in short, one or two sentence messages as if they were sending texts instead of emails.

> *I don't buy it. I think there's something more going on here.*
> *Helen*

I agree, but there's nothing we can do about it now. You can follow up with her if you want to, but I'm not going to worry about it.

Carla

I think we need to go over to her house and see her. That's what I would want you all to do for me.

Helen

So you would want us to stalk you if we didn't think you were telling the truth?

Carla

No. Not stalk, but I'd want you to show me how much you care.

Helen

Like she showed us how much she cared when she started visiting other churches without telling us?

Carla

I'm sure there's a good reason. I've tried to call her several times, but she's not answering or returning my calls.

Helen

There you go. She obviously doesn't want to talk about it. It's time to move on. We have work to do.

Carla

I can't just write her off. I won't. I need answers!
Helen

Amy decided it was time to jump into the conversation and do some damage control.

Good grief! You two have filled up my Inbox. Switching to text.
Amy

Amy: Helen, I know you want answers. So do I. I begged Joan to sit down with me.

Amy: She refused.

Carla: Time to move on.

Helen: I'll get through to her. She owes me one conversation at least.

Carla: Suit yourself.

Helen: What are we going to tell the others? They'll keep asking about her.

Carla: We'll blame it on the men. Just like she did. If anyone wants to know more, they can talk to her directly.

Amy: Joan asked that we not send anyone to her.

Amy: She doesn't want to keep explaining things over and over.

Carla: Sounds good to me.

Helen: I think it should be hard to leave a church. Especially when you've been at one as long as Joan has.

Amy: I don't disagree, but we have to respect Joan's wishes. She wants to be left alone.

Carla: Sounds good to me.

Helen: I'm not giving up.

Carla: On to more important business. Amy! What were you thinking?

Amy: About what?

Carla: Sending the letter to the elders without us.

Amy: I'm sorry. Are you mad?

Carla: A little, but I'll forgive you. Again.

Helen: I trust your judgment.

Carla: Have the elders responded?

Amy: Not yet. Ellis said it would take several days.

Carla: Let us know when you hear from them.

Amy: Of course.

Chapter 14

LATER THAT NIGHT, Amy and Tom were watching a movie on Netflix in their living room. They had been watching Sunday Night Football, but the game was a blowout, and they decided it wasn't too late to start a movie. Since she had slept most of the day, Amy was wide-awake.

She felt her phone vibrating on the couch next to her. She checked the number and thought she recognized it. She took a deep breath and answered.

"Hi Amy. It's Ellis. Do you have a minute to visit?"

Amy muted the volume on the TV. "Sure."

"Good. Thanks. I wanted to touch base with you at church today but didn't see you."

"I wasn't feeling well, but I'm better now."

"Glad to hear it. Listen, I'm calling because the elders met tonight to talk about your letter. We had quite a conversation."

Amy smiled. "I can only imagine."

Tom mouthed the words, "Who is it?"

Amy waved him off, threw the remote control into his lap, and left the room.

Ellis said, "As you know, the elders have been exploring the best way to expand leadership roles for women at South Barkley for some time."

"Of course I know that," Amy said. She walked through her bedroom and into the master bathroom. "You all have been saying it for years."

"You also know what a volatile issue this is for churches," Ellis said. "Some congregations have mishandled it and cut their membership in half. We don't want to make the same mistake."

"Is it ever a mistake to do the right thing?" Amy asked.

"It is if you do it at the wrong time."

"Some changes are too important to keep postponing." She stepped into the large closet adjoining the bathroom, as far from Tom as possible.

"Postponing," Ellis said. "You used that word in your letter. We don't think it's an accurate description of what we're doing."

Amy adjusted the hangers on the closet rack so they were equally spaced. "What would you call it?"

"We think it's better described as the incremental implementation of disruptive change. We know the process seems painfully slow to you, but we envision this change as a glacier--a slow moving force, which, over time, can move a mountain."

"What if your glacier melts before anything moves?" Amy said.

"It's not melting, Amy. It's just not moving as fast as you want it to."

"That's right," she said. "It's moving too slow to do any good. I think it's time for lightening to strike our old, slow moving glacier and start an avalanche."

"Avalanches bury people, Amy," Ellis said.

"Ellis, half of our church's talents are already buried."

"Not half," Ellis said. "There are plenty of women who are happy with the way things are."

"Do you have a list of their names, Ellis? Because I have a pretty long list of women who are ready for things to change."

"We both want the same outcome."

"Do we? Are you sure about that?"

"I am. We just have different strategies. But if we can get on the same page and work together, I think we can make some progress, though it probably won't be as much as you're hoping for. We still have to be careful, but it could still be more than we've made up to this point."

"So you're willing to negotiate?"

"I don't like the word negotiate," Ellis said. "Sounds unseemly. But I will say there's room for compromise."

"Okay," Amy said. "You go first." She wondered if it was really going to be this easy.

"I didn't call to make a deal with you, Amy. I called to invite you to a special elders' meeting on Tuesday night."

"So we can negotiate?" She used the word intentionally.

"So we can listen to each other and find a way to move forward without blowing up the church."

Amy sighed and examined the frayed cuff on one of Tom's shirts. "Ellis, when you talk about the church blowing up, you make it sound like it's a stick of old dynamite. Is our church really so fragile?"

"Old dynamite is quite unstable, and yes, it will blow up if it's not handled with care," Ellis said. "At least that's what happens on TV, but I don't think that's the right analogy."

"What is?"

"I think it's more accurate to say you've walked into a dynamite factory with a box of matches."

"Now you're being overly dramatic, Ellis," Amy said. "No one is going to blow up anything. There is a peaceful way through this." So long as the elders give us what we want, she thought.

"I'm glad to hear you say that. See you on Tuesday at seven."

"I'll be there. Anything else I should know?"

"Not that I can think of. Will anyone else be coming with you?" Ellis asked.

"I'm not sure," Amy said. "Do I need to bring back-up?"

Ellis laughed. "Hardly. Have a good night, Amy."

"Good night, Ellis, and thank you."

Amy slipped her phone into her pocket and stepped back into the bathroom. She looked at herself in the mirror and replayed the conversation in her head. She had always liked Ellis. He had a good heart, and she believed he meant well, but he was naive to think a few minor concessions would satisfy The Deborah Club.

She decided she didn't like the image of a lightening strike turning the elders' glacier into an avalanche. Lightening strikes are random and uncontrollable. Ellis was right. Dynamite was the better analogy. She doubted the elders appreciated how ready and willing she was to light the fuse if they didn't do the right thing.

She felt her spirits lift, and she smiled at herself in the mirror. Her conversation with Ellis had taken her mind off of Joan. Now that her attention had returned to her former best friend, there was, intermingled with her anger, a trace of pity. Poor Joan had lost her nerve just when things were getting good, and now she was going to miss out on all the fun.

Chapter 15

FOR THE SECOND night in a row, Amy didn't get much sleep, but this time it wasn't the heartache of being betrayed by a friend that kept her awake. Her conversation with Ellis had banished the twin demons of self-doubt and defensive rationalization into the abyss. She was on the brink of accomplishing her goal, and it charged her with the energy. She couldn't wait to meet with the elders.

From the beginning, she believed the elders would cave when forced to choose between doing the right thing and having the hardest workers in the church go on strike. She knew they wouldn't give in easily. They couldn't. But once they saw her resolve and understood how far she--how far The Deborah Club--was willing to go to break the chains of injustice, she expected them to relent. How could they do otherwise?

She remembered one of Dr. King's famous lines. Something like, "The moral arc of the universe is long, but it bends toward justice." Yes, that is what was happening at South Barkley. The arc of the universe was bending toward justice. But it wasn't bending by itself, was it? It was being bent. Bent by God, of course, but God was also using a specific person to do the bending. What a privilege it was to be chosen for such a momentous task.

The slow moving sun tested her patience. She was ready to get her day started. There was still so much to do. So many decisions to be made. Who would she take to the meeting with her? Not Carla. She talked too much, and if she didn't like the way the meeting was going, she might try to take over. Certainly not Helen. She was too much of a peacekeeper to follow through. She would melt at the first sign of resistance. Amy needed someone she could trust-- someone who would support her and follow her lead. Someone like Joan. But not Joan. Never again Joan.

She would have to go alone. It was the only way. The elders needed to hear The Deborah Club speak in a unified voice. This would only be possible if hers was the only voice they heard. She would wait and tell Carla and Helen about the meeting after their victory was already assured. How could they be angry and celebrate good news at the same time?

Chapter 16

THE BANK WAS closed on Columbus Day so the pile of paperwork Amy had put off on Friday was waiting for her when she sat down at her desk on Tuesday morning. She moved it to the side and promised herself she'd get to it that afternoon. She was surprised at how quickly the morning passed thanks to a long conference call and an unscheduled conversation with a potential client. When it was time to dig into the paperwork after lunch, she found the minutia in front of her unworthy of her attention. She needed to be preparing for one of the most important meetings of her life. By mid-afternoon, she was starting to feel the butterflies in her stomach.

While she was no stranger to meetings--attending, leading, and skipping them whenever possible was a way of life for her-- she had absolutely no idea what to expect at the elders' meeting. She had never been to one. Very few women at South Barkley had. She imagined a bunch of grumpy old men, wearing loose ties and wrinkled shirts with rolled up sleeves, huddled conspiratorially around a conference table in a smoke-filled room while plotting their next move to expand the borders of their empire.

She knew this was a wildly inaccurate, silly image. To her knowledge, none of the elders smoked, and most of them didn't wear suits or ties to work. Deep in her heart, she also knew they weren't power hungry despots who loved brainstorming new ways to squash their opposition. As individuals, they were all good, decent men with strong convictions who loved the Lord and wanted to do the right thing. But when they gathered as a group, they morphed into a band of hand wringers, prizing peace over progress. She planned to use their desire to keep the peace to her advantage. Once they realized how disruptive a strike would be, they would do the right thing. They had to.

She sat back in her chair, closed her eyes, and tried to visualize how the meeting would go. They would welcome her into the smoke-filled room. Why couldn't she shake that image? She would take her seat, and they would thank her for coming. Then they would spend some time in prayer asking for wisdom and guidance. After praying together, they would ask her to reconsider moving forward with the strike. She would smile and politely decline their request. They would ask how many other women were part of The Deborah Club. She would produce a list of names. The elders would be unsuccessful in masking their surprise. They would ask if she would be willing to extend the deadline by a few months to give them more time to pray and discern what to do next. She would smile pleasantly and tell them the time for discernment had passed. She would call them to action. After a few seconds of silence, one of them, maybe Ellis, would call for a vote. They would go around the table, and each man would express his regret for dragging his feet and agree it was finally time to set the women of South Barkley free. The vote would be unanimous. They would declare that from this moment forward, the women of South Barkley were empowered to serve in all leadership roles in the church with no exceptions. They would ask Amy to help them craft an announcement to be made at church the next Sunday. She would agree and volunteer the services of Carla and Helen to help. Ellis would be appointed to write the first draft and then email the rest of the group for feedback. They would close the meeting with a prayer and group hug. They would leave the room together—unified, equal and ready to get to work.

It was a compelling vision of things to come. It was so rich and vivid in detail that she wondered if it might be a gift from God, the Holy Spirit's way of setting her mind at ease and infusing her with courage.

Her phone beeped with a text notification. She was surprised to see it was from Craig. He hadn't said a word to her in weeks. She was impressed by how well he had been able to pretend The Deborah Club didn't exist. He seemed to be going along as if it were business as usual, with no hints of what might be coming in his sermons.

Craig: Can you come by my office at 6:30?

Amy: Why?

Craig: To visit about the meeting.

Amy: You're not going to talk me out of it.

Craig: I know. That's not why I want to meet. I want to help.

Amy: Really? I thought you wanted to stay out of it.

Craig: I do. But I would like to prep you for how the meeting will go.

Amy: How do you know how it will go?

Craig: I have been to hundreds of these things. They pretty much all go the same way.
Amy: Will you be there for the meeting?
Craig: Of course.
Amy: Are you going to sabotage me?
Craig: No.
Amy: Good. See you there.
Craig: So no pre-meeting meeting?
Amy: I'll be okay.
Craig: I hope so. Good luck.

So Craig was going to be at the meeting too. She hadn't seen him in her vision of how the meeting would go, probably because his presence was inconsequential. It wasn't his decision to make. He couldn't do any harm as long as he didn't say anything.

She typed a final text to Craig.

Amy: Just keep your mouth shut, and everything will be fine.

She regretted sending it as soon as she hit the button. It was too harsh, even if truthful, and it might provoke him into doing something stupid.

Craig: Will be happy to. Sorry I offered to help. Won't happen again.

Chapter 17

AMY ARRIVED AT the church building at 6:45. Despite her optimism, she was still quite nervous and wanted to give herself plenty of time to settle in before the meeting began. The door to the church library, which doubled as a conference room, was closed. She looked through the square window in the door and saw Craig and Ellis sitting next to each other. The seat to the left of Craig was open. She could hear someone else talking, but she couldn't see the other side of the table from her vantage point. She knocked on the door as she opened it and stepped inside.

Ellis looked up and said, "Sorry, Amy. Can you wait outside for a few minutes?" She apologized and backed out of the room awkwardly. Craig gave her a sympathetic half smile.

She leaned against the wall and waited in the hallway. It hadn't occurred to her that she would be joining a meeting already in progress. She berated herself for barging into the room uninvited. Her nerves had gotten the best of her and made her look like an amateur. And what was with the way Ellis had so quickly dismissed her? Her embarrassment turned to anger. She could hear murmurs on the other side of the wall but couldn't make out what was being said.

At 7:03, she was tempted to knock on the door again and ask if they were ready to begin, but she didn't dare run the risk of being kicked out of the room a second time. Five minutes later, Craig opened the door and invited her in.

The elders were sitting around a rectangular conference table made of cherry wood. It was by far the most expensive, and least used, piece of office furniture the church owned. It looked out of place in a room lined with cheap metal shelves, which were straining under the weight of old, dusty books.

Amy attempted to make eye contact with each elder as she walked in. All but one greeted her with polite smiles. The holdout was Barney Staples. He kept his eyes fixed on a sheet of paper in front of him.

The South Barkley Bible Church had five elders. Over the years, the number had varied from as many as nine, to as few as three. The church's bylaws stipulated that the board must always consist of an odd number of elders. The purpose of this rule was to ensure there would be no ties when voting on controversial issues. While the provision surely made sense to the church founders who authored and approved the bylaws, succeeding generations found it to be cumbersome. Every time an elder resigned, there was a scramble to find another elder to replace him. If a replacement couldn't be found, then a second elder had to step down. Years before, an elder with a sense of humor had moved to change the name of the elder board in the bylaws to "The Ark," since they could only come and go in pairs. His motion got a laugh, but not a second.

"Sorry to keep you waiting, Amy," Ellis said. "We had a few other items on the agenda to discuss."

"That's okay," she said, hiding her irritation with a smile.

An uneasy feeling settled over her as she took the seat next to Craig. This was not how she imagined things would be. When it appeared Ellis was going to launch straight into the conversation, Amy said, "Excuse me, Ellis. Sorry to interrupt. Would you mind if we spent some time in prayer before we begin?"

"No, not at all," Ellis said. "That's a great idea." He looked around the table. "Who would like to lead us?"

Amy didn't give anyone else a chance to respond. "I will," she said. "I was thinking maybe we could go around the room and give everyone a chance to pray."

For the first time since she had entered the room, Barney looked up from his notes. He cleared his throat and said, "Why don't I say one prayer on behalf of everyone, for the sake of time?"

Ellis may have been the chair of the elder board, but Barney was the alpha in the room. When he put his foot down in a meeting, the rest of the group deferred to him. He didn't build consensus. Consensus was built around him.

Everyone in the room, except Amy, automatically bowed their heads. When Barney began to pray, she bowed hers as well.

"Our heavenly Father, it is indeed a mystery why you love us as much as you do. Just like the Israelites in the Old Testament, we are a stiff-necked and hard-hearted people. We get caught up in petty little quests for power and prestige, wanting to make a name for ourselves like those who built the Tower of Babel. We covet things we think will be good for us, but in the end, we only damage the Body of Christ and hinder your church's mission in the world. Please forgive our sins of arrogance and obstinance. Where we disagree, bring us to unity. Where there is conflict, we ask for peace. As we consider what is best for this congregation, please give us the wisdom to know what to do and how to do it and the courage to know when to say yes and when to say no. Help us to love each other, even when we don't see eye to eye. And please protect us from this current attack from Satan, who is trying to destroy the good work your Son is doing through this church. In Jesus name, Amen."

The rest of the elders added their amens. Amy looked around at the others in confusion. Did they just agree with Barney's prayer?

Current attack from Satan?

Was he talking about her?

Ellis said, "I'm not sure how to best launch into this discussion. We have all read Amy's letter, and we've discussed it as a group. Amy and I have had a discussion about it as well. I asked her, for the sake of maintaining the unity of the church, to reconsider her proposal to organize a strike so we can have more time to discern what to do next. She didn't like that idea, and I suggested she meet with the entire group to see if we can come to an understanding for how to move forward peacefully. I'm wondering if--"

Barney cut him off. "It wasn't a proposal. It was a threat."

"Whatever you want to call it, we're here to discuss it and hopefully come to a mutually beneficial resolution," Ellis said.

"I don't like being threatened," Barney said. "Especially when it's an attempt to manipulate the way we oversee the Lord's work. In all my years, I've never heard of something so brazen. Does she really think she can hold this church hostage until she gets her way?

It's ridiculous and divisive. I'm not here to negotiate with a terrorist. I'm here to put an end to this nonsense."

Barney owned a large construction company he inherited from his father. He was used to being in charge and speaking his mind. In his world, there was no one higher up the food chain to settle him down. He was a natural leader with a dominant personality, and he was accustomed to getting his way through the sheer force of will. Some of the elders grumbled behind his back about him not being a team player, but Barney considered himself an excellent team player, as long as the team did things his way.

Ellis held up his hand as if he were a police officer trying to stop traffic. "Now Barney, I don't think it's fair to refer to Amy as a terrorist. That kind of labeling isn't going to get us where we want to go."

"It's alright, Ellis," Amy said. "When you've already been referred to as Satan in a prayer, being called a terrorist feels like a promotion. At least I know where Barney stands." She looked around the table at the others. They were all looking down at the sheets of paper in front of them. "How about the rest of you?"

The other elders looked at each other, ready to defer to the first one foolish enough to clear his throat. Ben Reeves, the newest and youngest of the elders, finally broke the silence. "Amy, I certainly understand why you're frustrated. We're frustrated too. We'd like to move faster, but we're not sure how to do it without dividing the church. While I can sympathize with your desire to get things moving, I don't think this is the best way to do it."

"Fair enough," Amy said. "Do you have a better idea for doing it differently?"

"I guess I'm asking you to trust us and to trust the process," Ben said. "We want the same outcome as you. We just have a different strategy for getting there."

"Trust the process," Amy said, impressed with how well they had all memorized the same script. "I wish it were that easy, but--"

"I don't want what she wants," Barney said. "In the past, I've been open to rethinking what the Bible has to say about women, but this Deborah Club nonsense makes me think Paul had good reason to forbid women to teach. I can certainly see why he told women to be quiet in church. Perhaps the Bible's limitations on women leaders isn't cultural but genetic. If you ask me, this is Exhibit A for why the Bible teaches male spiritual leadership. If she's the best the women of this church have to offer, then God help us." He waved his hand dismissively in Amy's direction. "She's out for her own glory, and it looks to me like she's willing to destroy the church in order to get it."

"That's enough, Barney," Ellis said.

"No, it's not. I'm just getting started."

Barney glared at Amy. "Did you really think this would work? Did you think you could get your way by withholding your service to this church like you get your way at home by withholding sex from your husband?"

"Barney!" Ben shouted.

"Shut up, Ben," Barney growled. "You haven't been an elder long enough to know what you're talking about. Let me handle this."

He turned back to Amy. "There is not going to be a discussion tonight. We're not going to hold hands and pray our way through this. You're not going to walk out of this room in triumph to tell all your lady friends how those stupid old elders finally saw the light. You want to show up and do nothing on Sundays? That's fine. We'll find a way to get along without you. I know for a fact my wife is ready to step up and fill your spot. She's not alone. I've been asking around and not every woman in this church is a part of your Jezebel Club. Rather than causing trouble here, why don't you find a new church where they'll let you do whatever you want? I'll even volunteer to help you look for one. You'll be happier, and our church will be healthier, not to mention more godly, the moment you leave."

"Barney, you are way out of line," Ellis said.

Barney slapped the table, causing everyone to jump. "Do not interrupt me again, Ellis!" He scanned the room, inviting someone else to challenge him. No one dared look him in the eye.

Amy looked around the table and felt the tears welling up within her. Not now. Do not cry right now. She looked over at Craig for support. She hoped he would come to her defense. Maybe even admit the strike had been his idea. He gave her a quick, shameful glance and then looked back down at the sheet of doodle-covered paper in front of him.

She was alone.

She stood up and said, "All this time I thought you were afraid of change. Now I see you're all just afraid of a bully. I'm not the one holding you hostage." Her voice broke, and she took a sharp breath. "He is," she said, pointing at Barney. "He's the only terrorist here."

She wanted to say more, to lash out at them, to call them cowards, to shame them for their behavior, to defend herself, but she knew she couldn't do it without breaking down. She wasn't about to give Barney the satisfaction of seeing her cry.

She turned and forced herself to walk out of the room at a controlled pace, even though everything within her wanted to sprint down the hall in a race against the tears, which were already beginning to flow.

Chapter 18

CRAIG WANTED TO catch up with Amy before she made it to her car, but he was no more successful in lifting himself from his chair than he had been in lifting his eyes from his doodle sheet when Barney was ripping into Amy. Except for the quick glance her way when she was desperately looking for an ally in the room, he had kept his head down.

He wished he hadn't looked at Amy at all. This would have spared him from seeing her bewildered expression as she was ambushed in what she had every right to assume would be a safe environment.

He kept telling himself he hadn't betrayed her. In fact, he had tried to warn her. He knew Amy had no idea what Barney was like behind closed doors in an elders' meeting. He also knew Barney wasn't going to let anyone bully him. Certainly not a woman. Still, Craig was surprised by the ferocity of Barney's personal attack on Amy. He hadn't just disagreed with her idea; he had assaulted her character and humiliated her in front of the other elders.

Craig appreciated how Ben and Ellis tried to intervene, but they were no match for Barney. Ben was too young, and Ellis was too nice. The other two elders played according to character. They typically didn't speak unless it was to weigh in on a trivial decision with nothing at stake--in those instances they were quick to comment. On important issues, they kept their silence and waited to hear Barney's position. They would nod their heads in agreement, as if he were articulating their thoughts word for word. At least this time they hadn't been nodding when Barney eviscerated Amy. They hadn't shaken their heads in disapproval either. Like bystanders who see an assault happening across the street, but don't want to put themselves at risk or be called on to testify at a future trial, they had chosen to look the other way.

After Amy left the room, they all sat in embarrassed silence until Barney said, "Ellis, do we have any more business to discuss?"

Ellis shook his head.

"Well, I guess we're done here," Barney said. "Ellis, do you want to follow up with Amy and see what her plans are now?" He was acting as if this had been just another ordinary meeting on a random Tuesday night.

Craig wanted one of the other elders to confront Barney and tell him how unacceptable his behavior had been. Someone needed to demand he step down as an elder immediately. But he knew it wasn't going to happen. None of them had the backbone to stand up to Barney. It was Craig's move to make. If he didn't man up and say something, Barney would leave this nightmare of a meeting believing he could get away with anything. Just like always.

Craig could feel the moment slipping away. He moistened his lips and said, "I'll talk to her, Ellis." It was all he could bring himself to say. He would later convince himself it hadn't been his place. It wasn't his job to hold Barney accountable for his behavior. It was up to the elders to police each other. He couldn't do it for them. It wouldn't work even if he tried.

"Thanks, Craig," Ellis said.

"By the way," Barney said, "if they do go on strike, my wife is willing to do whatever needs to be done to make sure we can still have church this Sunday. You might visit with your wives and ask them to do the same. I seriously doubt they will go through with it. It's a bluff, I'm sure, but I want to be prepared, just in case."

"My wife will be out of town," Ben said.

"That's okay," Barney said. "We don't need her anyway. I'm sure the other wives can handle it. Shall we pray?"

Barney led a brief closing prayer, after which the leaders of the South Barkley Bible Church scattered into the night without saying a word to each other.

⋆⟶⊙ ⊙⟵⋆

Craig sat in his car in the church parking lot staring at the screen of his phone. Why had he volunteered to reach out to Amy? What was he supposed to say? He was relieved when her phone went straight to voicemail. He didn't blame her for rejecting his call. He hung up without leaving a message and sent her a text instead.

> Craig: I'm sorry.
> Amy: Go to hell.
> Craig: Are u okay?
> Amy: What do you think?
> Craig: I guess not. Can we talk?

Amy: Is your voice working again?
Craig: I deserve that. Can we talk?
Amy: You knew what was coming, didn't you?
Craig: I'm sorry.
Amy: Sorry it happened or sorry you didn't say something.
Craig: I was told to keep my mouth shut, remember?

He couldn't believe he was piling on. *Stupid idiot. Knock it off!*

Amy: You're unbelievable.
Craig: What are you going to do?
Amy: What do you care?
Craig: I'm worried about you.
Amy: Careful. You're already a coward. Don't be a liar too.
Craig: He shouldn't have been allowed to speak to u that way. Someone should have intervened.
Amy: But no one did.
Craig: I'm sorry.
Amy: You know nothing about being sorry. But you will. You all will. I can promise you that.
Craig: What are u going to do?
Amy: You don't want to be a part of the plan, remember? The less you know the better, remember?

Craig stopped texting and called her. Once again, the call went straight to voicemail. Amy texted in response.

Amy: Stop calling me. I don't want to talk to you. And now I'm done texting.

Craig: Ur scaring me. Can we talk, please? I'll stop by the house if u want.

Amy: Don't even think about it. If you do, I'll call the police.

Craig: We really need to talk.

Craig: Amy?

Craig: Please respond.

Craig: Ur not going to hurt yourself are u?

Amy: You're an asshole. Leave me alone.

⋯⋯

Craig's wife was waiting for him at the kitchen table when he walked in from the garage. He dropped his keys on the counter and sighed.

"Where have you been?" she asked.

"Elders' meeting."

"On a Tuesday night?"

"It was a special occasion," he said.

"Dare I ask?"

Craig answered by walking over to the freezer and grabbing a half-gallon of ice cream. He picked out a big spoon from the utensil drawer and joined her at the table.

"Did you want me to get you a bowl?" she said.

"Nope."

"What happened?"

Craig told his wife very little about what happened in elders' meetings, just like he didn't forward her every critical email he received from someone in the church. The less she knew, the better, especially when someone was mad at him. She always took criticism of his work more personally than he did. In his experience, women held grudges longer than men. Grudges were one of the many luxuries a minister and his family couldn't afford. But this time he told her everything. He hoped she could help him reach out to Amy.

"And no one said anything?" she said, when he had finished.

He shook his head, unable to look her in the eye.

"Why didn't you say something?"

"It wasn't my place," he said. "It's not my job to hold elders accountable for not being Christians."

"Actually, I think it is your job," she said. "You should have defended her."

"My hands were tied. If I had tried to help, I think Barney would have punched me. I've never seen him that angry."

"I knew he was powerful," she said. "But I never imagined he could be such a bully. Have you checked on Amy?"

"I tried," he said. "But she won't take my calls. We had a scary conversation over text."

"What was scary about it?"

He read her the highlights of their text conversation from his phone. He left out the parts where Amy called him a coward and edited her last insult to read "idiot" instead of "asshole."

"She's right. You are an idiot," she said.

"I really am worried she may hurt herself," he said.

"Why, Craig? Because women are so weak their only response to someone like Barney is to go home, sit in a tub of warm water, and slit their wrists?"

"No, I guess not. It's just that her comment about all of us being sorry made me think she was going to do something drastic."

"I'm sure she is about to do something drastic, but it won't be to herself. She's right. You all will be sorry for the way you let Barney treat her."

Craig left his spoon stuck in the carton of ice cream.

"Any ideas about what she'll do?" he asked.

"Not a one," she said. "Did you forget I'm a silent member of the club? I haven't been to any of the meetings, to protect you. I didn't even know she was talking to the elders already. Why didn't you tell me?"

"It's not my job to keep you up to speed on what The Deborah Club is doing."

"You keep saying it's not your job to do blah, blah, blah," she said. "What is it your job to do, exactly?"

"It's my job to help the elders keep the peace," he said. "And after tonight, my job got much harder." He gave his wife a sad smile, hoping for some sympathy. "You know, I kind of wish you were more involved in The Deborah Club. I could use some behind-the-scenes information right about now."

"If I were involved, it wouldn't be so I could be your spy." She stood up from the table so fast her chair nearly fell over. On her way to their bedroom, she said, "Amy was wrong about you. You're not an idiot. You're an asshole."

Craig grabbed the spoon and resumed shoveling ice cream into his mouth.

Chapter 19

OTHER THAN CRAIG, who could go straight to hell for all she cared, Amy didn't have anyone she could talk to about what had happened at the elders' meeting. As much as she wanted to, she couldn't tell Tom. He knew she was going to a meeting--she was always going to meetings--but she didn't tell him what kind of meeting it was. The last thing she wanted to be was the kind of woman who ran to her husband when she was in trouble. If she needed a man to be her hero, she had no business leading The Deborah Club.

It had been a stupid move to keep Carla and Helen in the dark. Would Barney have behaved the same way if there had been more women in the room? Had she invited his wrath by coming alone? She envisioned Carla walking around the table and slapping Barney's face hard enough to make his double chin jiggle. If only.

She was up most of the night thinking about how to respond. She wondered if she would ever sleep again. In the quiet of the early morning hours, she seriously considered giving up. It wasn't worth it. It would be so much easier to leave and find another church where women weren't an issue to be discussed or a problem to be solved. There were plenty to choose from. Perhaps Joan was right, and she was causing trouble for all the wrong reasons. Damn you, Joan, she thought. I need you now more than ever.

She had just about talked herself into quitting when she checked her email. She was hoping to find something from one of the elders apologizing for not coming to her defense. What she found instead was a marketing piece from a non-profit organization raising money to drill water wells in impoverished areas around the world. She normally wouldn't have opened it, but the subject line piqued her curiosity.

"She stopped cooking, and he started listening."

She clicked on the email and read a story about a village somewhere in Asia. It told of how the women, in addition to taking care of their families, spent much of their spare time hauling potable water over long distances. It described how children were forced to bath in a nearby pond, which was contaminated with bacteria known to cause skin disease. None of the homes in the village had toilets. Since it was considered disgraceful for women to use the bathroom in daylight, the women had to wait until dark before they could relieve themselves. One day, the women heard about an organization offering to bring running water to nearby villages. With running water came cleansing baths for their children. It meant no long, backbreaking walks carrying heavy buckets. And it meant toilets! To qualify for the project, the entire village had to demonstrate its commitment through sweat equity. They would have to work for their water. While the women were willing do whatever was necessary, the men didn't see the need for such a luxury like running water. They refused to help.

The email went on to describe how difficult it was for the women to persuade the men to join their effort. One woman took the drastic action of refusing to cook for her husband until he agreed to help. Her courageous refusal to do what was expected of her gained her husband's attention, as well as his anger. She and the other women of the village endured harsh treatment from their husbands, but they stood together and after many meetings and discussions, they eventually wore the men down. The men and women of the village worked together until clean water flowed. Just like the organization's tagline said it would, water changed everything.

Amy wept as she read through the email several more times. Her pain paled in comparison to what women all over the world were enduring to secure basic human rights and bare necessities. Was she really going to give up this easily?

Not a chance.

She took a cue from the example of the women in the story and resolved to stop trying to go it alone. She admitted she was neither strong enough, nor smart enough, to do this by herself. It was time to invite as many people into the conversation as possible. No more private meetings behind closed doors.

The Deborah Club was going public.

⊶⊷⊙ ⊙⊶⊷

First thing in the morning, Amy called a meeting with Carla and Helen via text.

Amy: We need to meet ASAP. How about coffee in an hour?
Carla: I can't. I have a showing.
Amy: Can you cancel it? This is important.
Carla: No, I can't cancel it. This is how I make a living.

Amy: Sorry. How about meeting in my office over lunch?

Carla: That works for me.

Helen: Better for me too.

Carla: What's wrong?

Amy: Nothing. I'll see you at lunch.

Three hours later, they were in Amy's office, unpacking sub sandwiches that Helen had picked up at a nearby deli.

"Why the urgency?" Carla said, showing no interest in her sandwich.

"First, let me start with an apology," Amy said. "I'm sorry for going out on my own."

Carla narrowed her eyes. "What did you do?"

Amy told them about the meeting and what Barney had said, almost word for word--like she would ever forget--and then offered another apology. "It was a stupid mistake. I'm not sure why I thought it would be better if I went alone, but I was obviously wrong."

"Yes, you were," Carla said. "If I had been there, I wouldn't have let them, let him, get away with it." She punched her open hand.

"I know," Amy said. "I should have slapped him. I wish I had."

"If Barney had said those things to me," Helen said, pausing to think of an appropriate response. "I would never show up at church again."

"That's exactly what Barney wants her to do," Carla said. She leaned back in her chair and crossed her arms. "I'm not going to accept your apology until you answer one question."

"Okay," Amy said. She had expected Carla to make this as difficult for her as possible.

"Did it work?" Carla asked.

"Did what work?" Amy said.

"Did Barney's attempt to intimidate you work? Are you going to quit?"

"Absolutely not!" Amy said.

"Then I accept your apology and so does Helen."

"It would have worked on me," Helen said. "I don't know how I will ever look him in the eye again."

"That's why Amy didn't want us in the meeting," Carla said, looking at Helen. "I would have slapped his face, and you would have quit." She turned back to Amy and gave her a slight nod. "Maybe you did do the right thing."

Amy exhaled and said, "Thank you. Both of you. Now with your permission, I'd like to stop talking about what happened yesterday. It's no longer important. What matters now is how we choose to respond."

"Any ideas?" Helen asked.

"Oh yes," Amy said. "But we need to get moving."

Chapter 20

CRAIG KEPT TRYING to check on Amy the next morning, but she wouldn't answer his calls or texts. Over lunch, he asked his wife to reach out to her.

She rolled her eyes. "Will you just leave her alone? If she wanted to talk to you, she would answer."

"Just send her a text to make sure she's okay," Craig said. "Please?"

"Fine."

She typed a long text into her phone: Hi Amy. Craig wanted me to check and see how you're doing. He told me what happened at the meeting last night. I don't blame you for ignoring him. I think he's afraid you're going to show up at the church office and shoot him. He has a guilty conscious and for good reason. Can you confirm that you're okay, so that he'll leave both of us alone for the rest of the day?

Amy: I'm fine. Thanks for checking on me. Tell Craig he can leave his bulletproof vest at home.

Craig's wife showed him Amy's text. "See," she said. "Now go get some work done. Maybe write a sermon about how elders shouldn't abuse their power."

Later that afternoon, Craig was back in his office pretending to work on his sermon when his desk phone beeped. He usually ignored it and let it go straight to voicemail, but today it was a welcome distraction.

"South Barkley Bible Church, this is Craig."

"Hi Craig, this is Emily Branson from Channel 8 News. You're the Senior Pastor of the church, correct?"

"Yes, I am. I guess." He sat up straight in his chair as if a bolt of electricity had just shot down his spine. *Uh oh.*

"I'm doing some research on a story, and I'm hoping you can help me out with some information. Do you have a few moments to visit?"

"Visit about what?" Craig asked unnecessarily. He knew exactly why she was calling.

"I received an anonymous tip earlier today about a strike that could be happening at your church this Sunday."

Craig wondered if it was too late to hang up. "Okay," he said, not knowing what else to say. *Did she say this Sunday?*

"The tip said the women of your church are planning to go on strike from their usual areas of service to protest your church's discriminatory practices against women. Can you confirm this is true?"

"Which part? The possible strike or our church's discriminatory practices against women?"

Clever response big boy, but this isn't the time to be a smart ass.

"Both, if you can," the reporter said.

"Yes," Craig said. "I've heard talk of a potential strike, but I didn't know it was going to happen this Sunday. And, no, I would not describe South Barkley's practices as discriminatory."

"Is that your official response to those who are protesting your decision?"

"Wait. What? My decision?" Craig said.

"Yes, I'm assuming as Senior Pastor you're the one who made the decision to continue excluding women from leadership at your church."

"No," Craig said. "This is not my decision."

"Whose decision is it then?"

"That would be our elders," Craig said without hesitation.

"Elders? Who or what are elders?"

"Elders are the official leaders of our church. They make final decisions about our mission and vision, as well as our doctrinal positions."

"And you're not one of these elders?" she said.

"No, I'm not."

"Then what are you responsible for as the Senior Pastor?"

Craig thought she sounded more skeptical than confused. "I'm responsible for implementing our church's strategic vision, which the elders must approve."

"So you're responsible for implementing the elders' decision to exclude women from leadership?"

"I wouldn't say it that way," Craig said.

"How would you say it then?"

"South Barkley's position on the role of women in ministry and leadership isn't something we have to intentionally implement. It's just the way things are. The way things have always been," he said.

"And this is what the women are protesting? The way things have always been?"

"Yes," Craig said. "Or, I guess so. You would need to ask them that question."

"The elders?" she asked.

"No, the women who are threatening to strike," Craig said.

"It also sounds like I need to be talking to the elders."

That's a great idea. Craig said nothing.

"Do you think the elders will give the women what they want to avoid a strike?"

"That's a question only the elders can answer."

"Can you give me their names?" she asked. "And the best way to contact them?"

"Hold on one second," Craig said.

He muted the phone and placed the receiver on his desk. So this is what Amy meant when she said they'd be sorry.

Well played.

He didn't blame her. He blamed Barney for leaving her with no other option. He was tempted to give the reporter Barney's number, so he could become the face of South Barkley's idiocy. While exposing Barney would bring Craig great joy, he couldn't count on Barney to be properly embarrassed. It was more likely Barney would make them all sound like fools and would then wear the public ridicule as a badge of honor for service rendered in his ongoing fight against the liberal media. He couldn't give Barney that kind of platform. Ben was the most well-spoken of the elders, but he was too new to be put on the hot seat and possibly too sympathetic to The Deborah Club's cause to represent the other elders fairly. The other two elders would have to ask Barney what he wanted them to say before they could comment. Ellis was the only choice, and he would do fine, but Craig needed to prep him

He picked up the receiver and said, "Can I get your number? I'll have one of our elders call you later today."

She gave him her number, and Craig said, "Any idea when you will air the story?"

"Not sure. I still have a lot of work to do. Until you confirmed the existence of The Deborah Club and their threat to strike, I wasn't even sure there was a story. So thanks for that."

"You're welcome," Craig said and hung up.

Stupid idiot!

He had no clue how long she would wait for a call from Ellis. All she had to do was dig around on the church's website, and she would find a list of the elders' names and emails, but thankfully, no phone numbers. He was surprised Amy hadn't given her all the elders' names and numbers directly.

Before calling Ellis, he needed to find out if Amy really had moved up the strike to this Sunday instead of the first Sunday of November, as she had originally threatened in her letter. Now that she had taken her revenge against him and the elders by alerting the media, he hoped she would talk to him. He started with a text.

Craig: I just talked to a reporter from Channel 8. I need to talk to you ASAP. Please pick up when I call.
Amy: Okay.

He didn't waste any time when she answered. "I can't believe you called a reporter."

"I have no idea what you're talking about," she said.

"Whatever," Craig said. "I don't have time to play games right now. The reporter said the strike is happening this Sunday. Did you move it up?"

"Yes, I, I mean we, did," Amy said. "But the reporter didn't hear it from me. I didn't call a reporter."

"Whatever," Craig said. "Why did you move up the strike?"

"The elders have taken their position, and we're ready to take ours," Amy said. "Why waste any more time when it's obvious where everyone stands?"

"Because we need more time to work this out," Craig said.

"There is nothing left to work out. Barney made that, and much more, very clear."

"Barney doesn't speak for the elders," Craig said. "He was way out of line."

"Do you really believe what you're saying, Craig? Or have you gotten so used to lying to yourself that you no longer notice when you lie to others?"

Craig softened his tone. "You know he wasn't speaking for me."

"I know, but I also know you refused to speak for yourself. You gave up your right to play the victim card when you kept your mouth shut last night."

"Are you sure you all are ready to strike?" Craig asked.

"How hard do you think it is to make sure no one does anything?"

"What if other women step up and help?"

"There might be a few," she said, "but not enough, since I know how many women have joined The Deborah Club. We have the numbers, Craig."

"Amy, will you do me one favor? Please?"

"What?"

"Don't give the reporter any more information. Since you've already put her on our scent, make her work for the rest of the story. I need some time to try and talk some sense into the elders."

"Be careful, Craig. It almost sounds like you're about to get involved."

"No. My only goal is to keep this from destroying our church. I just hope it's not too late. Will you stay away from the reporter for a day or two? For the good of the church?" *And for the sake of my job?*

"I haven't spoken to a reporter," Amy said.

"Thanks for nothing," Craig said. He ended the call and immediately made another to Ellis.

What little sympathy Ellis felt for Amy vanished when he learned she had called a reporter. He was already angry with Barney and even angrier with himself for letting Barney be Barney. He took his frustration out on Craig, as if he were also to blame.

"Why in the world would you talk to a reporter?" Ellis said.

"I didn't know it was a reporter until I answered the phone," Craig said. "What did you want me to do? Hang up on her as soon as she told me who she was? Nothing guilty looking about that."

"You didn't volunteer any information, did you?"

Ellis had learned to be leery of reporters. Several years earlier, another company had sued his company for breach of contract. It was a frivolous lawsuit, and the case was dismissed. The local media had reported the lawsuit with great fanfare when the news broke. Their reporting made Ellis' company look guilty from the beginning. When the case was dismissed, the story was given a single paragraph buried deep inside the newspaper, and the TV stations didn't bother to mention it at all.

Craig chose not to tell Ellis how he had inadvertently confirmed the story and then referred the reporter to the elders. "She's eventually going to track down one of you guys," he said. "We can wait and see who wins the lottery, or you can call her and try to control the story. The last thing we want is for her to talk to Barney."

"That's for damn sure." Ellis paused. "Sorry for the language."

"Not a problem, Ellis. It's perfectly acceptable to curse in this situation. I'm glad no one has been following me around recording what I say."

"Be careful of what you say out loud," Ellis said. "For all we know, Amy has your office bugged."

Craig laughed.

"I'm not joking. After this, I wouldn't put anything past her."

"Are you going to call the reporter?" Craig asked.

"I guess so," Ellis said. "Unless you want to call her back and speak on behalf of the elders."

Craig wasn't sure if Ellis was serious. He hoped not. "I'm not sure that's such a good idea, Ellis. I don't know what to say."

"Like I do?" Ellis said. Craig faked a laugh, and Ellis kept talking. "I'll never admit this to anyone else, but when I first received her letter, I was ready to work with Amy to figure something out. I was on her side, but she's taking it too far. If they go on strike this Sunday and the media covers it, it will ruin our reputation in the community. We'll be more dependent on Barney than ever."

"We can't let that happen, Ellis."

"It may be too late," Ellis said. "If I ever find out who put this harebrained scheme in Amy's head, I'll shoot him."

Craig swallowed hard. "What makes you think it's a he?"

"I don't know," Ellis said. "Call me sexist, but this plan seems too cutthroat for a woman to devise. It just feels more like something a man would think up."

"You're right, Ellis. That is sexist. Please don't say that to the reporter."

"I'm mad, not stupid," Ellis said and sighed. "I guess I better call her."

Craig gave him the reporter's name and number and then got off the phone as quickly as possible, before Ellis could change his mind and delegate the task to him.

Chapter 21

DURING THE SIX o'clock news that evening, in the segment just before the weather, Dale Hutchens, Channel 8 news anchor, introduced a story about a controversy at a local church.

"Let's go to Emily Branson for more," he said.

The newscast cut to a live shot of a young reporter with shoulder-length, sandy blonde hair and wearing a blue, short-sleeved dress designed to show off her well-toned arms. She was standing in an empty parking lot with a traditional looking church building, steeple and all, in the background. At twenty-six years old, she was the least experienced reporter at Channel 8 and well aware of how her youth gave a lightness to every story she covered. She stared into the camera with an overdone somber expression, as if she were about to tell the world the President of the United States had been assassinated.

"Thank you, Dale. I'm standing outside the main entrance to the South Barkley Bible Church. It's a congregation with approximately 350 members, over half of which are women. Yet, none of these women are part of the church's leadership team, nor are they allowed to speak during the church's worship services. This has been the standard practice throughout South Barkley's history, but if a frustrated group of women, known as The Deborah Club, gets its way, all of that is about to change.

According to a member of The Deborah Club, these women plan to protest the church's discriminatory practices by going on strike from their usual areas of volunteer service this coming Sunday morning. Just a few minutes ago, I spoke with Ellis Monroe, Chairman of South Barkley's Board of Elders, about the threatened strike. He said the elders are in dialogue with leaders of The Deborah Club, and they hope to resolve this misunderstanding before it escalates into what he called, and I quote, 'An unnecessary and unfortunate public airing of a private church matter.'

He also said he believes this issue will be resolved before Sunday and that the church's ministries will continue to function with the full participation of all volunteers, both men and women. When I asked Monroe why he thought The Deborah Club felt it necessary to resort to such drastic action, he said he didn't know, but he hoped a spirit of peace and unity would prevail. For Channel 8 News, this is Emily Branson."

Spirit of Peace and unity

Chapter 22

CRAIG MUTED THE volume on his television after watching the report on Channel 8. He placed his cell phone on the arm of his easy chair and waited. It wouldn't be long. Five minutes later, Ellis called him. Five minutes after that, Craig was in his car headed to the church building for an emergency meeting with the elders. He was the last to arrive. The elders were already in full-on damage control mode when he made his reluctant entrance.

"Ellis, why didn't you tell us a reporter was asking questions," Barney said. "And why didn't you warn us about that report on TV tonight? I was sitting at my kitchen table eating dinner, and out of nowhere, I see the front door of our church building on TV. Sixty seconds later, my phone starts ringing."

"I'm sorry, Barney. I apologize to all of you," Ellis said. "I only spoke to her thirty minutes before the report aired. I had no idea it would happen so soon. I really didn't have time to reach out to each of you."

"That's okay, Ellis," Ben said. "It was a tough spot to be in."

"You could have at least reached out to me," Barney said. "I would have appreciated being asked for input about what you were going to say to her. Especially since you were speaking on my behalf."

"I tried not to be too inflammatory," Ellis said.

"And I thought you were too soft," Barney said. "You made it sound like we were negotiating with them. You gave them hope we were willing to compromise before Sunday. You should have said we have made our decision. We're standing our ground, and we will not be bullied by divisive church members or the liberal media."

"I don't think that would have gone over very well," Ben said. "I think what Ellis said was fine. This battle is already over in my opinion. We lost it as soon as the reporter used the word discrimination. Anything short of giving The Deborah Club what they want makes us look like sexist tyrants."

"Hogwash!" Barney said. "The first amendment gives us the right to run our church any way we see fit."

"That's not completely accurate, Barney, and you know it," Ellis said. "Besides, this is not a first amendment issue."

Ben said, "You know what drives me crazy? I basically agree with their position. I'm all for including women in more leadership roles. Yet, now I'm being portrayed as a chauvinistic pig. When my wife saw the report, she looked at me like I was an alien trying to take over her home world. I tried to explain the dynamics of the situation, but the more I talked, the more ridiculous I sounded. When I left for this meeting, she was calling Amy Brandt, and it wasn't to express her dismay with The Deborah Club. Later tonight, I have to walk into my house and crawl into bed next to a woman who is going to sit up and ask me what we decided. I say we get Amy up here so Barney can apologize, and we can sort this mess out tonight."

"I will do no such thing," Barney said, his voice low and menacing. "And if you all give into her demands, Wanda and I will start looking for a new church tomorrow morning."

There it was. Now that Barney had played the "do this and I'll leave" card, Craig knew how things would turn out. Because of his success in business, most church members viewed him as the most credible elder at South Barkley. He was their opinion leader. The best-kept secret at South Barkley was just how unpleasant Barney was to work with behind closed doors. New elders were often shocked at how Barney dominated discussions and bullied the group into agreeing with him. After his first few meetings, Ben met Ellis for lunch to complain about Barney. When he asked why the elders continued to put up with Barney's behavior, Ellis told him about the money.

Barney's weekly contribution funded almost thirty percent of the church's budget. His best friends and strongest supporters funded close to another twenty percent. Without their money, South Barkley would be crippled financially. Ministries would not be funded, and salaries would be cut. It would also put South Barkley in danger of defaulting on repayment of just over five hundred thousand dollars of debt the church took on to renovate the building four years earlier. Once Ellis explained the financial benefits of having Barney around, Ben understood why they always did things Barney's way.

"Why didn't you tell me this before I became an elder?" Ben had asked.

"Would you have still said yes if I had told you?" Ellis had said.

This was the first time Craig had ever heard Barney verbalize his threat to leave in a meeting. Barney knew the other elders knew just how indispensable he was, so he never had to say it. His willingness to do so now made it clear just how serious he was. He wanted them to choose between him and Amy Brandt, which was no real choice at all.

Ben said, "Well, I guess that settles it."

"What is that supposed to mean?" Barney asked.

"You know what it means," Ben said. "We're going to go with whatever you decide because your contribution check is more important than doing the right thing for the women of this church."

"I don't know what you're talking about," Barney said, feigning offense. "I'm just saying I can't in good conscience go along with what these women are asking for. And I will not be manipulated into going against my convictions. If you all don't see things the same way, I'm not going to force you to go along with me, but I also won't be able to go along with you. You should do what you think the Spirit is leading you to do."

Ben leaned forward, as if he were about to reach across the table and grab Barney by the throat. "Right now I sense the Spirit is telling me to resign and go find a church where Jesus is Lord, instead of the elder with the deepest pockets."

"Now Ben, let's not make any rash decisions in the heat of the moment," Ellis said, trying to regain some sense of order. "This isn't the time for anyone to be stepping down as an elder. Right now, our primary focus should be navigating the church through this media firestorm."

"How dare you insinuate such a thing?" Barney said to Ben. "I have never, nor will I ever, use my giving to exercise undue influence on the decisions we make as a group."

Ellis made another unsuccessful attempt to redirect the conversation, but Ben cut him off. "That's a bold face lie, Barney, and you know it."

"I will not stand for this," Barney shouted. "Who do you think you are, speaking to me this way?"

"As of right now, I'm an ex-elder." Ben turned to Ellis, "Ellis, I hereby submit my resignation as elder, and I withdraw my family's membership from this church. I would say it's been a pleasure serving on this board, but that would make me just as big a liar as Barney."

He stood and addressed the group, "Farewell gentlemen. And you too, Barney." It was a hackneyed insult, but Craig appreciated it all the same. On his way out of the conference room, Ben slammed the heavy door so hard the glass in the square window shattered. Everyone, except Barney, flinched and hunched their shoulders as shards of glass came crashing down.

Barney shifted in his chair triumphantly and took control. "That's a shame, but I have to wonder, how did a man with that kind of temper ever become an elder in the first place?"

Ellis coughed to clear his throat and said, "I'm sorry that happened. Do we need to take a break to clean up this mess?"

The other two elders looked to Barney for an answer.

"I'm fine," Barney said. "Let's press on."

Ellis nodded and said, "Does anyone else have any thoughts about how to proceed?"

Jake Thomas, one of the two elders who usually didn't have much to say, found his voice and said, "Barney, what do you think we should do?"

Barney sat back in his chair and looked up at the ceiling, as though this were the first time he had given the question some serious thought. "I think we proceed on Sunday morning just like we always do. Let's each call five men and make sure we have enough volunteers to cover our bases. My wife is willing to step up and fill a gap. If all our wives do the same, we should be fine. Once we show The Deborah Club that we can make it without them, they will see they're not nearly as powerful as they think they are."

"But what if they don't?" Ellis asked. "I'm sure we can cover one Sunday, but what about the next Sunday? And the one after that?"

"Let's not borrow more trouble than necessary," Barney said. "Let's take it one Sunday at a time. My prediction is they'll break sooner than you think."

"What about the media?" Ellis asked. "What do I, or we, say to the reporter if she calls again?"

Barney said, "Why don't we tell her the truth? That our decisions and convictions are based on our understanding of what the Bible says about the proper ordering of male leadership in the family and the church. Remember, our position is not unique, nor is it recent. We have church history on our side."

"But is this what we really believe?" Ellis asked. "After all the studying we've done, I thought our position is that women can be included in more public roles of leadership than we have traditionally allowed, but we want to be careful how we introduce any changes so as not to endanger unity."

"I remember discussing that as one of several options, but I don't remember us ever officially adopting it as our position," Barney said. "Personally, I'd like to see us stick to a more orthodox understanding of the Scriptures."

Even though he had vowed to keep his mouth shut, Craig couldn't resist the urge to ask a question. "Barney, we've talked about including more women in church leadership many times, and I've never heard you voice this kind of opposition before. In fact, I've always had the impression you were open to it. Did I misread you, or have you had a change of heart?"

Craig had never challenged Barney in a meeting, and he wasn't looking for trouble now. He was genuinely curious about what was behind Barney's vehement opposition to The Deborah Club, as well as his horrible treatment of Amy. It was too extreme, even for him.

Barney thought about the question for a moment, and Craig filled the silence with a clarification. "I'm not saying you don't have the right to change your mind. Nor am I saying I agree with the tactics of The Deborah Club."

More silence from Barney.

Craig couldn't stop himself. "Maybe this isn't the time to talk about it, but I am curious."

"It's a fair question," Barney said. "The truth is I'm not sure how to explain it. I'm not one to see the hand of God at work in every event, nor do I like to blame Satan every time something goes wrong, but everything about this feels sinister to me, like a Satanic attack. I'm not bold enough to say God has literally spoken to me about this, but I can say I sense God wants me to fight this darkness with everything I have."

Barney's tone softened. "I'm just trying to be obedient to God's will. I'm sorry if I've made things difficult for you guys. That was never my intention."

Jake said, "We know that Barney. You should never feel the need to apologize for doing what you think is right. We admire your courage and convictions. I think we all needed a wake-up call on this one."

Craig saw the thin ice in front of him. *Don't take another step.* But he couldn't resist. "What if Amy Brandt believes God has called her to do what she's doing?" *Quit while you're ahead.* "What if she too thinks she's being obedient to the will of God?" *Are you insane?*

Barney's eyes almost doubled in size as if the skin on Craig's forehead had suddenly split open to reveal a third eye. "She can think whatever she wants, but she has obviously been deceived," he said. His wide eyes narrowed. "I thought you were on our side."

"It was just a question, Barney. I meant no offense," Craig said. "I know you both love the Lord and want to please him. I just hate seeing Christians square off like this, especially with the world watching."

"Let it watch," Barney said. "I'm not afraid of a little publicity. What scares me is displeasing God. He is watching too."

"Well said, Barney," Jake added, breaking his personal record for most comments made during an elders' meeting.

They spent the next twenty minutes rehashing the details of Barney's strategy for Sunday. When they started repeating themselves, Ellis changed the subject back to Ben's resignation. "Should I ask Ben to reconsider?"

"Absolutely not," Barney said. He showed his true colors tonight."

"Then we'll need to find someone to replace him," Ellis said. "But I recommend we get through this crisis first."

"Don't worry about it," Barney said. "I have the perfect guy in mind. Let's pray and go home."

On his way out, Craig stopped and put the large pieces of glass in the trashcan by the door. As he handled the jagged shards, being careful not to cut himself, he saw it as a metaphor for what he was trying to do at South Barkley. What were the chances he could clean up such a nasty mess without bleeding?

Snowball in hell, stupid idiot!

Chapter 23

AFTER CLEANING UP the glass, Craig made a beeline for his car. He had parked behind the church building in case any reporters were staking out the front entrance. He felt zero guilt for not suggesting the elders do the same. They were big boys. Let them plan their own escape routes.

His self-congratulatory moment, a rarity these days, was interrupted by the sight of Carla's fancy Lincoln Navigator parked next to his clunker. It was a clear, crisp night with just enough breeze to warrant a light jacket. Moonbeams bounced off the shiny, black exterior of her vehicle. Carla was leaning against her front bumper, dressed in jeans and a t-shirt with her arms crossed to fight the chill, waiting for him to appear.

"You don't look like you're having much fun," she said as he approached.

"What are you doing here?" He was too preoccupied with the current crisis to remember to feel nervous in her presence and too emotionally drained to worry about what it would look like if they were caught talking to each other in a dark parking lot behind the building.

"And good evening to you too, sir. Things not go your way in there?"

"I don't have a way for things to go, unless all of it goes away."

"That's clever," she said, "but I don't see that happening anytime soon. Do you?"

"Nope. Especially not after the report on Channel 8 tonight."

She faked a sympathetic look. "I hope that didn't complicate things for you guys."

"Don't lump me in with those guys. I'm trying to stay out of it, just like I said I would."

"You know what I thought when Amy first showed me your email?"

"Here's a great opportunity to get our pastor fired," Craig said.

"Clever again, but no. I thought, finally, an idea that will work. It didn't bother me in the least that it came from a man. In fact, after reading your manifesto, I decided you were one of the few men in this world I'd be willing to follow, maybe even submit to, in certain situations."

Follow. Submit to.

Craig remembered to be nervous around Carla. He felt his face turn red and hoped it didn't show in the moonlight. Was this flattery or flirtation? Either way, he liked it. What began as an annoying obstacle to getting home now felt dangerous. But rather than making him want to run away, it was the kind of danger that drew him in for a closer look.

She went on, "So you can imagine how disappointed I was when you refused to lead us. Amy thinks you're a coward, but I disagree. I think you just lack the proper motivation."

With her auburn hair blowing in the breeze, her perfect skin glowing in the moonlight, and her dark brown eyes looking straight into his soul, Craig was transported back to his high school days. He didn't know how it was possible, but she was more stunning than ever.

Do not ask her what kind of motivation she has in mind. Walk straight to your car and drive away. Run over her if you have to. Do not look back. Do. Not. Say. Another. Word.

"What kind of motivation do you have in mind?" *You idiot!*

She smiled and squeezed herself with her crossed arms, enhancing the fullness of her breasts. "Oh, I have several ideas, each one more exciting than the next," she said.

Exciting.

"Is this one of them?" he said. "Waiting for me out here in the dark?" *Good idea. Stall her with stupid questions until your brain comes back online.*

"No, my first was to call Channel 8 and see if they'd be interested in telling our story. How did you and Emily Branson get along?"

"So you're the one who called her? Amy said she didn't know who did it."

"And she doesn't, at least not yet," Carla said. "I decided it was time for me to take the initiative. Amy's not the only one who likes being in charge. She thinks she knows what she's doing, but she's in way over her head. She's too proud to admit it, but I'm not. We need your help." She took a long breath and her chest heaved. "I need your help."

Craig fought to maintain eye contact. "Calling a reporter is a strange way to ask for help. She said you told her to talk to me."

Carla cocked her head to the side. "I thought it might wake you up to what was really at stake. I assumed you wouldn't let yourself be publicly identified with the good ole boys you privately despise."

"I told her it's not my decision," Craig said.

"Trust me, Craig. That's not the way people will see it. You're the pastor of this church. They'll assume you and the elders are on the same side. Why else would you still be here if you don't support their position? I did you a favor today. I gave you a chance to show everyone you're not one of them."

"That's ridiculous," Craig said. "And devious."

"I worked in public relations before I started selling houses," Carla said. "I know how this works. Don't confuse me with a timid housewife. I'm much more experienced than that."

Experienced.

Craig's mouth twitched.

He spoke carefully, trying not to stumble over his words. "Do you really think threatening me is the best way to get me to help?"

"I'm not threatening you, Craig. I'm trying to help you. I'm willing to do whatever it takes to get you to see how good we can be together."

How good we can be together.

"What do you want me to do?" His inner voice was shrieking. *If you're not going to run, at least shut up!*

Carla gave him a heart-melting grin. "Oh, there are a number of things I'd like you to do, Craig, but for starters, how about telling me what you guys talked about tonight? How are the elders planning to respond?"

"That's what you want, information?"

"For now, yes. I want you," she paused, "to be my spy." She gave him a sly grin and added, "on the inside."

"Your spy?"

"Just you and me," Carla said. "Amy doesn't need to know."

Amy.

He remembered his wife.

Craig was suddenly aware of how close he and Carla were standing to each other. Yet, she hadn't budged from her initial position in front of her SUV. Had he been inching toward her this whole time? He stepped back and said, "I'm sorry. I can't betray Amy like this."

Carla was mystified. "How is this betraying Amy?" Then her eyes widened as if she'd just solved the world's most complex mystery. "Have you two been working together all along?"

"I'm talking about the other Amy. My wife," Craig said.

"What does she have to do with this?" Another surprised look flashed across Carla's face, as if she'd just solved a riddle within the mystery. "What do you think is happening here? Do you think I came here to--oh you are an idiot and a pig--like I would ever--"

Craig held up his hands and stammered, "I'm sorry. I just thought that, well, it sounded like you were suggesting--"

"Well, I wasn't," Carla said. She sidestepped her way back around her SUV, careful to not turn her back on Craig. "I can't believe you." She felt for the door handle and pulled it open. She kept talking as she climbed in. "No matter what you write or what you say you believe or what kind of man you try to convince other people you are, when it comes down to it, you're just like all the rest of them."

She slammed the door and sped out of the parking lot, leaving Craig standing straight as a post and slack jawed, his arms dangling by his sides, looking as if he'd just been shot with a tranquilizer dart and was seconds away from toppling over.

When he regained the power of movement, he turned and looked back at the church building to make sure there were no witnesses before launching himself toward his car. He wanted to put as much distance between him and the scene of the crime as possible.

As he drove through the main parking lot on the other side of the building, he saw Ellis's car parked near the main entrance. He made an instant decision to run in and submit his resignation. There was still time to extract himself from this mess before he lost his soul. He could go home and tell his wife and kids they were moving. The next day they would load their stuff into a U-Haul van and head to the other side of the country. He would start over with a new church and do it right this time. Then he saw Barney's pick-up truck parked on the other side of the portico covering the main entrance, and just as quickly, Craig decided to go straight home.

He needed to talk to his wife, to hug and hold and tell her how much he loved her. But he could never tell her what just happened with Carla. He wasn't even sure what just happened.

One thing he did know for certain: Carla was not so pretty anymore.

Chapter 24

WHILE EVERYONE ELSE was scattering from the meeting, Ellis asked Barney to stay for a brief conversation. He wanted to take one last shot at convincing Barney to back down so he could work something out with Amy Brandt. Ellis was the only person, except for Barney's wife, Wanda, who had a chance of getting Barney to reconsider his position. Ellis knew from experience that it was best to have this kind of conversation with Barney in private. Barney didn't change his mind in front of others.

That's why, before the disastrous meeting with Amy, Ellis had scheduled a lunch with Barney to see how he wanted to respond to her letter. Barney was angry, but he also said he was open to compromise for the sake of unity. In an attempt to show The Deborah Club they were taking steps in the right direction, Ellis suggested they meet with Amy and come up with a list of relatively inoffensive activities--like asking women to read a scripture or make announcements on Sundays--that the elders were willing to implement over the next few months. Barney had reluctantly supported Ellis's idea, but not without first stressing how much he despised Amy's scorched earth tactics. Looking back on their conversation, Ellis realized he should have paid closer attention to the look in Barney's eyes when he agreed to go along with the plan.

When Barney ran Amy out of the room, it wasn't the first meeting he had hijacked. It was, however, the first time he had blindsided Ellis by flipping his position and deviating from a predetermined strategy. Ellis had never been closer to resigning than he was that night. He felt betrayed. Ellis didn't always have to agree with Barney for them to work together effectively, but he did have to trust him.

Ellis had been too emotional to confront Barney at the time. He made the wise decision to go home, calm down, and collect his thoughts. When his head cleared, he promised himself he would talk to Barney about his behavior. It didn't matter who Barney was or how much money he gave to the church. He couldn't be allowed to verbally abuse another human being in one of their meetings ever again.

When Craig called and told Ellis about the reporter from Channel 8, his priorities changed. The confrontation with Barney would have to wait. At this moment, his primary goal was to prevent further damage to South Barkley's reputation. The church might survive the strike, and The Deborah Club might eventually get their way. Or Barney might drive them out and use his checkbook to keep the church afloat. No matter what happened, Ellis couldn't imagine a scenario in which South Barkley would ever be a growing church again. Who in their right mind would want to join a church after this kind of public relations disaster? Ellis didn't understand why Barney couldn't see this.

After the room cleared, Ellis and Barney returned to the conference table. Barney sat on the edge of his seat and leaned forward. Ellis took the hint and wasted no time making his case.

"Barney, I'm really worried about the path we're on."

"Me too," Barney said. "I'm trying to do something about it."

"This reminds me of the mutually assured destruction policy we had with the Soviets during the Cold War. The way this is going, I don't think there are going to be any survivors, no matter who appears to win."

"Nonsense," Barney said. "We beat the Soviets fair and square. God was on our side."

Ellis shook his head. "Never mind the Soviets, Barney. You've taken a much tougher stance against The Deborah Club than we originally talked about. What's going on?"

"It's like I told Craig. The more I thought about it, the more I realized we had to take a stand or lose everything we stand for," Barney said.

"Yes, but what if taking such a hard position destroys our church's reputation in the community?" Ellis asked.

"Who cares what the community thinks? They're a bunch of liberals anyway. This is about standing for the truth, and the truth always wins. That's why Communism failed."

"Come on, Barney. Just a few days ago, you were willing to compromise with Amy to keep the peace. What changed?"

"I changed," Barney said. He leaned back in his chair, his go-to posture for pontification. "I realized how tired I am of doing nothing while our culture blurs the lines between right and wrong, good and evil, male and female. There was a time when everyone knew who they were and how to act. Now everyone is confused. Men act like women, and women act like men. When I was a kid, I heard stories about it happening in Hollywood. A few years ago, it appeared on TV, right before my very eyes. Next thing you know, it'll be happening in this church. It's a slippery slope leading straight to hell. Not on my watch, Ellis." He slapped the table, his go-to gesture for emphasizing a point. "And not on yours either."

Barney stood to leave. Ellis remained in his seat, dumbfounded. He made a futile attempt to retrace Barney's logic and gave up before he lost his way in a labyrinth of lunacy. Barney was almost to the door when Ellis said, "Barney, what in the world are you talking about?"

Barney turned back to Ellis with a pained look on his face, as if it hurt him to have to explain something so simple to a grown man. "The gays, Ellis. They're coming. And they're using The Deborah Club to get their foot in the door."

Ellis stifled a laugh. "Amy's not gay."

"Of course she's not," Barney said. "But she's doing their work. She doesn't realize it, but she's doing it." Barney turned and walked out the door, then stopped and stuck his head back in. "Trust me, Ellis. I know how they operate. I know."

Ellis waited until he was sure Barney had left the building before he prayed out loud, "Dear God, if you let that reporter talk to Barney, I'm switching to Buddhism."

Driving home, Ellis considered calling Craig and telling him he was resigning, but he couldn't stomach the thought of abandoning Craig in the midst of a crisis. This wasn't Craig's mess; it was the elders'. Their indecision helped create The Deborah Club. It was God's punishment for dragging their feet. Pulling into his driveway, Ellis wished they had done right by the women of South Barkley years ago when they had the chance, back before Barney lost his mind.

Chapter 25

CRAIG'S WIFE WAS sitting in front of the TV, not really watching it as she anxiously waited for Craig to come home from his meeting and tell her what the elders had decided to do. She had mixed feelings about the report on Channel 8. The publicity was good for The Deborah Club, which meant it was also good for her, but it was trouble for South Barkley, which meant it was bad for Craig, which meant, ultimately, it was also bad for her. Not as a woman, but as a wife. She hated this distinction, but it was a reality she couldn't afford to overlook as long as Craig insisted on being a pastor.

She couldn't remember another time in their marriage when their relationship had been so icy. Since gashing each other during their initial fight over her joining The Deborah Club, they had been unable to maintain a truce long enough for their wounds to heal. They had both said things they instantly regretted. They had both apologized, but when Craig came home later that day, he refused to look her in the eye. He was still hurt by what she had said about his lack of leadership, and she couldn't blame him. It was the meanest thing she had ever said to him, and it had hit too close to home. When she had cautiously approached him for make-up sex later that night, he had refused. "It's okay," he said, even though it wasn't.

He pouted for several days, giving the shortest answers possible to all of her questions. When she asked him how much longer he was going to punish her for what she had said, he pretended he didn't know what she was talking about. She forced the issue and before they could stop themselves, they were fighting about The Deborah Club again. They continued to repeat this pattern every few days. Just when things seemed to be getting better between them, they would draw each other back into the argument and rip off the scabs. While she couldn't point to the exact day on the calendar, she knew it had been over a month since they had had sex, their longest drought since the birth of their second son. She was missing it, but Craig showed no interest. She loved what The Deborah Club was doing, but she also feared it was destroying her marriage.

The ringing of the household phone broke her thoughts. It had made more noise this evening than in the past year and a half. A few years ago, she and Craig had considered canceling their landline altogether, but they decided to keep it so church members would have a number to call that didn't go directly to either one of their cell phones. Tonight she was seeing the wisdom of this decision. It seemed as though the entire church wanted to make sure Craig was aware that South Barkley was in the news. After answering the first three calls, she let the rest go straight to voicemail.

She glanced at the cordless handset on the coffee table in front of her and saw that the call was from Barney. He was supposed to be meeting with Craig. It made no sense for him to be calling Craig at home and on this line instead of Craig's cell. Thinking there might have been an emergency at the church, she took the call.

"Hello, Barney."

"Hello, Amy," Barney said. "How are you doing tonight?"

143

"I'm fine. Is everything okay?"

"Well, I guess the honest answer is no, everything is not okay. I'm really worried about our church."

She was relieved there wasn't an emergency. She also had zero interest in talking to Barney about church business. "I am too, Barney. Are you looking for Craig? I thought you two were at a meeting together."

"We finished up a few minutes ago. I'm on my way home. I expect he'll be home shortly as well. Truth is, I am calling to visit with you."

She turned off the TV and waited for him to continue.

"The elders are calling around to ask folks to help us pick up the slack on Sunday if The Deborah Club is foolish enough to go through with this strike. I would like you to cover the nursery on Sunday. I know it's been a while since your boys were in diapers, but I'm guessing it's like riding a bicycle. You remember the drill, right?"

She clenched her jaw and waited for the wave of anger to pass. Craig said Barney was a piece of work, but this was unbelievable. He hadn't asked if she was willing to help. He just assumed she was waiting for her orders to be handed down from on high. She thought of several different responses, but none of them were even remotely Christian.

Early in their marriage when they started working with their first church, Craig told her one of the hardest parts of being a pastor is you can't always say what you're really thinking. The same was true for a pastor's wife. She found this rule to be unfair, but she did her best to follow it.

She smiled into the phone, flexed her polite muscle, and in the most pleasant voice she could muster, said, "I'm sorry, Barney, I don't think I can do that."

"Is there another area where you'd rather serve? If so, that's fine. Just let me know where, and I'll mark it down. Just want to make sure we have all our bases covered."

She rolled her eyes. Her brother was a sales rep for a telecommunications company, and he loved to brag about the power of the assumptive close. It was his favorite technique to employ after making a presentation. Rather than asking the prospect to purchase the product, he assumes the sale is already made and jumps directly to the question of how much or how many. He said most people lack the ego strength to correct the salesperson's mistaken assumption. Some prospects may even think they made the mistake of giving the salesperson the false impression they're saying yes. Her brother claimed that enough suckers go along with the assumption and start negotiating the details of a purchase, which they never intended to make, to generate a monthly commission check large enough for him to put a swimming pool in his backyard.

This is exactly what Barney was trying with her. He assumed she was on his side and was ready and willing to help Craig's boss save face. The only detail left to discuss was where she'd be serving.

She concentrated on sounding pleasant. "I'm sorry, Barney, but there is not another area where I'd rather serve."

"Then there's no reason you can't handle the nursery. I need all hands on deck. I can't let you sit this one out. Just like Jesus said, 'You're either for us or against us.'"

She wanted to tell Barney he was quoting Jesus out of context, but she took the high road and lied to him instead. "I wish I could help, Barney. I really do. But I'm afraid I'm going to be out of town this Sunday."

"Oh, I'm sorry to hear that." He sounded genuinely disappointed. "Would you consider changing your plans? Craig really needs you to be here this Sunday."

"Craig will be just fine without me. It won't be the first Sunday I've missed."

"You and I both know this isn't going to be a typical Sunday. I'm worried about how it will look if you're not here to do your part on such a critical day. We don't want to give some people the impression you secretly support The Deborah Club and would rather be gone than stand against them."

"I seriously doubt anyone will assume all of that just because I'm not there. I appreciate you trying to protect us from *some people*, though." Easy does it, she thought.

"Oh, you'd be surprised what," he paused, "some people will assume. What's worse, it might raise suspicions about where Craig stands. Perhaps he told you to leave town because he secretly supports The Deborah Club. While I'm sure Craig would never undermine the authority of his elders, I would hate for others to question his loyalty."

"I would too," she said. "But I think it's a stretch to say my absence would lead anyone to such a ridiculous conclusion." Her polite muscle was burning. She wasn't sure how much longer she could hold it.

"When anxiety is high, like it is now, people are looking for an excuse to be suspicious of those in leadership. I'm sure you don't want to be the excuse people need to start taking shots at Craig."

She remembered what her yoga teacher had taught her and took a calming breath, inhaling through the nose and exhaling through the mouth. "Of course not," she said.

"So Craig can count on you to be here on Sunday to help in the nursery?"

"I really don't think I can change my plans," she said, trying to smile with her voice.

"Where exactly were you planning to be this Sunday?"

She noticed he said "were" instead of "are." Another assumptive close. His confidence was nauseating.

She hadn't thought this far ahead when she lied, and now she needed to stall while she came up with a believable answer. Her polite muscle relaxed for a split second, and her anger took over. "I'm sorry, Barney, but I don't see how that is any of your business."

"And I can't see why you would mind telling me," Barney said. "You and Craig aren't looking to move to a new church, are you?"

Part of Barney's manipulative genius was his ability to ask insinuating questions. Was he asking her if she was going on a scouting trip to look at a different church? Or was he telling her that she and Craig would soon be looking for a new church if she didn't start cooperating with him? She didn't want to give him credit for being this clever, but she knew she couldn't afford to underestimate him.

She reminded herself she was attempting to charm a poisonous snake and chose to answer the less sinister interpretation of Barney's question. "Of course we're not looking for a new church, Barney. We love it here. I can't imagine going anywhere else. Besides, what good would it do for me to go looking without Craig?

He's the head of our household. He'll decide when it's time to leave, not me." She crinkled her nose and hoped she hadn't taken that last bit a step too far.

"You're right," Barney said. "Craig is the head of your household, but he's not the head of this church. While it's accurate to say he can resign at any time, the decision for when it's time for you all to leave is not his alone to make. I'll remind you that he serves at the pleasure of the elders."

"And it's his pleasure to serve you," Amy said, while making an obscene gesture with her middle finger to the phone. It was something she used to do to her dad behind his back when she was a teenager. "He loves working with you."

"I'm glad to hear you say that," Barney said. "So I can mark you down for Sunday?"

Her anger at this man was growing into hatred. She didn't want to get Craig fired, but she also wasn't going to let Barney bully her into working for him on Sunday. She said a quick prayer for help and an idea popped into her head.

"No, Barney, you can't. I'm going to be out of town. Not that it's any of your business, but just so you know, I'm going to visit my sister and her family. Her oldest is getting baptized, and I want to be there for it."

She hung her head in shame. What lake of fire in hell was reserved for those who make up a story about a child's baptism as an excuse to miss church? If asked on the day of judgment to explain the rationale for committing such a grievous sin, she would hold up her hands and offer the world's oldest excuse: the devil made me do it.

Barney said nothing.

"Barney? Are you there?"

"Yes, I'm still here," he said. "Have a nice time with your sister. We'll miss you on Sunday."

"I'll miss you all too." The lies were coming easier now.

"And, Amy?"

"Yes, Barney."

"If we can't break The Deborah Club this week, and they try us again next Sunday, I'll expect to see you in the nursery. Understood?"

Amy heard the garage door opening. It was time to end this conversation. "We'll see. Have a nice night, Barney." Then she hung up on the devil.

Chapter 26

CRAIG PLODDED THROUGH the kitchen as if he were heading straight for their bedroom. He saw his wife leaning against the counter and nodded in her direction. He dared not look her in the eye.

"Another bad one, huh?" she said.

Something in her voice made him stop and give her a long look. "What's wrong?" he asked.

"What do you mean?"

"I mean you look like you just saw a ghost. You're white as a sheet. What's wrong?"

"It's nothing," she said. "Tell me about your meeting."

"My meeting went about like I expected. No surprises."

"Then why do you look like you just ran a marathon?"

"Running a marathon is nothing compared to seeing a ghost." He looked into the living room. "The boys in bed?"

She nodded.

"What did I just walk into?" he asked.

"I told you, it's nothing," she said and waited for him to talk. When he called her bluff and refused to break the silence, she filled her lungs with air and slowly exhaled. "I just got off the phone with Barney."

"Barney?" Craig said. "What did he want?"

She summarized the conversation up to the point where she lied about her niece's baptism. She saw no reason to confess this sin to her husband.

"So Barney thinks you're going to be out of town this Sunday?"

"Yep, but he also told me he expects me to be working in the nursery the Sunday after if the strike lasts that long."

"How do you feel about that?" Craig asked.

"I have no intention of working in the nursery."

"No, I'm talking about being gone this Sunday. How does that feel?" he said.

"I don't want to miss it," she said. "I want to be there and do nothing just like all the other ladies."

"Carla ambushed me in the parking lot after the meeting," Craig said.

His wife cleared her throat. "I'm sorry, what did you just say?"

"She was waiting for me by my car in the parking lot after the meeting," he said.

She crossed her arms. "What did *she* want?" she asked, emphasizing the word "she" as if pointing a finger at Carla in a perp line-up at a police station. *She did it, Officer.*

Craig carefully summarized his conversation with Carla, minus the part where he mistook her for wanting to have an affair with him. He saw no need to burden his wife with this information.

His wife ignored the content of the conversation. "Was anyone else there?"

Craig shook his head and tried to act like it was no big deal.

"How did it end?"

"I told her I wouldn't help and didn't want to be involved, and she drove off into the night."

"She'll try again," she said. "She thinks she can bend any man to her will."

"Not me," Craig said, a beat too quickly.

"Yeah, whatever. I know you think she's gorgeous."

"What? Me? No way!" Craig said. He tried to act appropriately offended without appearing to over-protest. It was a delicate balance to strike. He was sure he nailed it.

She held up a hand to block his nonsense. "Don't even try to act like it's not true. I see the way you look at her when you don't think anyone else is watching."

"I have no idea what you're talking about," he said, with diminishing confidence in his acting skills.

"Craig, it's okay. She's beautiful. She's the kind of woman who draws every eye in the room toward her. Except mine. When you're looking at her, I'm still watching you."

"That's creepy," he said.

"No, it's love, and I'd much rather look at you than her."

"That's sweet," he said and leaned toward her, hoping for a hug.

"And if you ever do anything more than look at her, I'll castrate you with a dull razor blade. Understood?"

He snapped to attention. "Yes ma'am." *Not quite hugging time yet*.

"Good, because she's not going to leave you alone."

Thinking back to how insulted Carla was when she drove away, he said, "I think she might."

"Trust me, she won't, and don't you dare let yourself get caught in another meeting with her all by yourself. Are we clear?"

Craig nodded like a guilty little boy being scolded by his mother for crossing the street without looking both ways. He was ready to change the subject. "Barney's not going to leave you alone either."

"No, I don't expect he will."

"What are we going to do?"

"We?" she said, her stern expression softening into a thin smile. "We haven't been a *we* in a long time."

"I know," he said. "But from this point forward, we're in this together. We have to be."

"Then let me take care of Carla," she said.

"I'm not sure that's such a great idea," Craig said. The last thing he needed was for Carla and his wife to have a conversation.

"Don't worry. I know how to take care of myself." She patted his chest. "And my husband."

Craig realized it had been a mistake to even mention Carla to his wife. He also knew there was no point in attempting to talk her out of whatever she intended to do. It probably didn't matter anyway. Barney was eventually going to learn that Craig's wife was a secret member of The Deborah Club, and that would be the end of Craig.

"What do you think I should do about Barney?" he asked.

"Is there anything you can do? He's the boss."

"He's not the only boss."

"Yes, but he's the big boss."

"He sure is." Craig thought of Ben storming out of the conference room. "He's the big, bad boss, and he's coming after you."

"I guess I'll go hide at my sister's."

"It won't do any good," Craig said. "Barney isn't giving in, and Amy isn't giving up. He'll come after you next week and the week after that. He's no dummy. He'll figure it out."

She bowed up, ready for a fight, the same fight they'd been having for a month. "Craig, we've been over this before. I will not stand against The Deborah Club."

Craig saw the defiance in his wife's eyes, and he thought of Barney and then Carla and then Barney again. *Screw it.* "I want you to show up and do nothing this Sunday, just like all the other women. If that's really what you want to do."

Her shoulders sagged as the tension left her body. "Thank you," she said. "But what will I tell Barney?"

"Tell him you're a member of The Deborah Club."

She fought to suppress her joy and tried to show the proper concern for Craig. "But then what will you tell him?"

"I'll tell him the truth," Craig said. "I'll tell him my beautiful wife is too strong and too smart to let me or any other man tell her what to do."

She beamed, and he knew it was finally hugging time. In the midst of a long and swaying embrace, he asked a final, pressing question. "Did you remember to buy more ice cream today?"

Chapter 27

AMY'S HUSBAND, TOM, hadn't seen the report on TV, but like everyone else at South Barkley, he heard about it minutes after it aired. Later that night, while in bed with Amy, he watched a video of it from Channel 8's website on his iPad.

Without looking up from the screen, he said, "So this is why you've been sneaking around."

"What do you think?" she asked.

"I'm relieved. I was beginning to think you might be stepping out on me."

"You really think I would do that?" she said.

"I hope not, but it did cross my mind. Why didn't you tell me?"

"Because I didn't want your help," she said.

He set the iPad on his nightstand and rolled over to face his wife. "And what's wrong with my help?"

"Nothing. It's just that The Deborah Club is a movement of women organized by women."

"And you're afraid I would take over?"

"No. Not you, but some of the other husbands might. Or even worse, try to stop us. So we decided to keep you all in the dark."

"Are you the leader of this club?" he asked.

"I guess so," she said.

"Look at you. Large and in charge."

"Are you mocking me?"

"Not at all. It's a big responsibility," he said. "Especially now that it's on the news."

"Tell me about it," she said.

"You don't sound thrilled."

"It's harder than I thought it would be," she said. "People I thought I could trust have let me down. There is always someone ready to take a shot at you. If it's not your enemies, then it's your allies who think they could be doing a better job."

Tom smiled. "That is precisely why I'm happy to sit in my pew every Sunday and do nothing. I see enough posturing and drama at work. I go to church to escape that mess, not step in it with both feet."

"You're a wise man."

"I must be," he said, "I married you. Are you sure you don't need my help?"

"Well, there is one way you could help me tonight," she said.

"Okay. Let's hear it."

She turned off her lamp and let the darkness settle over them. "Tonight, I don't want to be in charge of anything."

Chapter 28

When Amy had asked Carla to confirm her suspicion that she was the unnamed source in the report, Carla's response had been dismissive. "Of course I did it. Who else could have?" Carla seemed to think she was the only member of The Deborah Club clever enough to come up with such an idea. Maybe she was.

Amy didn't appreciate Carla reaching out to Channel 8 before running the idea by her, but she couldn't argue with the result. Using the media to turn up the heat on the elders was a stroke of genius. Why hadn't she thought of it?

Once again, Amy felt like Carla was trying to take The Deborah Club away from her, but what could she say? Amy had already acted on her own too many times to get snippy when someone else took initiative without first getting her permission. Carla wouldn't stand for such hypocrisy. Besides, she had neither the time nor the energy to bicker with Carla about who was in charge of The Deborah Club. At least not this week. There was too much work to do. They both needed to focus on making sure everyone was organized and ready for Sunday.

The South Barkley Bible Church had an official membership of just over 350 people, of which only 247 showed up on an average Sunday. And it was never the same 247. Several clusters of fifty inconsistent souls took turns attending each week. On special Sundays, like Easter, when everyone was there, attendance would swell to almost 400. Of the 350 members, seventy-five were under the age of eighteen. Of the remaining 275 adults, 150 were women, including several elderly widows too feeble to do much more than push their walkers through the foyer. When it came down to it, roughly 95 of the 150 regular women attenders really cared about what they were, or were not, allowed to do at church on Sunday mornings. The rest were either too busy working, traveling, or taking their kids to sporting events to do anything more than show up every third Sunday.

That seventy-two of the ninety-five eligible and able-bodied women had pledged their support to The Deborah Club bolstered Amy's confidence. Those who hadn't signed on were either elders' wives, and therefore hadn't been invited to a meeting, or women, like Jane, who didn't want to see other women step outside of her comfort zone. While Amy would have loved to have 100 percent buy-in, she didn't think she needed it. When seventy-two of the most active women in the church took their stand, or to be more precise, sat on their hands, on Sunday, it would make a difference, so long as everyone stuck to the plan.

To ensure this happened, Amy reserved the back room of a local coffee shop and invited every member of The Deborah Club to a meeting on Thursday night at 6 p.m. This would be the first time they were all together in the same room. Thanks to Emily Branson and Channel 8 News, they no longer needed to operate in stealth mode.

Amy arrived thirty minutes early to arrange the tables and chairs. She liked having something physical to do before the meeting. It burned off nervous energy. She made sure every woman would have a clear view of the stage in the corner of the room where unknown and marginally talented musicians played acoustic sets on open mic night and where, tonight, she would stand to rally her troops.

She bought a tray of assorted pastries and sat it on one of the tables next to the entrance. The manager of the coffee shop hadn't charged Amy a fee for reserving the room--he believed hosting community meetings was good for business. Amy wanted to make sure The Deborah Club bought enough food and drink to make it easy for the manager to say yes if they needed to reserve the room again next week.

At 6 p.m., with only five women in the room, including Carla and Helen, Amy quit worrying about boosting business for the coffee shop and started doubting herself instead. She did her best to mask her disappointment as she greeted the small group of ladies and told them they would delay the start of the meeting for a few minutes because others were still on their way. She hoped she was telling the truth. If no one else showed up, The Deborah Club would be dead, she would be humiliated, and Barney would win.

Her fears proved to be unfounded. The room slowly filled with the women of South Barkley. Much like the Sunday morning worship gathering, they regarded the official starting time for the meeting as more of a suggestion for when to leave home than when to arrive. By the time they all did their part to keep the coffee shop in business and stopped by the front counter to purchase a hot beverage, it was almost 6:30.

Amy didn't like starting the meeting late--she thought it reflected poorly on her organizational skills--but she was relieved to see forty-three of the seventy-two members of The Deborah Club crammed into the room. She scanned the group and tried to make eye contact with those who weren't engrossed in conversations at their tables. The room was abuzz with anticipation. Or was it anxiety? Amy couldn't tell the difference. She saw expressions of hope on a few faces, while others were clouded with concern. They were looking to her, their leader, to calm their fears. But first, she had to calm hers.

She took a deep breath. This was it. Now or never. She raised her hand to get the group's attention, and in her outside voice, said, "Thank you so much for coming tonight." Most of the women stopped talking and looked Amy's way, but a few kept chatting as if they hadn't heard her.

Amy tried again. "Alright. Okay. Thank you for coming. Can I have your attention please?" When the sidebar conversations continued, she clapped her hands crisply three times. This brought everyone to attention.

She said, "Again, thanks for coming. We have a lot to cover tonight, so let's jump right in. As I think most of you already know, the elders have responded to our letter by taking a hard line. Up to this point, they have been more interested in telling us how ashamed we should be for having the audacity to stand up to them, than in sitting down and having a meaningful conversation about our concerns. I, for one, am disappointed in how they have responded, but we knew from the beginning that a hostile response was a distinct possibility. My sense is that they don't believe we are willing to follow through on our threat to strike. They think they're calling our bluff. If they could only stand where I'm standing tonight and look into your strong, determined faces, they would realized just how wrong they are and start rethinking their position."

Amy wasn't expecting a standing ovation in response to this introduction, but she hoped it would merit an "amen" or perhaps a "whoop" from some of the more spirited ladies. All she got instead were blank stares, as if she were speaking in a foreign tongue. This threw Amy off her rhythm, and she struggled to find her next thought, transforming what could have been a dramatic pause into a moment of awkward silence.

She finally recovered and said, "You all have read the rules of engagement, right?" She waited until she saw a few nodding heads. "Our plan is simple and straightforward. We attend church just like always. The only difference is that we refuse to serve in our usual capacities. Any questions?"

Someone asked, "What will our kids do if none of us are back in the children's area?"

Amy looked at Sheila Webb, the volunteer children's ministry coordinator. "Will they just stay in the sanctuary with us the entire time?"

Sheila shook her head while she swallowed a half-chewed bite of pastry. "I got a call from Nate Jensen today, and he said the elders asked him to coordinate the children's ministry events this week. He had a few questions for me about how we usually do things."

A woman on the other side of the room interrupted her. "What does a middle-aged bachelor like Nate Jensen know about taking care of our kids?"

"He'll be fine," Sheila said. "He was an elementary school teacher back in his twenties."

Amy said, "You didn't help him, did you?"

"I certainly did," Sheila said. "I'm not going to throw him into that lion's den unprepared."

Carla stepped up onto the little stage with Amy and said, "You're thinking like a volunteer coordinator. You can't do that. If he calls again, you have to tell him he's on his own."

Murmurs of disagreement bubbled up from the group. Sheila looked at Amy for confirmation of Carla's instructions.

"She's right," Amy said, wishing Carla would return to her seat. "The point of this exercise is to let the men struggle without us until we get their attention."

"But Nate is such a nice guy," Sheila said. "He's not an elder. Why punish him?"

Carla pounced before Amy had a chance to think of an answer. "He may be a nice guy, but he's also supporting the elders by helping them out. He could have just as easily refused, to show support for us."

"I thought we didn't want any of the men helping us." This came from the back of the room.

"We don't want their leadership," Amy said. "But they are welcome to help us by refusing to volunteer at a church led by men who discriminate against women."

"I think I'll keep my kids in church with me," another woman said. "I don't want them back there with one man who isn't even married."

"Of course you should do whatever you think is best," Amy said, "but I'd encourage you to send them back to children's church as you normally do. If the elders are determined to go on with business as usual, let's give them all the business they can handle."

Sheila said, "I told Nate today that church policy says there must be two volunteers in the room with the kids at all times. They'll be safe. I also told him if he can't find a second volunteer, then the kids will have to stay in the sanctuary with us. I follow the same policy myself."

"I'm sure he'll find someone," Amy said. "The elders have been calling around and asking the men to step up."

"Barney called my husband late last night," someone said.

"What did he say?" Carla asked.

"He told Barney he'd be sitting next to me in the pew doing nothing. Just like every other Sunday."

The room erupted with laughter.

"What about the other women who haven't joined our group? Do you expect some will serve anyway?"

"Yes, I do," Amy said. "I expect all the elders' wives to cross our proverbial picket line to help their husbands save face."

"Bunch of scabs," Carla said. There was a smattering of restrained laughter, as if the ladies found the comment funny but refused to let loose and laugh because Carla had made it.

Betty Ravitch, one of the older members of The Deborah Club, said, "I don't think every elder's wife will be serving. I have it on good authority that Grace has already told Ellis she's going to be sick this Sunday."

Amy was surprised. "Who is your good authority?"

"Grace," Betty said. Everyone laughed again. Amy was pleased to see the room loosening up.

"I thought about inviting her tonight," Betty said, "but I wasn't sure if I could."

"I think it would have been fine," Carla said. "Grace is her own woman."

That's not your decision to make, Amy thought. She gave Carla the side-eye, hoping she took the hint to sit down.

"What about Amy, Craig's wife?" asked Kelly Hughes, a mother of three who brought her kids to church every Sunday while her husband stayed at home. "Why isn't she here? Is she not with us?"

"She's with us," Amy said. "But for understandable reasons, she's chosen not to be an official member of The Deborah Club."

"What reasons?" Kelly asked.

"She doesn't want to put Craig in a difficult situation," Amy said.

Jenny Malone, a twenty-three year old newlywed and one of the first ten women to join The Deborah Club, raised her hand. "What about Craig? What does he think about all of this?"

Amy wanted to answer the question truthfully. She was still mad at Craig for letting her get trounced by Barney in the elders' meeting, but she also felt bound by her promise to put as much distance between him and their group as possible.

"That's a good question," Amy said. "As you know, Craig is present at every elders' meeting. He was there when I met with the elders. I'm guessing he was at the meeting the elders had after the news report, assuming they had one." She was stalling for time and hoping someone would interrupt with another question and change the subject.

"They did," Carla said with an emphatic nod. "And he was there."

Amy noticed the certainty in Carla's voice and shot her a curious look. "When I met with the elders, Craig didn't say anything," she said. "I think he'd rather not get involved."

"That doesn't surprise me," Kelly Hughes said. "He strikes me as more of a politician than a pastor."

Several heads nodded in agreement.

Carla said, "You may be right. If we're successful, he'll probably go around telling everyone the strike was his idea."

"When we're successful, not if," Amy said. "And we're not here to talk about Craig. We're here to make sure we're ready for Sunday."

A voice from the back of the room said, "If you really mean that and promise to stop talking about my husband, I'll come in and join the meeting."

Every head in the room turned and saw Craig's wife standing in the doorway.

⊷⊷⊶ ⊷⊶⊶

Carla had no idea how long Craig's wife had been standing there or how much she had heard. She shifted her gaze from Craig's wife over to Amy, whose face was frozen in a smile. Carla had seen this expression on Amy's face before when she had been under attack from Jane Gilmore.

Seizing the opportunity, Carla looked back at Craig's wife and said, "Are you sure you want come in? It could be dangerous for Craig if the elders find out." She hadn't meant it as a threat, but when she heard herself say it, she liked the ominous tone it set.

Craig's wife stepped into the room. "I'm not worried about Craig. He'll be fine as long you stop ambushing him in the parking lot late at night."

It was as if she had hit the mute button on a remote control and silenced the room. It was easy to identify the many conflict avoiders. They decided now was a good time to inspect their nails to see if it was time to schedule a manicure or to look down and see how clean the floor was beneath their feet. The few who willingly embraced conflict and relished a good fight looked up at Carla and waited for her response. Amy side-stepped away from Carla, as though to reduce her chances of being hit by a stray bullet. Had a tumbleweed blown across the room, no one would have questioned its presence or timing.

Carla felt her face flushing. She tried to will it away, but it was impossible to hide her embarrassment. She twisted her face into a confused expression and said, "Excuse me?"

Craig's wife put her hands on her hips. "You heard me. Craig told me how you tried to recruit him to spy on the elders Tuesday night. It must have been a shock when he said no. I bet you're not used to hearing that word from men, except maybe your ex. That'll be Craig's answer the next time as well, so save your breath and stay away from my husband."

Carla's reliably tart tongue was glued in place. She couldn't deny she had tried to recruit Craig, but the way his wife had emphasized "stay away from my husband" added deeper meaning to the threat. The silence lasted long enough that even the conflict avoiders looked up to see what Carla would say. She scanned the group hoping to see a few sympathetic faces, but she knew better. All she saw instead was a roomful of jealous women who wanted her to stay away from their husbands as well.

She heard Amy clear her throat and say to Craig's wife, "If you're here to make sure we don't involve Craig, I can assure you--"

"That's not why I'm here," she said. "I'm here because Barney pissed me off. Assuming you all are done talking about Craig, I'd like for you to forget I'm his wife and treat me like any other woman who is tired of being bullied by men who claim to be Christians."

Amy smiled and said, "I think we can do that." She opened her arms in a welcoming gesture and addressed the group, "What do you all say?"

Everyone in the room applauded, except for Carla. She returned to her seat and didn't say another word for the rest of the meeting.

When one of the women asked Craig's wife what Barney had done, she recounted her phone conversation with him, choosing once again to leave out the part where she lied about her niece's baptism.

When she finished, Mary Andrews, a quiet soccer mom, raised her hand. She said, "I have a confession to make. I came here to-night with the intention of talking you all out of this crazy idea. I thought we were just trying to get the elders' attention. When they called our bluff, I assumed we would call off the strike. But after hearing about that phone call and the way Barney tried to manipu-late you, I have changed my mind. Pardon my language, but I'm sick of this crap, and I say it's time we do something about it."

The women of The Deborah Club whooped and hollered and gave each other a standing ovation. Amy watched with great satisfaction. They were ready. She also made a mental note to include some coarse language in her next motivational speech. It seemed to fire these church ladies up like nothing else.

Chapter 29

IT HAD BEEN a slow news day. That was the only reason Emily Branson had followed up on the tip about the latest conflict at a local church. She wouldn't have normally been interested. Christians were always fighting about something, especially the conservative, evangelical churches her mother had warned her about.

When her source--presumably one of the women at the church--told her about the impending strike, it piqued her curiosity. She had never heard of such a thing happening at a church. Since she didn't have anything else to report that day, she did some digging and found enough meat on the bones of the story to convince her producer to go with a live shot in front of the church. The same night Emily's report aired, a city councilman was arrested for driving under the influence of a controlled substance. Emily believed a busted politician was far more interesting than a church fight and her producer agreed, so she moved the South Barkley story to the back burner.

On Friday afternoon, three days after the report aired, Emily was sitting at her desk, eating a take-out salad and catching up on the comments below the video of her South Barkley report, which had been posted on the Channel 8 website within an hour of its airing. Emily monitored the comments for every one of her reports posted on the site. It was her least favorite part of the job. Comment sections on media websites were typically littered with brain droppings from some of humanity's worst bottom-feeders, courageous enough to share their offensive opinions only when their true identities were cloaked behind anonymous screen names.

Emily had learned to sift through the detritus, ignoring the crackpots and trolls whose sole talent was to post incendiary comments meant to provoke others into doing the same. Rather, she was looking for comments from those who claimed to have a personal connection to the story. It didn't happen often, but sometimes, especially when the story involved some form of discrimination, or a sexual scandal at a church or school, an insider would comment in defense of the accused or to pile on with additional information.

When these rare comments appeared, Emily accessed the login credentials of the commenter, which were required from everyone who posted on the site. The credentials included a public screen name and a private email address, visible only to the website administrator. Most commenters gave fake email addresses that bounced back immediately. Even when an address turned out to be legit, there was no guarantee of a reply. Emily had never run the numbers, but she guessed less than ten percent responded to her requests for more information. She had learned not to get her hopes up.

The first few comments on the South Barkley story were as off-the-wall and offensive as expected.

ScienceWinsEveryTime: Why would you waste your time reporting on stories about a squabble between a bunch of people who still believe in the great sky fairy? I say let them keep eating their young until their kind is completely extinct.

ShutUp&ManUp: I hope the men in this church stand strong against this onslaught of Femi-Nazis. They won't be happy until they teach every boy in America to pee sitting down. This will be our culture's downfall. Mark my words. The Amazons thought they had it figured out. Where are they now? Fight on men of South Barkley Bible Church!

DetachablePenis: ManUp should take his own advice and ShutUp. Having experienced our culture as both a man and a woman, I can tell you that while men have more power, women have more fun! Here's to my Sistas over at the South Barkley Bigot Church. I may have to visit this Sunday to show my support. LOL.

ShutUp&ManUp: Do the good folks at the South Barkley BIBLE Church a favor: stay at home and play with your lego penis.

ScienceWinsEveryTime: Maybe we should all go and watch them eat each other. Sadly, we can't throw them to the lions anymore, but this may be the next best thing.

JesusIsWeeping: This is exactly why the atheists are winning right now. As long as Christians keep fighting in public like this, more people will keep converting to atheism.

HairlessMonkey: Hey weeping jesus, you don't convert to atheism. You de-convert from christianity. If you're interested in being *unbaptized, let me know, and I'll show you how. It only costs $150 to file the paperwork. I take cash!*

GodHatesChurches: Wouldn't it be great if this church just withered up and died? One less church on the streets would make our community that much nicer. We could convert their empty building into a bar or strip club. Maybe DetachablePenis would dance for us!

Detachable Penis: I'm dancing in front of my computer right now. Wanna watch?

Emily scanned through these comments unfazed. While these nuggets of idiocy added nothing to the conversation, they were still signs of life. There was nothing more disappointing than spending hours or days working on a story only to watch it die a commentless death online.

Early Friday morning, after almost twenty-four hours without a new comment, someone using the screen name "Deb" joined the conversation.

Deb: Is anyone still watching this story? You should be. It's about to get interesting.

Another comment appeared an hour later.

Deb: The strike is on! Come to the South Barkley Bible Church on Sunday morning and watch us do nothing.

DetachablePenis: I'll be there with heels on but not much else. Hee Hee.

Emily clicked on the link at the bottom of Deb's comment and entered a password to access Deb's profile. She clicked Deb's email address and sent her a quick note. There was no sense in wasting time on the first email since so many of them bounced back.

Deb,
I saw your comment about the strike on the website. Are you a member of The Deborah Club? If so, I'd love to visit with you.
Emily Branson
Channel 8 News

Five minutes later, Deb replied.

Emily,
Yes, I'm a member of the club. I don't have anything to say except you should be there on Sunday morning. It is going to be glorious.
Deb

Emily sent another email asking Deb for a phone conversation. Deb's reply was almost instant.

No. See you Sunday.

When asked on questionnaires about her religious affiliation, Emily had recently started checking the "none" box, even though she was raised Catholic. Her mother made Emily and her four siblings go with her to Mass every week, while her father stayed at home, read the paper, and listened to weekly news programs like *Meet the Press* on TV.

When she was eleven years old, Emily found her mother in the kitchen and asked her why the Church didn't have any women priests.

"That's the way things have always been," her mother said, while peeling a potato. "It goes all the way back to the twelve Apostles. They were all men."

"That doesn't seem fair," Emily said. "I bet women are just as good at being priests as men are."

"That doesn't matter," her mom said, carefully dropping a naked potato in a pot of boiling water. "What matters is faithfully attending Mass and receiving the Sacraments. That's all you need to worry about."

When Emily asked why her dad didn't go to Mass with them, her mother said, "He's not Catholic. He's Baptist."

"What's a Baptist?"

"Go ask your dad."

When she marched into the living room where her dad was watching TV and asked him what a Baptist was, he said, "A Baptist is a kind of Christian who doesn't like Catholics."

Emily looked into the kitchen to see if her mom had heard him say this. "Why did you marry mom then?" she whispered.

"Because I'm not a very good Baptist," her dad whispered back, never taking his eyes off the TV.

"How come you never take me to the Baptist church?" Emily asked.

"Because I never go the Baptist church," he said. "Plus, your mom would kill me if I tried."

"Does the Baptist church have women priests?"

Finally looking at his daughter, he said, "The Baptist church doesn't have priests. They're called pastors, and they're nothing like priests."

"Does the Baptist church have women pastors?"

"Not the Baptist church I grew up in," he said.

"What do women in the Baptist church do then?"

"They do lots of things, I guess," he said. He reached for the remote control.

"What about during Mass?"

"Baptists don't call it Mass. They call it a worship service," her dad said.

"And what do women do in the worship service?"

He used the remote to mute the volume on the TV. "Why are you so interested in what happens at a Baptist church?" he asked.

"Because I don't like what happens at mom's church," Emily said. "I think women should be able to do what men do. I don't understand why the Catholics won't let them."

"You're wasting your time barking up the Baptist tree," he said. "At the Baptist church where I grew up, on Sunday morning the women were expected to sit still and keep their mouths shut. And they all wore hats. Ugly hats. They wore them every Sunday."

"Why?"

"Why the hats, or why were they expected to keep their mouths shut?"

"Both, I guess."

"I think it's because that's what the Bible says women are supposed to do. Not really sure. I never questioned it as a kid, and now I don't really care. Like I said, I'm not a very good Baptist."

"Is that why you don't go to the Baptist church anymore, because women have to keep their mouths shut?"

"No, honey. But I guess that would be as good a reason as any to stay away. I don't go to church because I don't need to spend time with a bunch of hypocrites to feel closer to God. Sitting in church doesn't make you a Christian any more than sitting in a hen house makes you a chicken."

Emily laughed. She liked this line and kept repeating it to herself the rest of the night until she had it memorized.

At her mother's insistence, Emily attended Mass until she graduated high school. During her first semester away at college, Emily decided she liked her dad's way of being a Christian more than her mom's. She was busy having fun with her friends. She also couldn't see herself sitting quietly in church for the rest of her life. She had a voice, and she wanted to use it.

Emily hadn't attended a church service of any kind in almost ten years. After reading Deb's email, she could feel her streak about to end. She thought through the complications of attending church as a reporter. Could she take her cameraman in for the service? Probably not. The church had the right to keep cameras out of their assembly. The parking lot was as close as he would get. This too bad. She would love for the women of The Deborah Club, not to mention the men who were oppressing them, to see her standing in their church building speaking into a microphone while being filmed by a man. While the men were preventing the women in their church from speaking, a woman would be telling the world about their stupidity. Of course, the sweet taste of this delicious irony would no doubt be lost on the numbskulls running the church. Did these guys not realize how far behind the times they were?

Even more puzzling than the hardheaded men leading the church was the number of good-hearted women who had tolerated it all these years. Why did they stay? This was one of the first questions she wanted to ask Deb.

She sent another email to Deb asking if she was the leader of The Deborah Club.

When Deb said no, Emily asked if Deb would put her in touch with whoever was.

Deb wrote, "I'll pass your email on to her, and she'll reach out to you if she wants to visit."

"Thanks," Emily responded, not really expecting to hear anything else for the rest of the day.

Emily wondered if there were similar movements afoot in the Catholic Church. Other than hearing the occasional sound bite from the new Pope and the seemingly endless revelations of sex scandals among priests, she hadn't paid much attention to what was going on in the Church. She couldn't believe priests were still forbidden to marry, even though such an archaic practice all but guaranteed even more sex scandals in the future.

When she was just out of college and ready to conquer the world, she asked her mom how she could continue to belong to a church still stuck in the Dark Ages. Her mother, taking no offense, shrugged and said, "I'm Catholic. Where else would I go?"

"Mom, that makes no sense."

"You're Catholic too, Emily," her mom said. "The Church will be here waiting for you when you're ready to come home."

Emily looked around the kitchen where she and her mom were sitting. She said, "This is my home. If God is everywhere, then I don't need to go to Mass to find him, do I?"

"You're right; God is everywhere. But he's in the Church especially."

"I don't see how that can be," Emily said. "Not when the Church is so full of hypocrites."

Her mom laughed. "Now you're starting to sound like your dad. Do you know what it means when you let a hypocrite come between you and God?"

"What?"

"It means the hypocrite is closer to God than you are."

"Mom!"

"Listen to me," her mom said, turning serious. "If you don't learn to see God at work in all things, including the hypocrites in the Church, you'll never find him."

"Who says I'm looking?"

"Everyone is looking," her mom said with absolute confidence. "Even the atheists."

That was the last time she and her mom had had a serious conversation about the Church. For the next few years, her mom would occasionally ask if she was attending Mass, usually around Christmas or Easter. Emily's curt responses made it clear she had no interest. Her mom eventually got the message and stopped bringing it up in their conversations, choosing instead to ask how things were going at work and when Emily was going to settle down, get married and give her a grandchild.

What would her mom think if she knew she was going to attend a protestant church, even if only for professional reasons? The thought of telling her mother made her nervous. More nervous, in fact, than the thought of walking into a strange church run by idiot men.

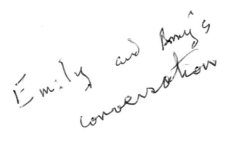
Emily and Amy's conversation

Chapter 30

FIRST THING SATURDAY morning, Emily checked her email on her phone before getting out of bed. It was a terrible--and apparently unbreakable--habit that prematurely launched her into work mode and amped her anxiety levels so high she couldn't enjoy a hot shower or her first cup of coffee. But this morning her bad habit paid off. Waiting in her Inbox was an email from Amy Brandt, with the subject line: The Deborah Club.

Emily rubbed her blurry eyes and tapped it open with her thumb.

A friend of mine told me you wanted to speak with someone from The Deborah Club. I'm available for a quick visit today if you're still interested. If you send me your phone number and a time to call, we can talk.

Thanks,

Amy Brandt

Emily was impressed by the cautious nature of the email and responded with appropriate caution of her own. She had no idea who Amy Brandt was or whether she really was a member of The Deborah Club. For all she knew, "Deb" could be just another twenty-something, pajama-wearing, unemployed cretin holed up in his mom's basement getting his jollies by messing with a TV reporter. It had happened before. So instead of giving "Amy" her cell number, she gave her office number and said she would be available at 10 a.m. Depending on how the call went, Emily might ask for a face-to-face meeting later that day.

She sent her reply, rolled out of bed, and launched into her morning routine. She checked her email fifteen minutes later and read Amy's reply: *I'll call you at 10 sharp.*

Emily hustled to get dressed and eat a decent breakfast before heading to her office to wait by the phone.

Her desk phone beeped right on schedule.

"Hello, this is Emily Branson."

"Hi Emily, this is Amy Brandt. Is this still a good time to talk?"

"Absolutely," Emily said. "Thanks for calling. I hate to sound so suspicious, but how do I know you really represent The Deborah Club?"

"The first person you called when you were following up on an anonymous tip--which did not come from me, by the way--was our pastor, Craig MacPherson. He told you he wasn't responsible for the decision and referred you to our elders. To my knowledge, the only elder you've spoken with so far is Ellis Monroe. That enough verification for you?"

"That'll do," Emily said. "Can you confirm that the strike is going to happen tomorrow?"

"First things first," Amy said. "Please don't use my name in any of your reports. This is not about me. I don't want to be the focus of this story, okay?"

"That's fine," Emily agreed. "I'll say I spoke to a representative from The Deborah Club. How's that?"

"That'll do," Amy said. "And the answer to your question is yes. We're ready to strike tomorrow morning. Unless, of course, I hear from the elders before then."

"You sound confident. Do you expect to hear from them?" Emily asked.

"No, I don't. They have zero interest in compromising. In fact, their initial response has made things much worse than necessary."

"How so?"

"It doesn't matter now," Amy said. "It's in the past and not worth talking about."

Emily took Amy's refusal in stride. "Okay, let's talk about The Deborah Club. My first question is, and forgive me if I'm missing something embarrassingly obvious, who is Deborah and why does she have a club?"

"That's a fair question," Amy said. "Unless you're familiar with the Old Testament, it probably doesn't make much sense. Deborah was one of the few women leaders in Israel's history. You can read her story in the Book of Judges. The CliffsNotes version is that God used Deborah to save his people. She was wise, smart, strong, and courageous. She's the ultimate example of a capable woman leader in the Bible."

"Interesting," Emily said and scribbled the phrase *Book Judges* on her notepad. "I grew up Catholic, and I have never heard of her."

"It's not a popular story in churches dominated by men," Amy said. "Deborah is not the only strong woman in it. There's another woman, Jael, who offers hospitality to the villain in the story. While he's asleep, she drives a tent peg through his temple."

"Ouch," Emily said.

"Exactly. That's what most men say when they read it as well. It's like a stake driven into the heart of their precious little kingdoms. They don't want to be reminded of what the Bible shows women doing."

"So they just ignore it?"

"Not completely. But when they do mention it, it's as a negative example to point out the necessity of male leadership in church and home."

"Wait, I'm confused," Emily said. "How do they get that from a story about a woman who is a strong leader?"

"Oh, you'd be surprised how creative men can be when twisting the Scriptures to prop up their empires. I once heard a pastor say that when God has to use a woman to lead his people, it is proof of just how badly all the men in the land have failed. He also said the only reason *the women's issue*--that's what they all call it--was becoming such a hot-button topic in some churches is because the men in those churches were neglecting their God-given responsibility to lead their families. He said the reason the story of Deborah is included in the Bible is to show how in the absence of God-ordained male leadership, women are forced to go against the created order and attempt to fill the void. He said it wasn't a story to be celebrated and certainly not imitated."

"Pastor Craig said all that?" Emily asked.

"No, no, no. Craig would never say something like that. This was thirty years ago in the little church where I grew up. The pastor was nearly seventy years old at the time."

"Yes, but I'm assuming things haven't really changed that much since then," Emily said. "Otherwise, there would be no need for The Deborah Club."

Amy was silent for a moment before answering. "Yes and no. The conversation has changed. More churches are willing to talk about women in leadership without blaming it on the men for failing to lead."

"How do you account for the change?"

"The more educated and exposed to diverse interpretations Christians are, the more open they are to reading the Bible differently."

"Read the Bible differently?" Emily said. "Doesn't it mean what it says?" Emily had always assumed the Bible was a straightforward book, irrelevant to her life, but straightforward. She had never considered there might be more than one way of reading it.

"Yes and no," Amy said.

"That's the second time you've said that."

"I promise I'm not trying to be evasive. It's complicated. Today we have a better understanding of the way ancient cultures influenced how women were treated in the early church and how they were described in the Bible. Since we no longer live in a patriarchal culture, we have to filter everything the Bible says through an interpretive grid to account for the cultural difference."

"Translation, please," Emily said. "If I don't understand it, I can't repeat it on camera."

"Sorry," Amy said. "I told you it was complicated. It means we don't have to take everything the Bible says about women, especially what they can't do in church, literally. There's a way to take seriously the overall message of the Bible—God's enduring love for humanity—without getting hung up on all the specific details that sound like nonsense to people living in the modern world."

Emily was fascinated by this new way of reading the Bible. "I have never heard anyone talk about the Bible this way," she said. The truth was it had been years since she had heard anyone talk about the Bible at all.

"I'm not doing it justice," Amy said. "You should hear Craig explain it. Several years ago, I was just about ready to dismiss the Bible as an interesting but useless relic from a bygone era. Then Craig became our pastor, and he recommended a few books that caused me to fall in love with the Bible all over again."

"Why is Craig opposing you if he believes the Bible can be read differently?" Emily asked.

"It's complicated, and I wouldn't say he's opposing us."

"But he's not supporting you either. At least not publicly."

"That's true," Amy said.

"What is he doing then?"

"That's not my question to answer. You'll have to ask him."

"I'll do that," Emily said and scrawled in big letters across the top of her notepad: GET PASTOR CRAIG TO TALK! "But here's what I don't understand. If there's greater openness to reading the Bible differently, why are you protesting the way women are treated at your church? Why make a ruckus if the conversation has changed?"

"You don't go to church, do you?" Amy asked.

"No, I don't," Emily said. The question embarrassed her, and she wasn't sure why. "I hope you won't hold that against me."

"Not at all. But if you went to a church like South Barkley, you'd know why a changing conversation means next to nothing."

"Help me understand then."

"Here's how it works. Every week in churches across the country, Christians gather in classes, study circles, and small groups to read the Bible and talk about what they think it means. Do you know what seasoned church-goers call these gatherings?" Amy asked.

"No idea," Emily said.

"We call them D and D classes. Discuss and dismiss," Amy said with a chuckle. "Isn't that great?"

"I don't get it," Emily said.

"We read the Bible and discuss what it means. We may even go so far as to talk about how our lives would be different if we actually practiced what we are discussing. Then we run out of time, class is dismissed, and we go on with our lives as if the discussion never happened. We show up the next week, and we do it all over again. Discuss, dismiss, do nothing. Rinse and repeat."

"That sounds frustrating," Emily said. "Especially if you are hoping things will change."

"It is frustrating. It's also why saying the conversation has changed isn't necessarily anything to get too excited about. I'm sad to say Christians spend a lot of time talking about things that have absolutely no impact on how we live."

Emily wondered if Amy was exaggerating the futility of these conversations and asked, "Yes, but don't you think if you keep talking about it, things will eventually get better?"

"Yes, but who has time to wait and see how long that will take?" Amy said. "Plus, for years the elders have used their willingness to have a conversation to placate those of us who are wanting to see some real progress. When we ask them when we're going to take a step forward, they say, 'We're talking about it,' and ask for more time. That used to be enough to make me happy, but I've reached a point where I think Elvis was right. A little less conversation, a little more action, please."

"Aren't there other churches out there where women are already free to lead?"

"Sure," Amy said. "Some churches have women pastors and elders. They make no distinctions between men and women."

"Then why wait? Why not just leave and go to one of those churches?"

"Easier said than done. This is my church. It's home. I don't want to leave, and I'm not sure where I would go if I did."

Amy's explanation reminded Emily of her mother. She couldn't understand why they were so loyal to their churches. "Can you foresee a time when you feel like you will have no other choice but to leave?"

"I thought I was going to leave a few days ago," Amy said. "But a stubborn woman from Indonesia talked me out of it."

"Huh?"

Amy told her the story about the women who decided it was time to bring clean water to their village.

"What a great story," Emily said. "Do you really see your cause in the same light as theirs?"

"Yes, I do," Amy said. "Not necessarily for me but for the little girls who are growing up in this church and for the little boys who will marry them. I grew up believing God loves boys more than he loves girls, because even at a young age, the little boys were asked to say prayers and read Scripture in church, while the best we poor little girls could do was sit in the pew and silently cheer them on. I'm staying and fighting for them."

"Do you have kids?" Emily asked.

"One daughter," Amy said. "She's away at college."

"What does she think about The Deborah Club?"

"She doesn't know. Or, at least, I haven't told her."

"How do you expect her to respond when you do tell her?"

"I'm not sure," Amy said. "She's not super interested in church right now. She's pledging a sorority this semester."

"What about your husband? How does he feel about what you're doing?"

"He's supportive. He also believes the time has come to move beyond conversation."

"So he won't be doing anything at South Barkley this Sunday?"

"Not a thing," Amy said. "But that's not out of the ordinary. He quit playing the church game a long time ago."

"What would you say to your critics who describe what you're doing as nothing more than a selfish power play and an embarrassment to the church?"

"I would say that my critics haven't read the Bible carefully enough. At least we're not threatening to turn over the communion table and knock over pews."

"Is that in the Bible?"

"No, but Jesus did something similar to get the attention of the religious leaders in Jerusalem."

"Oh, I see, but if memory serves, it didn't work, did it?"

"Yes, it did," Amy said. "In fact, it worked so well they crucified him a few days later."

"It sounds like you're prepared for the possibility that this story won't have a happily-ever-after ending."

"I am, but remember, what appeared to be Jesus' demise was actually his greatest victory. This particular effort may not work, but that doesn't mean God won't use it for good."

"How so?" Emily asked.

"Other women at other churches may hear our story and decide to try something similar. Or it may inspire a better idea in someone else. Who's to say what will come of this?"

"But you believe it will work, don't you?" Emily asked, hoping Amy said yes.

"Of course, I do. I wouldn't be talking to you right now if I didn't."

"Can I tell you something, off the record?" Emily asked.

"Isn't that something I'm supposed to say to you?"

"Normally, yes, but this is a special case."

"Okay, then. Off the record," Amy said.

"That means you won't tell anyone I'm telling you this."

Amy laughed. "I watch TV. I know what it means."

Emily said, "I hope it works. I hope it works so well at your church that it works at other churches too."

"Thanks," Amy said. "So are you going to be there tomorrow? I'd love for you to be my guest."

"Yes, I am," Emily said. "But not as your guest. I'll be there as a reporter, and unlike you, I won't be sitting on my hands doing nothing to make a point. I'll be working my butt off trying to make sure the world hears this story."

"Good," Amy said. "We'll see you tomorrow. And thanks for taking the time to visit with me."

"No, thank you."

Emily hung up and pondered their conversation. Most of it wasn't usable in a story, but it was helpful background information. She found Amy to be a fascinating woman. The kind she wished her mother had been when she was filled with doubts and questions. Like her mother, Amy loved her church and was loyal to it, and yet, she was willing to critique it and fight for change. She was easy to root for.

Emily didn't know anyone who still believed in the myth of media objectivity. Journalists were never neutral observers of unfolding events. They shaped every story they told by choosing which words to say, which facts to include, and which details to omit. What separated the good reporters from the hacks was that the good ones knew how to tell their stories from a particular point of view, while maintaining the appearance of objectivity.

Emily knew she would have to work hard to keep her personal feelings in check, especially if The Deborah Club was successful. There was nothing she would enjoy more than telling the story of how another pole holding up the sagging tent of chauvinism had been knocked down by a group of courageous women who had finally had enough.

Professional objectivity be damned. For the first time since she was a little girl, Emily was actually looking forward to going to church.

Chapter 31

CRAIG WAS NOT an early riser the other six days of the week, but he had no problem waking up before dawn every Sunday morning. The task of facing a congregation of over-entertained and all-too-easily bored listeners, who evaluated his sermons like judges at a figure skating competition, provided ample motivation to get up and practice his sermon out loud several times. He did this to keep from accidentally preaching heresy or messing up the punch line of a joke, although in truth he usually worried more about the jokes than the heresy.

On this particular Sunday morning, Craig's eyes popped open two hours earlier than usual. It was pointless to try going back to sleep, so he quietly slipped out of bed and tip-toed into the kitchen to make a pot of coffee and prepare to deliver the most important sermon of his career.

Between bouts of self-flagellation for his absolute incompetence as a leader, Craig had let himself entertain the possibility he could somehow preach his way out of this mess. He knew this to be a common fantasy among embattled pastors. He also knew it almost never worked. He was, however, quite proud of the sermon he had written. If he nailed the delivery, which he had every intention of doing, then maybe the gospel would solve this problem. It was only a paper-thin shaving of hope, but who was he to place limitations on the Holy Spirit? This thought sustained him through his first cup of coffee.

On the way to refill his cup, he stopped at the kitchen sink and stared out the window. The shroud of darkness covering his back-yard in the predawn hours enveloped his heart. Try as he might, he couldn't envision a positive outcome. If the strike worked and the elders gave in, then Barney and his friends would leave, crippling the church financially. If Barney and his band of manly men were able to outlast The Deborah Club, then some of the best and bright-est young families would likely give up and go elsewhere, leaving Craig stuck with a bunch of sticks in the mud.

Who was he kidding? Even if he preached his best sermon ever, Craig could see the writing on the wall. He was done at South Barkley. This made him sad. South Barkley was far from a perfect church, but he knew he could do much worse. He also loved living in this part of the country. The quality of life was phenomenal-- never too hot or cold, with countless outdoor activities available four seasons of the year. The schools were top notch. It was the kind of city in which people made sacrifices to live, including learn-ing to tolerate tyrants like Barney so they could keep their jobs.

The thought of being forced to move his family depressed him. With his luck, they would end up back in the south, melting in the summer, or even worse, someplace up north where they would spend their winters digging out from blizzards. He would probably have to take a smaller church, which meant a smaller salary and bigger problems. Pastors who left their church in the state of disarray about to descend on South Barkley moved down, not up, the career ladder. Unless they fell off it completely. This is what scared Craig the most. Being a pastor was all he knew how to do. If his original email to Amy ever came to light, which it surely would, the word would spread, and he would never be able to convince another elder board to trust him again. Craig surmised it might be easier for a pastor to come back from committing adultery than from destroying a church. He let out a heavy sigh. *You're screwed no matter what you say. Ain't no sermon gonna save you today.*

He poured his second cup of coffee and went back to the kitchen table to brood. As soon as he sat down and read through his sermon notes again, he felt hope return. In just a few hours, the South Barkley Bible Church would gather. Thanks to the coverage from Channel 8, it would be standing room only. Those who came hoping to see some fireworks would be disappointed. There might be some chaos before the service as Barney and his boys scrambled to take care of a few unforeseen details. Since women aren't allowed to do anything in the service anyway, once it was underway everything would feel relatively normal, except for the anticipation hanging in the air when Craig stepped behind the podium to deliver his sermon. At that moment, everyone would lean forward, ready to hear what he had to say.

Would he play the hireling and pander to Barney and his cronies by thanking the men for their extra work? This is what Barney wanted him to do. Or would he play the rebel by expressing support for The Deborah Club, while simultaneously saying goodbye to his job? Or would he play the coward and say nothing about the strike at all?

Craig had given much thought to these options while writing his sermon and had decided the best way to address the situation wasn't head on but from the side. The gospel did its best work when coming in at an angle. One of his preaching professors in seminary had repeatedly quoted Emily Dickinson's line, "Tell all the truth but tell it slant." This was exactly what he intended to do. He would let the gospel pose a challenge to those on both sides of the conflict by reminding them of the sacrificial, self-giving love displayed by the crucified Christ, who found a way to defeat evil while dying for his enemies. Perhaps the example of Jesus would soften hearts and stir imaginations and inspire both sides to change their tactics. If the gospel worked its magic, which in his experience it seldom seemed to do anymore, he believed South Barkley could be saved. And if it didn't, then all would be lost, but this would also be the outcome if he picked a side or kept his mouth shut. He had nothing to lose, and everything to gain. Skimming over his notes one last time, he was once again impressed by how good his sermon was. Today the South Barkley Bible Church was getting neither a hireling nor a rebel and certainly not a coward. The good people of South Barkley were getting a preacher, armed with the gospel. It might not work, but it couldn't hurt.

Craig took a sip of cool coffee from his cup. He wanted to warm it up with a refill, but he dared not walk past the kitchen window again.

Chapter 32

CRAIG'S WIFE ROLLED over and reached out for him. Finding his side of the bed empty, she checked the time: 5:16 a.m. Fifteen years of marriage had taught her there were only two reasons for Craig to ever be awake at this hour: one was to catch an early flight and the other was because he was worried about losing his job. He kept saying The Deborah Club would be the end of his ministry at South Barkley, but she thought he was being overly dramatic. Now she knew he really believed it. She felt a tinge of guilt for not sharing the burden of her husband's anxiety, though not enough to squelch her anticipation for the day ahead.

Though Craig wouldn't want to hear it--and after what she had said about his leadership, he probably wouldn't believe it--she was proud of him. It was his idea, and even though he had distanced himself from The Deborah Club, none of this would be happening if he hadn't thought of it. She also believed it had been God's will for him to send his email to Amy Brandt instead of her. If she had been the first to read it, it would have never seen the light of day. She would have patted her affirmation-seeking husband on the head for coming up with such a brilliant idea and commended him for being an advocate for women and that would have been the end of it. But God had other plans for Craig's email, and it landed in front of the only person at South Barkley capable of doing something with it.

This was going to be one the most important days of her life, and she couldn't wait to watch it unfold. She just wished Craig wasn't so twisted with worry. If only he could relax and enjoy watching God show up and show off.

She was also looking forward to seeing Barney's face when she arrived for church. *Why yes, Barney, I'm here. No, Barney, I have no intention of working for you in the nursery. Have fun changing diapers, and don't forget to wash your hands.*

More than any other man she knew, Barney needed to suffer a good case of disappointment at the hands of a woman. He needed to come up against an untamable spirit who refused to submit to his domineering personality, which for too long he had yielded like a sledgehammer in a glass factory. Though she would never admit it to anyone, not even Craig, this battle was just as much about beating Barney as it was about setting women free. That both could be accomplished at the same time made it so much sweeter. Even if Craig's worries were justified, and they had to leave South Barkley, defying Barney would be worth the sacrifice. Win or lose, stay or leave, her time serving under Barney was over. No matter the final outcome, she already felt free.

Chapter 33

Barney sat at his kitchen table eating his traditional Sunday morning breakfast of French toast sprinkled with powdered sugar and drenched in maple syrup, with four slices of bacon on the side. Wanda had been making the same breakfast every Sunday morning for the past thirty years, ever since their kids were old enough to sit at the table and eat real food with utensils. When she first began the tradition, Barney had asked why they didn't eat their syrupy treat meal on Saturday mornings like most other families did. Wanda had said she wanted the kids to think of Sunday, not Saturday, as the most special day of the week because it was the Lord's Day. The logic made perfect sense to Barney, and he was thankful to be blessed with a wife who thought in such a way.

Wanda continued the tradition, even though it had been over ten years since Mitch, their youngest, had lived with them. When he left for college, Barney had suggested it was no longer necessary for her to go to the extra trouble of making him a special breakfast on Sunday. A bowl of cold cereal and a cup of strong coffee would suit him just fine. Wanda wouldn't hear of it and told him it was her way of keeping the memories of all those Sunday mornings with her kids alive and well in her heart. When it came to her own cherished traditions, she could be just as stubborn as Barney. So every Sunday morning, before heading off to oversee what happened at South Barkley, he took his place at the table and allowed her to send his insulin levels through the roof.

Barney had always taken his responsibility as an elder of the church seriously. He believed he was accountable for everything said and done during the worship service. If he allowed anything to happen that didn't please God, he was certain he would have to answer for it on the Day of Judgment.

Growing up in church, he heard one preacher after another repeatedly describe what kind of worship God demands from his people. They imbedded phrases like "in Spirit and in truth" and "decently and in order" deep in his soul, long before he was old enough to understand what these serious sounding phrases meant.

As a young man, he assumed the kind of worship God desired and the way his home church worshipped were one and the same. As he matured, he had come to the begrudging conclusion that naming and describing proper worship from God's perspective was more complicated than the over-confident preachers of his youth had made it sound.

While Barney still believed there were wrong ways to worship God, he could no longer say with confidence there was only one right way to do it. Although he initially resisted, he finally permitted the worship at South Barkley to become more informal and less predictable. During Craig's first year, he kept surprising Barney by deviating from the usual order of worship. Sometimes his sermon was at the end and sometimes he moved it to the beginning. Craig also fancied himself as an "innovative communicator." This meant occasionally showing a clip from a popular movie or bringing a prop on stage to make a point.

Barney didn't like any of it, but the younger people in the church did and so did Wanda. Or, at least, she liked the idea of the young people liking what was happening at church. "If we don't change a little bit, we're going to lose them all," she said. It took some doing, but she finally talked him into letting it go, but the one thing he refused to tolerate was being surprised on a Sunday morning. He liked knowing what was coming, not only for his own peace of mind, but also because he liked being able to tell others he knew what was coming. A surprised elder was an elder who wasn't really in charge. So he and Craig struck a deal. Craig would let Barney know in advance when he was planning something out of the ordinary, and Barney wouldn't fuss about the changes as long they served a purpose other than just trying to make people uncomfortable. Barney saw no sense in change for change's sake. If it didn't need fixing, why break it?

This was one of the biggest reasons Barney had resisted the move to include more women in church leadership roles. He never saw it as a problem in need of fixing. Churches had been doing just fine for centuries with an all male leadership structure. What problem was it solving to have women pray out loud or serve as ministry leaders or deacons or elders? In his estimation, these changes would only end up creating bigger problems in the long run.

His daughter, Sherri, had never mentioned being bothered by the way women were treated at South Barkley. That she was just as capable to pray out loud or read scripture or make decisions as her little brother wasn't up for debate. She was a natural leader who, from the moment she could walk and talk and tell other people what to do, never shied away from taking charge of a situation.

Her little brother was a different story. Barney had recognized the problem early on. Even though they were only two years apart, Sherri was so confident and outgoing, she overshadowed Mitch in all situations. If he or Wanda asked one of the kids to volunteer for a task, Sherri would step up and do it, and Mitch would disappear into the background and let her.

So Barney started pushing Mitch to be more assertive. He made him order his own meals in restaurants, even though Sherri was always willing to do it for him. He would ask Mitch to pray before family meals, and they would sit in silence until Mitch squeaked out a few sentences of gratitude to God. In one legendary stand-off, Barney asked Mitch to pray, and Mitch refused. The family sat in silence for ten agonizing minutes waiting for Mitch to say something. Sherri volunteered to do it several times, and Barney said no. When Mitch said, "Just go ahead and let her do it, so we can eat," Barney slammed his hand on the table, rattling the dishes and sending his family through the roof. "I don't want to hear her voice," he said through clenched teeth. "I want to hear yours." Mitch finally relented and said a quick prayer, and Barney ate his cold food with the satisfaction of knowing he was forging Mitch into a strong young man.

As the kids grew older, it was almost as if they swapped personalities. Sherri became more quiet and shy and less willing to speak up, especially in front of her dad. Meanwhile, Mitch became more outgoing. By the time he was in high school, Barney no longer had to prod his son to pray at the table. He was eager to do it. After Mitch moved out of the house, Barney learned it had all been an act. Mitch had been pretending to be something he wasn't to keep Barney off his back. As a father, Barney's deepest regret was that he hadn't started training Mitch for manhood sooner. He waited too long and took action after the damage had already been done.

Barney's failure with Mitch had shaped his philosophy of church leadership. He believed boys needed to be pushed into leadership roles at the earliest age possible, especially in the spiritual realm. Otherwise, they would grow into passive men. Over the years, he had noticed how more and more men at South Barkley were acting like Mitch had when he was a little boy. They were sitting on the sidelines content to let bolder, more aggressive women volunteer to fill the void created by their laziness. The only way to motivate these men was to reserve leadership roles in the church exclusively for them. When they realized no one else was going to step up and take their spot, they would finally become the leaders God created them to be. Barney was convinced this would never happen in a church where eager women were allowed to fill these leadership roles first.

Let the feminazis complain all they want about the lack of opportunities to use their gifts. Barney wasn't budging. Not with this much at stake. Couldn't women like Amy Brandt see how their selfish ambition was giving the men around them permission to invest their energy in far less spiritual pursuits than church leadership? Maybe they didn't care as long as they got their way. This was all the evidence Barney needed to confirm his belief that these women weren't fit to lead in the first place.

When a few young liberals began pressuring the elders to include more women in roles of church leadership a few years back, Barney wanted to squash them like bugs, but he let Ellis and Wanda talk him out it.

"If we don't address their concerns," Ellis had said, "we're going to lose a lot of our young people to more progressive churches."

Barney didn't like giving in to the demands of those too young and inexperienced to know the way the world really works, but he also didn't like seeing kids who had grown up at South Barkley join other churches.

"What's the harm in talking about it?" Wanda had said. "Maybe we've had it wrong all these years."

Barney was quite certain he wasn't wrong. Plain as day, the Bible said women were forbidden to exercise authority over men by teaching or speaking when the church was gathered for worship or by filling the God-ordained leadership offices of elder or deacon.

When Ellis suggested the elders begin to study the issue for themselves, Barney went along with it, believing he had both the truth and time on his side. He knew how long it would take a group of busy men with full-time jobs to study and discuss such a controversial topic in their spare time. In his mind, when the elders finally got around to finishing their study and shared their conclusions with the church--conclusions that would support the traditional position of male leadership--the young people Ellis so badly wanted to placate would be older and wiser and less interested in stirring the pot.

But as the study progressed, Barney was alarmed to see how willing the other elders were to entertain bogus interpretations of Scripture from feminist scholars hell-bent on rewriting the Word of

God to support their liberal agendas. Had he known they would be so easily swayed, he would have stuck to his original bug-squashing strategy. Since it was too late to halt the study--they had made the mistake of telling the church they would study the issue and report back to them--Barney redoubled his efforts to stall any further action.

When one of the elders would suggest they responsibly open up more opportunities for women to use their leadership gifts at South Barkley, Barney would request more time for study and prayer. The other elders knew they couldn't move forward without Barney's support, so they kept indulging his requests, believing them to be sincere. When one of the elders announced his resignation because he and his wife were moving to be closer to their grandchildren, Barney recruited Jake, one of his long-time friends, to replace him. At Jake's first elders' meeting, Barney suggested they take a few months to review what they had studied so far to bring his friend up to speed. Jake turned out to be even more studious and prayerful than Barney. Barney's strategy was working like a dream until Amy Brandt decided she wanted to be in charge.

Barney sopped up what remained of the syrup with the last bite of French toast and shoved it into his mouth. It was time to go do the job of an elder and protect his flock from a wolf. He pushed away from the table and stood with purpose like a soldier answering the call of duty. Amy Brandt was about to experience the futility of challenging him. He tilted his head from side to side. His neck made a cracking sound. He loved stand-offs. He lived for them. He had never lost one. Just like the role of women at his church, this wasn't about to change. He marched out of the kitchen, leaving his dirty plate on the table for Wanda to deal with later.

Chapter 34

AMY BRANDT LOOKED at herself in the mirror and considered skipping the eyeliner. Her hands were trembling, and she feared she'd look like a Panda after applying it. She couldn't remember ever being this nervous, not even before her wedding. She had no reason to feel this way. She wasn't in the South taking on the KKK or in North Korea publicly defying the supreme leader. She wasn't even preparing to stand in front of a hostile crowd to deliver a controversial speech. She had one job today: show up at church and do nothing. This was hardly a reason to be overcome with nerves.

Her churning stomach wasn't buying it. Amy wasn't just another member of The Deborah Club. She was the leader who had given Emily Branson an interview. Emily would be there today, watching everything and taking notes. She would ask Amy for a comment, maybe an on-camera interview in the parking lot. Amy was about to be the face of their movement, which was why she couldn't skip the eyeliner.

Over the weekend, her biggest worry had been that a few soft-hearted members of The Deborah Club would have compassion on a struggling man and help him in his time of need. She had sent out a final email yesterday emphasizing how important it was for everyone to stick together. She even broke out Ben Franklin's famous admonition given to his fellow revolutionaries: "We must all hang together, or assuredly, we shall all hang separately." Last night, she called a few of the women she was most concerned about to see how they were doing. They all assured her they were ready. She could stop worrying. There was nothing left for her to do but sit back and watch Barney squirm.

Barney. That man. Not a man, a bully. A cornered tyrant who wasn't going down without a fight. The memory of his round face, red with anger in the elders' meeting, sent a chill through her. She had done everything possible to prepare her ladies, but who could guess what Barney had planned? She remembered one of Tom's favorite sayings: "No battle plan survives first contact with the enemy." This, she realized, was why her inner pep talk wasn't working. She did have cause for worry. Her pounding heart, upset stomach and trembling hands were warning her of impending danger. She didn't have the luxury of showing up and doing nothing today like the other ladies. She was their leader, and she had to be ready to respond to whatever craziness Barney brought with him to church.

This realization allowed her to reclassify her feelings. She wasn't suffering from a bad case of nerves. It was dread. A voice deep inside was telling her something was going to go horribly wrong today. Something she wouldn't be capable of handling. She thought of Joan's refusal to follow her and Carla's constant challenges to her authority, and though she tried to ignore it, she heard Barney's voice saying, *"If she's the best the women of this church have to offer, then God help us."*

She was ashamed of her feelings. This was supposed to be their day of victory. This is what she had told everyone to expect, but she couldn't escape the sense of doom looming over her. Not knowing what else to do, she prayed for peace. As she did, her dreadful feelings increased. She wondered if God was trying to get her attention. Should she call off the strike? She imagined trying to explain her decision to Emily Branson. *I called off the strike because God told me to.* Then she saw herself sitting in her living room, watching Emily repeating her explanation on Channel 8. Amy would look like a religious kook who, just before the moment of truth, lost her nerve. This was an unacceptable outcome. If God wanted her to call the strike off, she needed something more definitive than feeling like she was about to throw up. And why was she attributing these negative feelings to God? God loved to set people free from tyrants. Now that she had taken a moment to doubt her doubts, she was able to discern the true source behind her crisis of confidence. She was being attacked by Satan. Nothing would please him more than seeing the women of South Barkley remain in bondage.

It took two tries, but she finally got her eyeliner right. It wasn't perfect but good enough to call it quits. She finished getting dressed and discovered that for the first time in their marriage, she was ready for church before Tom. Unable to enjoy the accomplishment, she paced through the house until it was time to leave.

Chapter 35

EMILY BRANSON WAS watching for Mike, her cameraman, to pull up in front of her duplex in the Channel 8 van. She was out the door and halfway down the sidewalk before he came to a full stop. She climbed into the seat next to him and said, "Did you get me some coffee?"

"No," he croaked.

Emily looked him over. "What's wrong, Mikey? You stay out too late last night?"

"Maybe," he said.

"You need coffee," she said. "I need coffee. Let's get some coffee."

He rubbed his right eye with the palm of his hand. "We can stop on the way."

"Okay, but let's hurry," she said. "I want to get there and get set up before they start to arrive."

"You want coffee or not?"

"Grumble, grumble, grizzly bear."

"I hope this isn't a waste of time."

"It won't be. I gotta feeling," she said.

"Of course you do. Do you think the church leaders are going to let us stand by the door and harass people as they walk into church?"

"The worst they can do is kick us off the property," she said.

"Or stone us."

"I think churches stopped stoning people a few years ago. Too much negative publicity." Her eyes lit up as if she had remembered some good news. "But I do think they still burn witches at the stake."

"Hope your outfit is flame retardant," he said.

She punched him awkwardly in the arm with her left hand. "How dare you!"

"I'm not saying you're a witch. I'm just saying they're going to treat you like one."

"If they do, I'm going to say you're my loyal servant who gathers the toadstools I use in my potions. You're going up in smoke too, buddy."

Mike grunted and said, "I think I would rather get stoned."

"It wouldn't be the first time," she teased.

"Hilarious," he said. "If reporting doesn't work out, you should try stand up."

She rubbed her hands together in anticipation. "Yep, I have a good feeling about this one."

"You say the same thing about every story we cover," he said.

"I know, but this one is different. I don't know why, but I think this one is going to be big."

"How big?" he teased.

"I don't want to jinx it, but it's got all the right ingredients. Religious oppression. Gender discrimination. Civil disobedience. We just need something wack to happen to take it to the next level."

"Wack?" Mike said. "What did I tell you about using street slang you don't know the meaning of?"

"Of which I don't know the meaning," Emily corrected. "Keep dangling your prepositions like that, and you'll never get out from behind the camera. And wack means something unexpected and exciting, a surprising turn of events."

"No, it doesn't. It means something lame or inferior. As in, if nothing exciting happens today, this story is going to be wack. And one doesn't dangle prepositions. One dangles participles. I can't believe they let you in front of a camera."

"Okay, okay," she said, holding up her hands in surrender. "My bad. I still think something is going to happen today to blow this story sky high. When it does, I'm going to have a front row seat."

"So you're still going inside?" he asked.

"Yep. You still refuse to come with me?"

"I am the cameraman. My camera is my baby. If they don't want my baby inside their church, they don't want me."

"You're not curious to see what happens? Not even a little?"

"Nothing that happens inside a church is of interest to me," he said. "I'll be happy to stand street-side and capture drive-by footage of those too smart to turn into the South Barkley parking lot."

He slowed the van as they approached a Starbucks on their right.

"Don't wander too far away from the van," she said. "Just in case we need to make a quick exit."

"Sure thing, Broom Hilda."

The van swerved as he tried to dodge another punch.

Chapter 36

"I CAN'T BELIEVE you're playing sick today," Ellis said as he slipped on his dress shoes. "I could really use your moral support."

"What you could use is enough common sense to get back in bed and play sick with me," said Grace, his wife of twenty-nine years. She was still in bed after diagnosing herself with a highly contagious, but short-lived, illness. She had assured Ellis she'd be feeling better by lunch.

"You know it's not that simple," he said.

"Oh, it never is when Barney's involved. Sometimes I wish he would get mad enough to go somewhere else and leave the rest of us alone."

"No, you don't," Ellis said. "The church would go bankrupt, and I'd be grumpier than I am right now."

"That's hard to imagine. What has he got you doing today?"

"I'm preparing communion. Shouldn't be too hard."

"Try not to spill any on your white shirt," she said. "Or better yet, just change into a red one."

"You're enjoying this a little too much. Sure you don't want to come and watch the show?"

"You sure you don't want to stay here with me?"

"Of course I do," he said. "But you know I can't, and I wish you wouldn't either. You know he's going to ask about you."

"Sorry, honey, but you and your friend Barney are on your own today. I'll just stay here and pray that everything goes well."

"Goes well for the church or well for The Deborah Club?" His keys rattled as he put them in his pocket.

"We both know there shouldn't be a difference between the two," she said.

Ellis looked at her and sighed.

"I'd pray against Barney if it didn't mean I had to pray against you too," she said.

"Go ahead and pray against him," Ellis said. "I'll do my best to dodge the debris if the ceiling falls in on him."

Chapter 37

CARLA WAS SITTING on her couch, in her pajamas, ignoring the chatter from a Sunday morning news show on TV. She had already decided to skip the worship service at South Barkley, which would start in little over an hour. She was still fuming over the embarrassing exchange with Craig's wife at the coffee shop on Thursday night. She no longer cared about the strike or helping The Deborah Club accomplish its goals. Her new mission in life was to run Craig and his stupid little wife out of town.

She had learned as a teenager that no one wants to hear a pretty girl whine about how hard it is to be beautiful. She was accustomed to keeping her frustrations to herself. Whether it was school, work, church, or the PTA, she always found herself in the same predicament.

Other women resented her. They attributed her accomplishments to her looks, rather than her talent, intellect, or hard work. When they weren't making snide comments behind her back about how much easier everything is for the beautiful people of the world, they were spitting and hissing in her face like cornered cats, as if Carla's only goal in life was to steal their men.

Of course, it would be easier to convince other women she posed no threat to them if their husbands and boyfriends could keep from scanning her with elevator eyes every time she walked into a room. It didn't seem to matter how she dressed or how little attention she paid to the idiots who tried to flirt with her in front of their wives. It was her fault for being beautiful.

If trying to befriend jealous women wasn't hard enough, she also had to protect herself from guys who were never satisfied with just being friends. She envied other women when she heard them talk about their platonic friendships. While she believed such relationships were possible, she had never experienced one for herself. Every boy she teamed up with for a school project and every man she worked closely with at the PR firm eventually made a move on her. She had even had a family man proposition her in a closet during a home showing, all while his wife and kids were checking out the rest of the house.

In college, the animals couldn't keep themselves from grabbing her ass. She was not afraid to slap a wandering hand, or if she really didn't like the guy, a face. The grown boys she had worked with at the PR firm were more professional and sophisticated, but no less aggressive. They bombarded her with verbal come-ons, cloaked in just enough innuendo to be explained away as an innocent misunderstanding in the event she parried their advance, which she always did with enough biting sarcasm to warn them against trying it again. Even the men who made a big deal about how committed they were to their wives made her uncomfortable by refusing to be alone with her or avoiding eye contact during meetings. She had learned the harder a man worked to ignore her, the more attracted to her he really was.

While she had never used the physical act of sex to her professional advantage, she was an expert at using her sex appeal to manipulate her co-workers. It worked particularly well with the holier-than-thou-avoider types. When she took the initiative, they turned to putty in her hands. Though it was a dangerous game to play, and it made her feel like a hypocrite, she learned to use the same tricks men used on her. Only she was much better at it than they were.

This was why her failed attempt to play Craig had left her so rattled. No man had ever been more obvious in his efforts to ignore and avoid her than he. In situations where he was forced to talk to her, he fumbled through their conversations like a tongue-tied junior high boy. During his sermons, he let his eyes linger on her a split second longer than anyone else in the congregation. She understood why. It was the only time he could look at her without getting into trouble with his wife. Sometimes, she could feel him watching her at church events. She'd bet a million dollars he thought about her while having sex with his run-down wife.

In the church parking lot, when she had hinted at what might be possible between them if they formed a secret alliance, she expected him to pledge allegiance to her like an Eagle Scout standing before Old Glory. Once he gave her the information she wanted, she'd turn cool and cut off contact with him. What was he going to say? To whom could he complain? If he confronted her, she had carefully covered her tracks with double meaning and innuendo, just like the boys at the office had taught her. It was a foolproof routine. Or, at least, it had been on every other fool she'd worked with. But Craig turned out to be more than a fool--he was a pastor with a conscience, who loved his wife more than he let on.

A simple "no" to her request for help was all he had needed to say. She would have pressed a little harder and stepped closer to the edge, but if he had stuck to his original commitment to remain uninvolved, she would have relented and left him alone until a more opportune time. That's how it would have worked at the office. Both men and women knew how to reject an unwelcome advance in such a way as to let the initiator save face.

But not Craig the idiot pastor. He articulated out loud his interpretation of what she was hinting at, which confirmed her suspicion she had been playing a starring role in his fantasies, while leaving her no room for a graceful retreat. Her only option was to act mortified and pretend there had been a terrible misunderstanding. It was the quickest way out of the parking lot, but it didn't take the sting out of Craig openly accusing her of trying to seduce him. She'd never been so humiliated. When she raced out of the parking lot, she hoped he was just as embarrassed as she was and would never say a word to anyone about their conversation. But then his wife showed up at the coffee shop and told her off in front of the group.

What kind of man goes home and tells his wife that a woman he's obviously attracted to just made him an offer he didn't want to refuse? One who has forgotten that the woman he just humiliated knows a nasty secret about him.

Craig's fate was sealed on Thursday night. She left the meeting knowing she was going to tell Barney that Craig was behind The Deborah Club's big idea. What she couldn't decide was when. The timing was crucial. If she waited too long and The Deborah Club prevailed, Craig might end up being treated as a hero. If she revealed the secret too soon, it would sabotage The Deborah Club's efforts. Craig would lose his job for sure, but The Deborah Club would also lose.

But did she really want to be part of a woman's movement orchestrated by a man too cowardly to stand by his own idea? Of course not. Did she even want to be part of The Deborah Club anymore?

When Craig's wife embarrassed her in front of the other women, she could feel their approval, even as they tried to fake their shock. They loved seeing another woman put her in her place. It was a fantasy come true. When no one came to her defense, not even Amy, an old, wretched truth rose up and slapped her in the face with its bony hand--a truth that hadn't changed since high school. She didn't belong, and these women would never accept her. At that moment, she ceased to be a member of The Deborah Club. No, the truth was she had never been, nor would she ever be, a member of their club.

Carla sprung from the couch and over to a bookshelf in her living room. She pulled out her church directory and turned to the page that listed the contact information for the elders. Barney's cell phone wasn't listed, but his home phone was. She hoped he hadn't left for church yet. She was cutting it close.

Chapter 38

CRAIG PULLED INTO the church parking lot and saw the Channel 8 van parked in the far corner. Emily Branson was sitting on the passenger side next to a scruffy looking guy in the driver's seat. He considered telling them to move their van off of church property. But then they'd bring out their camera, and Emily Branson would start asking questions, which he would refuse to answer, and he would appear to be an overly paranoid pastor with something to hide. If the elders wanted them off church property, they could do it themselves. He drove around to the rear of the building to his customary spot, slipped in through the back door, and immediately went and hid in his office, hoping to be left alone until it was time to preach.

→→☲◑ ◐☲←←

Emily and Mike saw the blue Ford Taurus drive through the parking lot and around to the back of the building.

"I'm pretty sure that's Pastor Craig," Emily said.

"Do you want to pull around and catch him when he gets out of his car?" Mike asked.

"No. He won't talk." She looked across the parking lot at the empty spaces between the van and the front door. "Besides, I don't want to lose our great parking spot."

Mike sipped his coffee. "Tell me again why we're here this early."

"Because I have no idea when people will start showing up for church. Better safe than sorry."

Thirty minutes later, a red pick-up truck pulled into the parking lot and took one of the spots closest to the entrance.

"Here we go," Emily said as she opened the front door and sprinted for the entrance. Mike scrambled to grab his camera from the back of the van and ran to keep up with Emily. The man, tall and skinny and dressed in starched blue jeans and a tan sports coat, was almost to the door.

"Excuse me! I'm Emily Branson from Channel 8 news. Are you a member of the South Barkley Bible Church?"

The man didn't stop walking. "Yes, I am," he said.

"How do you feel about what The Deborah Club is doing? Do you think it will work? What do you expect will happen today?" She squeezed in as many questions as possible before he reached the door.

"No comment," he said and walked inside the building.

Over the next fifteen minutes, thirty-two men pulled into the parking lot and walked into the building without giving Emily one usable quote. Most of them said nothing more than "No comment." They had been coached, and they were sticking to the game plan. The only exception was a young man who, when Emily asked why so many men were showing up so early, said, "We have a meeting."

"Be quiet and get inside," barked an older man, as he approached the door.

The young man held the door open for his elder. "Sorry, Mr. Staples."

Emily had studied the names of the elders listed on the website and recognized this one. "Barney Staples? Is there anything you would like to say on behalf of the elders?"

Barney stepped through the door, turned around, and looked at her with contempt. "You have five minutes to get off of church property, or I'm calling the police."

Emily hoped he was bluffing. Either way, she wasn't worried. It wouldn't be the first time she had been asked to leave a gathering held on private property. If the police showed up, she'd have Mike move their van to the street. In the meantime, she planned to stay put and see if she could get someone to talk.

Chapter 39

Barney's wife answered the phone after the third ring.

"Hi Wanda, this is Carla Tanner from church. Is Barney there?"

"No, he's not," Wanda said. "May I ask why you're calling?"

Carla couldn't blame her for being suspicious. She and Barney weren't regular conversation partners. "There's something he needs to know before church starts."

"What is it? I can tell him when I get there. I'm leaving in a few minutes."

Carla appreciated the impatience in Wanda's voice. She was in a hurry too. "I appreciate that, but this is something he needs to hear from me. May I have his cell number?"

"If this is about the strike, you're wasting your time unless you're going to apologize," Wanda said. "He's not going to give in. You all should be ashamed of yourselves. This is not the way to get what you want."

"It's not about The Deborah Club," Carla lied. "But it is something he needs to know. Today. Before church starts. May I please have his number?"

"It won't do any good," Wanda said. "He turns his phone off when he gets to church. He thinks it's terrible when people let their cell phones ring in the middle of the service. So do I."

"May I have his number anyway?" Carla said, faking desperation. "It never hurts to try."

"Okay," Wanda said, "but I'm warning you. He doesn't need any added pressure today."

"No pressure," Carla said. "I'm doing him a favor. He'll like hearing what I have to say."

⇥⊨⊙ ⊙⊨⊣

Barney was looking out one of the windows in the classroom where the men were gathered to go over their responsibilities one last time before the service started. The Channel 8 van was still parked in the corner of the lot. He grabbed his cell phone and thumbed through its settings. He usually turned it off as soon as he stepped into the building, but with all the moving parts to keep track of this morning, he had left it on, just in case.

He wondered if dialing 9-1-1 was the appropriate way to notify the police of someone trespassing on church property. Or should he just dial the police station and speak directly to the dispatcher? It wasn't technically an emergency, but he did want the van gone before more people arrived. He decided it would be okay to dial 9-1-1. If they couldn't send a car to the church, then he would call the station. He was in the process of double tapping the "1" button when his phone lit up and vibrated with an incoming call.

He didn't recognize the number and hesitated to answer, but it might be one of his foot soldiers calling to let him know he was running late. If it wasn't from someone he wanted to talk to, he would quickly end the call and get back to taking care of business.

"This is Barney."

"Hi Barney, this is Carla Tanner. Do you have a few minutes to talk?"

"Not really," he said. "I was just about to step into a meeting."

"This won't take long," she said. "There's something you need to know. It's about where the idea for this strike came from."

"It came from the deepest pit of hell," Barney said.

"That may be true," Carla said. "But someone had to go there and get it. I think you'll be shocked when find out who it was."

"We'll see," Barney said. "Make it quick."

Carla made an exception in this instance and did exactly as she was told. She skipped the part about the accidental email and Craig pleading with them to ignore his idea. The way she told it, Craig had called the first meeting and laid out his plan step by step.

Barney chewed on the inside of his right cheek as he listened. By the time she finished, he could taste blood in his mouth. He made her wait for a response as he gave her story silent consideration. Finally, he said, "Why are you telling me this? I thought you were part of their club."

"I was," Carla said. "But I've had a change of heart. I think Craig is more interested in stirring up trouble than in helping women. I no longer want to be a part of his plan. Please accept my apology for the trouble I've caused."

Never one to miss an opportunity, Barney said, "Would you be willing to come help us this morning? When the other women see that you've defected, it will break their spirit."

"I can't do it," Carla said. "I'm too ashamed of letting Craig dupe me. I can't dare show my face there today. I don't ever want to be in the same room with that snake again."

"I understand," Barney said. His jaw muscles pulsed with tension. "Right now I feel the same way."

He ended the call and turned away from the window, forgetting about the Channel 8 van and his interrupted call to 9-1-1. The room was packed with men waiting for the meeting to start.

"Where is Craig?" Barney growled, without addressing anyone in particular.

When no one answered, he raised his voice. "Does anyone in this room know where Craig is?"

The room fell silent. The men looked at each other and hoped someone else had an answer to the question. No one was willing to venture a guess and risk giving Barney inaccurate information.

"No wonder the women want to take over this church," Barney said as he stormed out of the room. "You're all pathetic."

Chapter 40

Amy and Tom Brandt arrived much earlier than she had planned. When Tom asked if she wanted to go on up to the church to see what was happening, she was already walking toward the car before he finished the question. She needed to be there, to see who was showing up, to watch the men scurry around making preparations, to hear what people were saying, and yes, to make sure no one from The Deborah Club forgot the meaning of the phrase "do nothing."

Walking into the building, Amy recognized Emily Branson standing next to the Welcome Center in the foyer while skimming a promotional brochure designed to highlight all the good things South Barkley was doing in the community.

"Hi Emily, I'm Amy Brandt. We spoke on the phone yesterday. I'm glad to see you made it."

"I wouldn't miss it for the world," Emily said. She returned the brochure back to its plexiglass holder sitting atop the Welcome Center counter. "I'm glad someone showed up who will actually talk to me."

"The guys not treating you well?" Amy asked.

"They're treating me fine. They're just not saying anything. I came inside to look around while my cameraman walks around the building to get some B-roll footage. I'll go back out when more women start arriving. They'll talk to me, won't they?"

"No one has told them not to," Amy said.

"Good. These men are well coached."

"Not all of them," Amy said. "Let me introduce you to my husband, Tom."

"Nice to meet you, Tom," she said as they shook hands. "What's it like being married to a modern day Joan of Arc?"

Tom made a show of looking around to see if anyone else was listening. "Off the record?" he asked.

Emily gave Tom a disarming smile and said, "Unless you say something really good. So far, I don't have much to choose from."

Tom chuckled and said, "Well, I'm not sure she wants to be put in the same category as Joan of--"

Shouting from the far end of the foyer drowned out the rest of Tom's response. "I warned you! Get out of this building and off our property. Right now!"

They all turned in unison and saw Barney marching toward them with wide, maniacal eyes.

⭒⭒⭒

Craig was finishing up the final run-through of his sermon and still feeling good about what he planned to say when he heard shouting coming from the foyer.

He double-timed it down the hall toward the noise. He stepped into the foyer and saw the Brandts staring at Barney, their mouths agape, as he bellowed at Emily Branson, who was holding up her hands defensively and shaking her head.

Craig heard Barney say, "You are not welcome here. You will leave this instant!" Then he saw Barney take an aggressive step toward Emily.

Craig sprinted across the foyer and stepped between the two of them. He reached out to place a hand on Barney's shoulder to stop his forward progress and said, "Calm down, Barney, calm down."

Barney paused and stared at Craig. The fog of rage seemed to delay his ability to recognize who was touching him. He blinked hard and then slapped Craig's hand away and resumed shouting. "And you can leave with her! I know what you've done! I will not let you destroy this church!"

Craig kept his voice low and steady. "Barney I have no idea what you're talking about. Just settle down, please."

"You are fired!"

Craig surveyed the foyer and accounted for each witness to Barney's tirade. Amy was holding her hand over her mouth as if watching two cars careen toward one another. Tom was stepping forward to help restrain Barney. Several men who had shown up early were racing around the corner from the education hallway on the opposite side of the foyer. And the saucer-eyed reporter was standing there taking it all in, like a life-size recording device.

"Barney, let's step into my office and talk. This is crazy," Craig said. He tried to put his arm around Barney and steer him out of the foyer. Barney knocked his arm aside and roared, "Don't you dare touch me!"

⊷⊶

Barney was a boiling cauldron of fury. In front of him, he saw the hostile reporter standing in the foyer of *his* church, hoping to dig up dirt on the Bride of Christ. He saw Amy, the Jezebel who had stirred the other women into a rebellion, regarding him like he was a rabid dog. He saw Tom, her prissy husband who couldn't control his wife, moving forward as if he were strong enough to restrain him. And then there was Craig, the lowlife, backstabbing preacher who had betrayed the elders, trying to grab him and tell him what to do.

He would not have it. They all had to leave. They had no place in his building. Let them say what they wanted about him. He wasn't going anywhere. South Barkley would survive this attack. He would make sure of it, no matter what. He did not lose stand-offs.

"I'll have you all arrested for trespassing!"

Craig made another attempt to touch him. Barney stiff-armed him and knocked Craig back a step. Barney held out his left hand, his open palm facing Craig as though to warn him to come no closer, and reached with his right hand into the inner breast pocket of his blazer. This time he had no doubt whom to call.

He felt the phone in his pocket, but he couldn't make his throbbing fingers close around it. The smooth surface of the phone was cool to the touch, as though it were made of ice. He looked at Craig and cocked his head in recognition--something wasn't right. He opened his mouth to speak but couldn't find the words. He was suddenly aware of how suffocatingly hot the foyer was. And then just as suddenly, he was aware of nothing at all.

Chapter 41

THE DOCTORS IN the emergency room would later say that Barney was dead within minutes of hitting his head on the hard tile floor in the foyer. The story around town was that he died of a massive heart attack, but the more specific cause of death was sudden cardiac arrest, which doctors love to point out is technically different than a heart attack. In the moments immediately after his collapse, such a distinction was meaningless to the members of the South Barkley Bible Church.

Wanda walked into the building at her usually brisk pace. Preternaturally skinny and powered by a supercharged metabolism, Wanda always seemed to be moving twice as fast as everyone around her. She walked across parking lots, through doors, and into rooms with a sense of urgency. When she saw Craig leaning over her husband and performing CPR, she stopped and took in the scene. When she moved forward again, it was with slow, halting steps. She was in no hurry to have her worst fear confirmed. With one look at Barney's face, she knew it was too late. She kneeled down next to her husband of forty years and placed her hand on his warm forehead and whispered in his ear. When the paramedics arrived a few minutes later, Wanda stepped back to give them room as they took Barney's nonexistent vitals and loaded him onto a gurney.

Wanda noticed Amy Brandt standing among the swelling crowd. "I hope you're happy," she said, spitting her words across the room. She pointed a quivering finger at Amy. "You did this to him."

Amy wanted to say she was sorry; she wanted to defend herself. She tried to speak, but there were no words. Not at a moment like this. Not after what she had just witnessed. She pushed her way through the crowd and hurried into the ladies' room.

Wanda walked next to Barney as the paramedics rolled him through the glass doors of the church entrance and lifted him into the back of the ambulance, which was parked underneath the portico. Several of Barney and Wanda's closest friends, along with Craig, followed them out the door. Everyone else remained inside and stared through the glass with grim expressions. Mike, the Channel 8 cameraman, was standing off to the side and filming the procession.

The paramedics invited Wanda to ride with Barney and helped her into the back of the ambulance. The others hurried to their cars to follow the ambulance to the hospital. Craig walked back into the building to address the stunned crowd.

⟶⊨◉ ◉⊨⟵

Amy was hiding in a stall in the women's restroom, using the toilet as a chair. She texted Carla.

Amy: Where are you?

Carla: I'm not coming. Don't feel well.

Amy: I think Barney just fell over dead in the middle of the foyer.

Carla: What?

Amy: Call me.

Carla called five seconds later, and Amy described what happened from the moment she had walked into the building until Wanda had accused her of killing Barney.

"Did he really try to fire Craig on the spot?" Carla asked.

"Yes, Carla. Not the main point though. He had completely lost his mind. I thought he was going to hit Emily Branson."

"What did Craig say when Barney tried to fire him?"

"It doesn't matter!" Amy said, her voice echoing in the empty restroom. "Barney just died while making an ass of himself in the foyer of our church, in front of Emily Branson."

"And Wanda was mad at you, not Craig?" Carla said.

Amy said nothing, unable to make sense of Carla's sudden interest in Craig.

"Is church going on as planned?" Carla asked.

"I don't know."

"Is the strike still on?"

"I don't know what's happening. I'm in a stall in the bathroom."

"You better go find out," Carla said. "I'll be there as soon as I can."

"I thought you weren't feeling well."

"I'll push through it. Get out there. Now."

Amy hung up, left the stall, and opened the restroom door. Everyone had their heads bowed, and Craig was praying.

⋯⟫ ◎≡⟪⋯

Before Barney, Craig had witnessed two other people die. The first had been when a church member asked Craig to be in the room when they took her elderly mother off life support. Craig didn't know the daughter well and had never met the mother. Still, it was eerie to be in the room when the old woman took her last breath.

The second was an old man dying at home. He had been grumpy in a lovable way, always giving Craig a hard time after his sermons. The family believed the old man was afraid to die. They asked Craig to come and pray over him and tell him it was okay to let go. Craig showed up, said a prayer, and whispered in the old man's ear, "Otis, you can go home now. There's nothing to be afraid of."

Fifteen minutes later, while Craig was standing next to the bed visiting with Otis's family, the old man moaned, took a final breath, and died. His family was relieved, and Craig was amazed. The old man had finally taken something he'd said seriously. Craig considered both experiences to be two of the holiest moments in his ministry.

There was nothing holy about Barney's death. Craig would never forget the way Barney's eyes, blazing with rage, flattened and then went blank, as if an invisible hand had flipped a switch on the back of his head and turned him off. His final moments were spent in anger, saying and doing things that made him look like a petty little man with a tinier mind. His final words were filled with hate and intended to harm. It was a horrible way to die and an awful last memory to leave in the minds of those who watched it happen.

When Craig had walked back into the foyer after the ambulance pulled way, he saw two different reactions from those looking to him for guidance. Those who hadn't seen it happen, who had arrived during the futile attempt to revive Barney, were quietly weeping or fighting back tears. Those who saw Barney collapse and had heard what he was saying, had the somber look of witnesses to the execution of a guilty prisoner on death row.

Over the next few days, multiple interpretations of Barney's death emerged. Some said it was a regrettable consequence to unjustifiably bad behavior. Had he fallen in Bible times, these same people would have described his demise as God's judgment for losing his temper in the House of God. Over coffee with their closest friends, a few women quietly wondered if Barney's death was God's way of showing support for The Deborah Club. Grace Monroe was tortured by the possibility that Barney's death could have been God's grotesque answer to her prayers. Craig's wife worried there was something wrong with her for not feeling even the slightest bit of sorrow over his death. Craig did his best to combat the bad theology running rampant through South Barkley. He maintained Barney's death was a freak accident and nothing more, but he secretly wondered if it was a sign of God washing his hands of the whole lot of them and turning them over to Satan until they came to their senses.

↔≫≡◉ ◉≡≪↔

Ellis arrived just as Craig was finishing his prayer. He was running fashionably late for the men's meeting, hoping to miss as much of it as possible. He walked through the front door and stopped dead in his tracks. He could tell from the tears, the bowed heads, and the pained expressions that something terrible had just happened.

He placed his hand on Craig's shoulder, a polite way of announcing his presence without interrupting the moment. Craig surprised him with a hug. As they embraced, Craig whispered in Ellis's ear, "Barney just fell over dead in the foyer. We need to cancel the service."

Ellis leaned back from the embrace to look Craig in the eye and verify what he had just heard.

Craig said, "You heard me right. He's dead." The color drained from Ellis's face as he processed the information with a slow nod.

Craig turned to the group and said, "In light of what just happened, I can't imagine proceeding with our worship gathering. If you want to go into the sanctuary and spend some time praying for Barney, I know the family would appreciate it. Can someone volunteer to meet people as they arrive and tell them services have been cancelled? Ellis and I need to go to the hospital to be with Wanda."

⭑⭑

Amy Brandt was standing at the back of the crowd when Craig asked for a volunteer. She almost raised her hand and told Craig she would do it, but then remembered the strike and caught herself. She looked around to see if any other women were volunteering but didn't see any raised hands. Several women were looking her way, either waiting to follow her lead or asking for permission to deviate from their plan. She didn't have time to think through all the implications of her decision. She kept her hands down by her side and looked at the floor to avoid eye contact with those looking to her for leadership. She didn't want them to misinterpret anything in her eyes. After a few seconds of silence, several men volunteered. Craig thanked them, encouraged everyone else to keep praying, and then he and Ellis left for the hospital.

As the group broke up, Emily Branson stepped toward Amy and said, "I noticed there weren't any women who volunteered to help."

"Are you okay?" Amy asked. "I was afraid he was going to hit you."

"There for a second, I did too," Emily said. "What impact do you think this is going to have on The Deborah Club and the strike?"

"I don't know. It may have changed everything."

Emily powered up to full-on reporter mode. "How so?"

"God may have just picked a side," Amy said without thinking. She saw the shock register on Emily's face and was horrified by her own words. "I shouldn't have said that. I didn't mean it. Please don't quote me. That was off the record."

"Of course," Emily said.

Amy realized how many people were standing within earshot of their conversation. "Let's continue this outside."

Tom caught up with them as they left the building. Amy turned to him and said, "We're going to visit out here for a minute. Meet you at the car?"

"You okay?" he asked.

"I'm fine, for now."

He looked at Emily before walking to the car. "It was nice to meet you. I'm so sorry that just happened."

"Me too," Emily said.

Tom headed toward their car, and Amy and Emily went the opposite way toward the Channel 8 van.

Mike ran up to Emily. "Holy cow! What happened in there? I filmed what I could, but it was hard to see through the glass from the outside."

"We'll talk about it in the van," Emily said. "Can you give us a minute?"

"Are we leaving? Don't you want to hang around and ask some questions?"

"No," she said. "We're done here. Start loading up."

"You're the boss," he said and headed toward the van. Amy and Emily followed at a much slower pace.

"What happens now?" Emily asked.

"I honestly don't know," Amy said.

"You're hopeful aren't you? His death changes things, doesn't it? Do you have a next step in mind?"

"I'm sorry, Emily, but it doesn't feel right to talk strategy just minutes after Barney keeled over. We weren't friends, and only the Lord knows how ugly things between us were about to get, but now is not the time to talk about The Deborah Club."

"I'm sorry," Emily said. "Just doing my job. I guess I have enough for today anyway."

"Will you do an update on the news tonight?" Amy wasn't sure what answer she wanted to hear.

"Probably, although I'd rather wait until tomorrow. No one watches the Sunday night news."

"Any idea what you will say?"

Emily cocked her head to the side, looked up at the sky, and said, "Something like--" She looked back at Amy as if she were in front of a camera and continued, "In a strange--" Emily paused, shook her head and started over. "In a tragic turn of events, what was supposed to be a silent protest by the women of the South Barkley Bible Church became a moment of silence for a church leader who collapsed in the lobby. Members were shocked, church services were cancelled, blah, blah, blah."

"Are you going to talk about the confrontation in the foyer?" Amy asked. "That's what we call it. Foyer, not lobby."

"I don't see how I can keep from it," Emily said. "I'd rather not become part of the story, but without the confrontation, there isn't much to report."

"I guess that's true." They were almost to the van. Amy stopped and said, "Maybe you could say you witnessed him berating one of the members of The Deborah Club."

Emily grimaced and said, "That's not exactly true. He exploded when he saw me."

"I know, but it would keep you out of the story."

"And it would generate some sympathy for The Deborah Club," Emily said.

"Yes," Amy said, "It certainly would."

"Are we still not talking strategy?" Emily asked.

"I know. I'm sorry," Amy said.

"Are you sure you're comfortable with that version of the story?" Emily asked.

Amy said, "I can tell by the look on your face you're not. It's just a suggestion. You're the one with the microphone. You get to do what you think is best. Just like the men at our church."

"Wow," Emily said. "I don't think I've been guilt tripped like that since the last time I talked to my mom."

Amy raised her hands in surrender. "I'm sorry. I'm a mess. I don't know what I'm doing. Forget everything I just said."

"It was off the record, so I already have," Emily said as she opened the door to the van. "But don't be surprised if I call you tomorrow with a few on-the-record questions."

"I'll be ready," Amy said.

Emily said something to Mike as she shut the door. Amy turned and saw Tom driving across the half-empty parking lot to pick her up. On the way home, she remembered Carla and sent her a text telling her that the service was cancelled, and there was no need for her to come to the building. But Carla came anyway.

She wanted to see where it happened.

Chapter 42

CRAIG DESCRIBED THE scene for Ellis on their way to the hospital.

"Are you sure he was dead?" Ellis asked. "You're not a doctor. Maybe you were mistaken."

Craig took his eyes off the road long enough to look Ellis in the eye. "Ellis, unless Jesus himself works at this hospital, Barney is gone."

"And the reporter saw the whole thing?"

"No, the reporter was in the middle of the whole thing," Craig said. "It looked like Barney was about to attack her when I interrupted them."

"Then he attacked you?"

"No, he fired me," Craig said, intentionally overdoing the incredulity. "It was the craziest thing I've ever seen."

"Good Lord," Ellis said. "There's no telling how the reporter will spin this."

"There's not much to spin, Ellis. Barney couldn't have been a bigger jerk right up to the very end."

"Do you think--"

"I have no idea," Craig said before Ellis could finish. "But I'm guessing everyone else is wondering the same thing."

They pulled into the Emergency Room parking lot, and Craig parked his car in the spot reserved for clergy. Before getting out of the car, Craig turned to Ellis and said, "Listen Ellis, Wanda was really upset. She accused Amy Brandt of being responsible for Barney's death. I have no idea what state of mind she'll be in. Barney was furious with me before he died. She may treat me like I'm the devil. If she does, I'll excuse myself, and you can visit with her. Okay?"

"Whatever you think is best," Ellis said. "You're the pro in this situation."

They walked into the waiting room. Almost every seat was taken by someone from South Barkley. They asked for an update, but no one had heard anything new. Craig and Ellis went to the front desk, and Craig flashed his clergy credentials. The attendant buzzed them into the back. Craig flashed his credentials again at the nurse's station and asked where he could find Barney Staples. The nurse pointed to a trauma room down the hall to her right and said, "His wife is with him now, saying goodbye."

Craig forced himself to walk down the long, white hallway. He was a step ahead of Ellis, who seemed to be hanging back intentionally and letting Craig lead the way. The trauma room was divided into two smaller areas by a yellow curtain. The right half of the room was empty. Craig stuck his head inside the curtain to his left. Wanda was sitting in a chair on the far side of the room next to a gurney with Barney's body. She waved him in, and he and Ellis stepped behind the curtain.

Craig walked around the gurney, ready to give Wanda a hug, but she kept her seat and extended her hand instead. He stepped back. Ellis stepped forward to shake her hand, but Wanda sprung from the chair with open arms.

Message received.

She returned to her seat, and Ellis joined Craig at the foot of the bed. "The good news is he didn't suffer," Wanda said, her voice trembling. "The doctor said he probably didn't feel a thing."

"I'm so sorry," Ellis said. "He was a good man and great friend."

"He was a grumpy man," Wanda said, "but I loved him." She paused a moment, looked at Barney's body and sighed. "He didn't deserve to go like this, fighting uppity women like Amy Brandt."

"It was bad timing," Craig said. He had both hands stuffed into his pockets. "There was so much going on this morning. He must have been under tremendous pressure."

"He thought he was ready for it," Wanda said. "He tried to act like it wasn't a big deal, but I could tell he was worried." Another long pause. "She killed him."

Ellis ignored her last comment and said, "I know he loved the church. He was doing everything he could to protect it."

Wanda nodded. "Yes, he was. And I don't want his death to be in vain. Ellis, I want you to promise me something."

"Anything you want," Ellis said.

Craig wished Ellis would stop talking. He didn't know what Wanda was about to ask of Ellis, but he knew it wouldn't be good.

"Please promise me you will do whatever it takes to keep Amy Brandt from getting her way," Wanda said. "Do not let her win, no matter what."

Craig jumped into the conversation before Ellis could do more damage. "You know we'll continue to do everything we can to bring this disagreement to a peaceful end. Protecting the unity of the church is our number one priority."

"That's not enough," Wanda said. "I don't want you to negotiate or compromise or make a deal with her. I want you to destroy her, just like she destroyed Barney." She returned her gaze to Barney's body and sighed again. "He didn't deserve this."

"Wanda, I know you're upset," Craig said. He ducked his head and leaned in, trying to make eye contact. "But revenge won't bring Barney back." Wanda refused to look at him. He kept talking anyway. "It will only destroy our church--Barney's church, the church he loved and worked to protect. Do you really think he would want--"

Wanda interrupted him without looking up. "He would want you to win this war. Just like I do. You must not let that woman win. Do I have your word you will not let my husband's death be in vain?"

"We'll certainly try," Ellis said. "But The Deborah Club has a lot of support, and with the attention our church is getting in the media, compromise may be our best option."

In a flash, the grief in Wanda's moist eyes dissipated and was replaced by a cold, hard stare, which she pointed at Ellis like a laser. Her countenance changed, as though she were channeling the words of another being. She leaned forward in her chair and said, "You're not hearing what I'm saying. If you let that woman get her way, I'll leave South Barkley and take my husband's hard earned money with me. Is that clear enough for you two peacekeepers?"

Craig and Ellis nodded.

"Good," she said. The sad expression returned to her face. She leaned back in her chair and resumed the posture of a grieving widow.

"We'll do the best we can," Ellis said. "For you and for Barney."

They stayed with her, mostly in silence, until her daughter Sherri arrived. Craig offered to say a prayer, and Wanda allowed it. Once Sherri was settled, they excused themselves.

Walking back to the car, Craig said, "For a minute there, I thought she was being inhabited by Barney's ghost, but then I remembered we don't believe in that kind of voodoo."

"I'm sorry," Ellis said. "I should have kept my mouth shut."

"She's in shock," Craig said. "She may wake up tomorrow morning having forgotten the entire conversation."

"Does that really happen?"

"Sure it does," Craig said. "But I bet we're not that lucky."

Chapter 43

EMILY BRANSON WAS sitting at her desk in the newsroom trying to figure out what to do. She tinkered with a pile of paperclips as she went over her options, hooking them together and dragging them across the surface of her desk like a train. If only she could connect the thoughts bouncing around her head in a similar fashion. Then she'd have a train of thought. Was that what the expression meant? She would have to look it up on the Internet to check the etymology of the phrase. Did phrases have etymologies or just words? Would she ever use the word etymology in one of her reports? What would her producer say? Not about the word etymology, but about what happened earlier that morning at the South Barkley Bible Church. They were meeting in fifteen minutes. What was she going to tell him? That the threatened strike never happened because the church cancelled its worship service after a man fell over dead in the foyer? Did these details even merit an update?

But there was much more to the story than her cursory summary implied. It wasn't just any old man who had died. By all accounts, he was the church's most influential elder. And he hadn't simply been walking through the foyer on his way to worship. He had threatened her for being on the premises and then fired the pastor when he tried to intervene.

She didn't completely understand South Barkley's leadership structure. It was very different from the way the Catholic Church was organized. It seemed to be more like a stand-alone mom-and-pop business than a global franchise with a formal hierarchy where rules were passed down from HQ.

How could such an emotionally unstable man end up being the most powerful leader of a church? She didn't have to speak this question aloud to recognize how ridiculous it was. The Catholic Church's history was peppered with leaders whose lives had no resemblance whatsoever to the ideals espoused by the Church. Why would a protestant church be any different? People are people and power is power and only fools trust people in power, especially when power comes cloaked in the guise of service to a religious institution.

Because of their roguish nature with no outside accountability, what if churches like South Barkley were more vulnerable to even greater abuses than what some in the Catholic Church had tried to hide? She shuddered at the thought. Was she prepared to dive all the way to the bottom of the craziness these religious nuts were hiding? Or should she just let it go? Could she let it go? What about Amy Brandt? She liked Amy, and Amy wasn't crazy, just desperate for change.

Emily thought of a recent report she had seen on a national news program about what life is like for women in Saudi Arabia. They aren't allowed to drive or work or wear what they want. The religious authorities, all men, impose their wishes--rooted in their interpretation of their holy book--on every woman in the country.

Outsiders see their religious laws for what they are, barbaric and oppressive. Emily wondered what it would be like to live in such a world where self-righteous men decide what women could and could not do. But she didn't have to go all the way to Saudi Arabia to find out. A trip to the South Barkley Bible Church, where women were not allowed to speak during the public worship service or occupy formal positions of leadership, was far enough.

The way she saw it, both groups existed on the same spectrum. While the good Christians at South Barkley joined her in condemning the way women were treated in Saudi Arabia, they voluntarily belonged to a religious community in which women were not allowed to fully participate.

It struck her as complete and utter madness that a man like Barney Staples could hold a position of authority at South Barkley, while a woman with obvious leadership gifts like Amy Brandt wasn't even allowed to speak during the worship service.

This story was worth telling, primarily because Amy and her followers were challenging an oppressive system. Like toxic mold growing in the damp, dark basement of an old home, this fundamentalist lunacy needed to be exposed to bright light and fresh air.

But how best to tell the story? Should she do as Amy suggested and shape the story to generate even more sympathy and support for The Deborah Club? Or would telling such an unbalanced story backfire? What impact would Barney's sudden death have on his followers? Would they solidify their opposition or scatter into the wind? Would the way he died inspire loyalty or cause them to regret putting their trust in a lunatic? So many questions.

She remembered what her first producer at Channel 8 would say to her at least once a week. "It's not your job to manage or manipulate the outcomes of your stories. They're impossible to predict, so don't even try. Just tell the story, and let the outcomes take care of themselves."

Enough overthinking. There was a story to report, and that's what she was paid to do. Just tell the truth and let the chips fall where they may. If Amy Brandt couldn't figure out how to use it to her advantage, she wasn't the leader she appeared to be.

Chapter 44

Ten minutes into the six o'clock newscast on Monday night, Dale Hutchens said, "Last week, we broke an exclusive story about an escalating power struggle at the South Barkley Bible Church, where a group of frustrated women are threatening to go on strike to protest what they describe as discriminatory leadership practices. Emily Branson was at South Barkley yesterday morning and witnessed a tragic event. She joins us here in the studio to give us an update."

The camera zoomed out to show Emily sitting at the news desk next to Dale. She had ditched her usual wardrobe, bright, breezy, sleeveless or short-sleeved dresses, for a conservative gray dress with long sleeves. The expression on her face was as serious as her attire.

Dale said, "Tell us about what happened yesterday morning."

Emily gave Dale a nod and then looked into the camera. "Yesterday morning, a group of women known as The Deborah Club, named after a heroine in the Bible, arrived at the South Barkley Church with the intention of abstaining from their usual areas of volunteer service. But instead, all Sunday morning activities were cancelled after one of the church's elders, Barney Staples, collapsed in the church foyer. He was taken to the Emergency Room at St. Joseph's Hospital where he was pronounced dead on arrival."

Since she could no longer claim to be an unbiased observer of what happened at South Barkley, Channel 8 management decided it would be better for Emily to share her experiences in an interview format. They believed it would be more powerful and dramatic if it appeared Dale was pulling the information from her, rather than having her deliver it via a scripted monologue.

Dale asked the second of several questions he and Emily had rehearsed before going on air. "What were the circumstances leading up to his collapse?"

Emily paused, as if she were considering the question before answering. "I was in the foyer speaking to one of the leaders of The Deborah Club when Mr. Staples confronted us. He was visibly upset and moving toward us in an aggressive manner. That's when Craig MacPherson, the pastor of the church, intervened and attempted to direct Mr. Staples to his office. Mr. Staples resisted and began shouting at Pastor MacPherson. That's when he collapsed. My first impression was that he had fainted, but he never regained consciousness."

While she spoke, Channel 8 ran the footage Mike had shot of Barney being loaded into the ambulance. The scene cut back to Dale and Emily for the next question. Dale said, "That must have been awful to see. You said he was moving toward you in an aggressive manner. Were you afraid for your safety?"

"No. I wasn't afraid for my safety, but I was worried about the safety of the woman to whom I was speaking. Mr. Staples didn't want me there yesterday; that was obvious. As a reporter, it wasn't the first time I have been asked to leave an event. And I was ready to comply. But Mr. Staples didn't want her there either. He accused her of trespassing."

"But isn't she a member of the South Barkley Bible Church?" Dale asked.

"Yes," Emily said. "She's been a member and active volunteer at the church for almost twenty years."

Dale frowned, as if he couldn't make sense of what he'd just heard. "So she had every right to be there?"

"Yes," Emily said. "But Mr. Staples was determined to remove her, remove us, from the premises." Dale looked as though he were about to ask another question, but Emily kept talking. "And if he hadn't collapsed, I don't know what he would have done next. He seemed angry enough to be capable of anything."

There. She said it. That was enough about Barney's behavior.

Dale must have felt the same way. He steered the conversation in a different direction. "How has the church responded to this tragedy?"

"Most people are in shock. Mr. Staples was an influential leader and long-time member."

"Has there been any indication from The Deborah Club of their intentions moving forward?" Dale asked.

"No. Right now their primary focus is helping the Staples family through this difficult time." Emily made this part up. Amy Brandt hadn't returned her phone calls from earlier in the day, so she really didn't know what The Deborah Club was planning, but it seemed like a safe thing to say.

"Well, everyone involved is certainly in our thoughts and prayers. Thank you, Emily." The camera zoomed in on Dale, and he segued into a teaser for an upcoming story about an alarming outbreak of an unidentified skin rash at a local high school wrestling tournament. "We'll have that story next, after this commercial break."

Emily waited for the "all clear" sign from the production team and then exhaled in relief. Dale gave her a thumbs up and said, "Nice job. I think you nailed it."

She hoped so. It was tricky striking the right balance. The facts were that Barney Staples had fallen over dead while throwing a tantrum. He hadn't been acting like a Christian when he died. Out of sensitivity to the family, she couldn't come out and say it this way. She had to trust the audience to connect the dots. Now that it was over, and despite Dale's affirmation, she felt the heaviness of regret settling in on her. She feared she had said too much.

Across town, Amy Brandt was watching TV from her couch and smiling. Craig was also watching and dreading his meeting with Wanda the next morning.

Chapter 45

WHEN SETTING UP the meeting to plan Barney's funeral, Craig offered to come to Wanda's house to meet with the family, but she refused.

"We'll be at your office at nine in the morning," she said. "I don't expect it to take long. We could probably do it over the phone if you prefer."

This would have been fine with Craig. He preferred keeping as much distance between Wanda and himself as possible, but for all he knew, she was setting him up so she could accuse him of being a distant, insensitive pastor later on.

"See you then," he said. "Who all will be coming?"

"Just the kids and me," she said.

Sherri and Mitch hardly qualified as kids anymore. Sherri attended South Barkley with her parents a couple of times a year, usually around the holidays. Single and in her mid-thirties, Barney had talked about her as though she were still a member, although everyone knew better. Where she spent the other fifty Sundays of the year was a topic of conversation no one dared broach with either of her parents.

Craig had never met Mitch. He didn't know where he lived or what he did for a living. When Barney had spoken of him, it was almost exclusively in the past tense, usually when telling a story about when the kids were still at home. At the hospital on Sunday, Craig had asked Wanda if Mitch was on his way. She had said no without offering an explanation.

Wanda and her kids arrived at Craig's office a few minutes early. Craig was ready for them. Barney had lived by the rule that if you're not at least five minutes early for a meeting, you're late. Craig assumed Wanda was of the same mind. He had never known her to show up late for anything, with or without Barney.

Wanda led the way into Craig's office, followed by Sherri and then Mitch, whom Sherri seemed to be dragging behind her with an invisible leash. Mitch looked like a younger, fitter version of Barney, with slightly more hair but not for long. The biggest difference was in the face. Almost every one of Barney's facial expressions was a variation of fierce, which gave the impression he was always ready for a fight. Mitch's face was softer, but not with fat. It was the look in his eyes. It reminded Craig of a cowed dog who had been mistreated as a pup. Craig shook his hand and was surprised by the strength of Mitch's grip. It was Barney's handshake, confident and assertive. But the eyes told a different story.

They all took their seats and looked at each other. Normally, Craig would take charge of the meeting and guide the conversation with a series of questions about what to include in the service. Not with Wanda. He sensed she had already planned every detail, and the purpose of this meeting was to give instructions, not to answer questions.

"Thanks for coming in," Craig said. "I know this is a difficult time."

Fire flashed in Wanda's eyes. "You have no idea," she said. "I suppose you heard what that reporter said about Barney last night."

"I watched it," Craig said and shook his head in disbelief. *She told the truth.*

"There are two sides to every story, and since Channel 8 isn't giving our family any airtime, we'll have our say tomorrow."

Craig didn't usually try to tell families what to do at funerals. It was their service and for their benefit, but he questioned the wisdom of using it as forum for a rebuttal against a reporter.

Wanda misread the look of concern on his face. "Don't worry," Wanda said. "I'm not going to ask you to speak for us. You're off the hook. In fact, I want you to keep your remarks about Barney to a minimum. Just read his obituary, and let those who knew him best say a few words."

This plan suited Craig just fine. It was much better than being forced to say nice things about Barney he didn't mean, and which at least half the people in the room would never believe.

"I'll do whatever you like," Craig said. "Whom do you have in mind to speak?"

"I want Mitch to say something," Wanda said.

Mitch squirmed in his seat but nodded his head to confirm his mother's wishes.

"Anyone else?" Craig asked.

Wanda gave him two other names: one was Barney's golfing buddy and the other was Ellis.

Craig looked at Mitch. "Do you or Sherri want to say anything?"

Sherri said, "Thanks for asking, but I don't think--"

"I want Mitch to speak on behalf of our family," Wanda said. Her tone indicated the matter was settled.

"Okay," Craig said, eager to get them out of his office. "That should just about do it. Is there anything else you want to make sure does or doesn't happen or is or isn't said during the service?" This was a question Craig always asked the family when planning a funeral.

"Just make sure you read every word of his obituary," Wanda said. "I'll have it ready for you by tomorrow morning." She narrowed her eyes. "And Craig, I mean every word."

"I look forward to reading it," he said. It was a ridiculous thing to say. Who looks forward to reading an obituary? It was also a lie, but one so minor compared to his other deceptions, it didn't bother him in the least.

Chapter 46

WHEN THE SOUTH Barkley Bible Church hosted funerals, a team of women usually coordinated a luncheon for the family before or after the service. Amy Brandt was the leader of this ministry team, not because she was a great cook, but because she was a fantastic organizer. After his meeting with Wanda and her kids, the first item on Craig's "to do" list was to call Amy and confirm that her team would take care of the luncheon. He would have normally delegated this task to his part-time assistant, but it was a good excuse to reach out and see how Amy was doing.

Amy answered her phone and skipped the pleasantries. "I figured I would be hearing from you sometime this morning."

Craig said, "I just wanted to call and confirm that your team is working on the luncheon for the family before the service tomorrow."

"Really?" Amy said. "Silly me for thinking you might be calling to see how I'm doing after nearly being attacked by a mad man at my place of worship on Sunday."

"I was trying to get him out of there," Craig said. "Just before he died." He felt his pastoral concern give way to aggravation.

"Which took my attention away from how badly he hurt your feelings, you know, before he fell over dead."

"Yes, you did try to help, and I appreciate that. But be honest, if Emily Branson hadn't been there, would you have tried to stop him? Do you only take stands when a reporter is watching? I guess I should have brought her with me to the elders' meeting."

"Come off it, Amy. I'm not calling to rehash the elders' meeting. Let's move on, especially since the offending party is now dead. I'm calling because the church needs your help."

"What's wrong?" Amy said. "Can't find any men to coordinate lunch for their fallen hero's family? All they need to do is put together several dozen sandwiches and a couple of pies. It's not hard."

"No, Amy, I haven't asked any men to help. I don't want to make this any harder than it has to be. I'd rather not subject a grieving family to the hospitality of a bunch of men whose idea of organizing a luncheon is ordering a stack of pepperoni pizzas. That won't go over well with Wanda."

"But isn't that what Barney wanted?" Amy said. "For the men to step up and show how unnecessary women are to the proper functioning of a church? This seems like a great opportunity for them to prove he was right."

"Please don't tell me you're going to use Barney's funeral to make a point," Craig said.

"And please don't tell me you think The Deborah Club is no longer on strike just because Barney is dead."

Craig squeezed the handset of his desktop phone. He was glad he hadn't called Amy on his cell. The temptation to smash it against the wall would have been irresistible. The truth was he had assumed there would be a truce until after the funeral. It was the right thing to do. As impossible as Barney was to work with, and as mad as Craig was about the way he had tried to intimidate his wife, Craig still felt Barney deserved a decent burial, absent of the controversy that helped put him in the grave.

"Well, Amy, if I'm being honest, I guess I was hoping you and the rest of The Deborah Club would set aside your differences with Barney and help us show his family how much we love them. That's not too much to ask, is it? It may even be the Christian thing to do. You know, the bit about loving your enemies and helping your neighbors during their time of need?"

After a long pause, Amy said, "In just about any other circumstance, I would agree with you. But this is the exception. Barney was crystal clear in expressing his thoughts about me, my leadership, and those dumb enough to follow me. I can't imagine he would want anyone associated with The Deborah Club to prepare a meal for his family with our unclean hands. After all, we might contaminate his loved ones with our liberal agenda."

Craig sighed. "Is that your final answer?"

"Sorry, Craig, but we will not be distracted by a funeral. As Jesus said, 'Let the dead bury the dead.'"

"Not only are you letting your cause twist your heart, but you just quoted Jesus out of context," Craig said. "Maybe Barney was right about how ill-prepared you are for leadership." He stopped himself a sentence too late. She was misquoting Jesus, and he was quoting Barney. They were racing each other to the basement.

Before he could apologize, Amy said, "Be careful, Craig. The last guy who said that ended up flat on the floor. God is watching, and for all you know, he's taking sides."

Rather than swallow his pride and say he was sorry like the mature adult he wanted to be, Craig slammed the handset down on its base and found it to be a far more satisfying experience than pressing a red button on a glass screen. Yet another reason he was glad he hadn't used his cell.

⟶▭ ◖▭⟵

Craig was certain he could find a few women willing to defy Amy and help prepare the luncheon. But he didn't have time to make multiple phone calls seeking them out. He also didn't have time to recruit a bunch of men to replace Amy's team. So he made an executive decision to solve the problem with a call to a local catering company.

He worried he might be setting a dangerous precedent for future funerals. Would every bereaved family expect a catered meal from this point forward? He talked himself into it anyway. He congratulated himself for so easily sidestepping Amy's effort to ruin his day. In his opinion, it was the best five hundred dollars the church had ever spent.

Wanda didn't see it the same way. She called him the next morning to specifically ask about the details of the luncheon. What time? In what room? And who would be providing the food?

When he told her the meal was being catered, Wanda asked a question to which she already knew the answer. "Don't we have a team of women who normally coordinate these meals?"

"Yes, we do," Craig said. "But I decided to go with a caterer this time."

"Why?"

"Because with everything going on this week, it seemed like the best thing to do," he said.

"And who is the leader of our luncheon ministry team?" Wanda asked.

Craig knew she wasn't looking for new information. She just wanted to hear him say it out loud. He closed his eyes and braced for impact. "Amy Brandt."

"Did that woman refuse to coordinate a meal for my family?"

"I'd rather not say."

"You don't have to," Wanda said. "Couldn't you get someone else to coordinate it?"

"I'm sure I could," he said. "But this seemed like the simplest way to get it done."

"Heaven forbid you be inconvenienced by my husband's death. It's not like you have to spend your precious time writing a eulogy."

"I'm sorry, Wanda. I'm doing the best I can."

"I want you to cancel the order with the caterer and get some other women in the church to coordinate the meal."

Sure, Wanda. I'll call a few ladies and ask them to put together a luncheon with two hours notice. I'm sure they have nothing better to do. "The food will be great, I promise," Craig said.

"That's not the point. The point is that you have allowed that woman to disrespect my husband one last time. My family won't be attending the luncheon."

"But the luncheon is for your family," Craig said.

"Then there is no need for a luncheon."

Craig asked her to reconsider, but there was no response. She had hung up on him.

Craig called the caterer and tried to cancel the order, but it was too late. He arranged for the food to be delivered to a homeless shelter instead.

An hour later, Wanda emailed Barney's obituary to him. He had to read it out loud several times before he could make it all the way through without cringing.

Chapter 47

THE SANCTUARY WAS full. Half the crowd was from South Barkley. The other half was from Barney's business and community connections. Craig sat in the front pew a few minutes before the service was to begin. He was looking over his minimal notes. Wanda wanted him to play the role of a glorified emcee and nothing more. It was an easy job. Still, he wanted to flee the sanctuary and disappear, perhaps to go eat with the homeless at the shelter where he had sent the catered food. The thought of becoming a nameless, faceless person roaming the streets appealed to him. No more conflict. No more drama. No more Deborah Club. No more Wanda.

Craig had presided over a number of funerals and graveside services. Some were for strangers who required nothing more from him than a few generic niceties and the usual scriptures about life, death, and life after death. Others were for people he loved so much that he had to fight back tears as he stood next to their open casket. This was the first service he had ever conducted for someone he did not like. Were he to explore his heart and put a more precise label on his feelings, he would say he hated Barney. He kept telling himself this funeral wasn't for him, it was for his family, but after going a couple of rounds with Wanda, he wasn't feeling much sympathy for her either.

So Craig kept directing his thoughts back to Sherri and Mitch. He couldn't imagine what it must have been like to grow up in a house ruled by Barney. With both of his parents still living, he also had no idea what it was like to bury a parent, especially one who had died in such an awful way. Putting himself in their shoes, Craig found the compassion he needed to care about Barney's funeral.

Craig came to attention when he heard the opening notes of "How Great Thou Art" playing over the sound system. It was the cue to seat the family and start the service. When the song was over, Craig stepped behind the podium in the center of the stage and made his opening remarks. He thanked everyone for coming to honor Barney, and he expressed his condolences to Barney's family on behalf of everyone in attendance. Then, just as Wanda had asked him to do, he read Barney's obituary word for word.

It was an expanded version of the one published in the local paper. Wanda had added several paragraphs to flesh out Barney's interests, accomplishments, and contributions to the community and to the church. Barney had been a mover and a shaker, and his wife had written an obituary to make sure every one in the room knew it.

The last paragraph was the most difficult to read. Wanda had included it to make sure everyone knew she was standing with Barney in his fight against The Deborah Club. Craig wanted to defy Wanda's wishes, skip the final section altogether, and move right into a prayer thanking God for Barney's life and legacy, but he had no interest in further inciting her wrath. So when he came to it, he steeled himself and read every word with careful precision.

"Barney died protecting the church he loved from a decadent culture relentlessly waging war against the everlasting Truth revealed in the Scriptures. He was a man of integrity, honor, and principle. Barney refused to let the changing times change him. His enemies despised and disrespected him for standing firm, but his friends and family admire him for holding fast to his convictions. May his passing be a wake-up call to those who have strayed. May they return to the path of righteousness while there is still time. May his sacrifice inspire more of us to honor his memory by joining in the battle against those who are still opposing him."

In the margin of his copy, Craig had written, "Take that Amy!" Too bad she wasn't there to hear it.

Just as Craig knew it would, the last paragraph had a chilling effect on the room. He tried to repair the atmosphere with a prayer emphasizing God's goodness instead of Barney's faithfulness. After his prayer, Craig introduced Barney's golfing buddy, whom Wanda had asked to say a few words about what it was like to be one of Barney's friends.

The transition couldn't have been more awkward. Even with Craig's prayer as a buffer, Barney's golfing buddy had come prepared to talk about what a terrible golfer Barney had been. "The only thing uglier than Barney's swing was the plaid pants he wore on the course." The audience laughed politely at the tone-deaf joke, but their hearts weren't in it. It was hard to make light of someone who had given his life for the everlasting Truth of God's word.

Ellis was up next. Wanda had asked him to brag about Barney's work as an elder. Given what was being said about Barney's death on Channel 8 and Ellis's familiarity with Barney's manipulative style of leadership and conspiratorial view of the world, this was not an easy task. But Ellis, ever the peacemaker, did his best to make Barney come off sounding like the Thirteenth Apostle. He spent five minutes describing someone Craig had never met. It was an amazing performance.

After Ellis, the program said Mitch would speak on behalf of the family, but Mitch didn't move from his seat. Craig turned and looked across the aisle at him as if to say, "Your turn," but Mitch wasn't looking to him for a cue. He was looking at his sister. They were holding hands. Mitch released his grip and patted Sherri on the knee. She stood and shuffled sideways past her mother and into the aisle. Before Wanda could reach out to grab her arm or stick a leg out to trip her, Sherri stepped onto the stage, notes in hand, and approached the podium.

She was tall and slightly overweight, with straight blond hair cut in a bob that made her face appear larger than it really was. She was wearing a knee-length black dress and an elegant string of pearls. Her shoes were flat and sensible and gave the impression she wasn't accustomed to dressing up. Craig glanced over at Wanda. She was staring at her daughter in confusion. Mitch was smiling.

Sherri placed her notes on the podium and said, "My brother, Mitch, apologizes for not being able to share his thoughts with you today. He was afraid his emotions would get the best of him, and he wouldn't be able to make it through what he planned to say, so he asked me to speak in his place."

She paused, looked down at her notes and fidgeted with her hair. "I love my dad, and I have never for a second doubted that he loved me. That doesn't mean he was always easy to live with. As my mother noted when she wrote his obituary, he was a man of deep conviction. He believed there was only one way to live and that was his way, which he believed was God's way. Growing up, I resented how he enforced his will on our family, but now that I'm older, I understand where he was coming from. I'm not saying I agree with him; I'm just saying I understand. Perhaps a few stories will help you see my dad as I see him now.

I remember when I was ten years old. Mom and Dad took us to the State Fair. Mitch and I were interested in different rides, so Mom and Mitch went one way and Dad and I went another. We were waiting in line to ride the giant ferris wheel. I wanted to see the city from the very top. The line was long, and we soon wished we had chosen to spend our time elsewhere, especially when the group of four guys waiting behind us started using vulgar language.

Dad and I both pretended not to hear them at first. We hoped it wouldn't last. But they kept going, and I made a face to show my discomfort. Dad leaned down and asked me if I was okay, and I suggested we go wait in line for a different ride. That's when my dad turned around and politely asked them to watch their language in front of his ten-year-old daughter. One of the guys apologized, and they stopped talking.

A few minutes later one of them started with the vulgarities again. My dad turned around and told him to knock it off. The guy told my dad it was a free country, and we could let them cut in front of us if we didn't want to overhear their conversation. My dad put his finger in the guy's chest and explained in clean, but blunt, language why he and his friends needed to go wait in line somewhere else.

All four guys were probably still in college and thought they were invincible. The truth was they were still boys, and my dad was a grown man with a daughter to protect. They melted away into the crowd. We crossed paths with them several times throughout the rest of the day--each time they turned and headed the other way. I remember being so proud of my dad, and I remember how special he had made me feel. He was my knight in shining armor.

I look back on that story now and realize how much easier it would have been for us to step out of line and find another ride, but that's not who my dad was. He never backed down. Ever. While this is a wonderful trait to have in a father who is defending you from dirty jokes and obscene language, it's not quite as enjoyable when you're a bit older, and you're the one he's staring down.

When I was sixteen, I emerged from my room on a Saturday night dressed in a t-shirt and tight jeans. My dad took one look and deemed the outfit inappropriate for a girl my age. I told him he was overreacting. I was only going over to a friend's house to watch a movie. He told me I wasn't leaving the house until I changed into something more modest. To make a long story short, I didn't change my clothes that night. I also didn't leave the house. As usual, he didn't back down. I hadn't told him the whole truth about my plans for the evening. My friend had invited some guys over to her house to watch the movie with us, and I was dressed to impress. I remember being so angry with my dad--I was certain I hated him. But now I understand. He was protecting me, just as he had when I was ten.

If I were to use one word to describe my dad it would be the word *protect*. He believed the world was a dangerous place, filled with people and powers looking to harm the weak. He also believed it was up to the strong to protect the innocent from these malevolent forces. As is so often the case, my dad's greatest strength was also his most glaring weakness. He believed the world was simple. The truth was black and white. He was able to categorize people in his mind as either good or evil. If you agreed with him, then you were good. If you didn't see things his way, then you were evil."

A few people laughed.

Sherri smiled. "That wasn't a joke. He believed the Bible was easy to understand and not nearly as hard to obey as many people made it out to be. I know this because he loved to say, 'It's easy to buy into fancy new interpretations of the Bible once you decide the old fashioned truth is too hard to obey.'

My dad was raised to believe it was his duty as a Christian to read the Bible and do what it says, without, as he would say, 'looking for loopholes or exceptions.' That is exactly what he strived to do. In other words, he always tried to do what he thought was the right thing, and that's what he taught Mitch and me to do as well. For this, I am so grateful. Even though I made my share of mistakes growing up, I can honestly say I did more right than wrong, mainly because the last thing I ever wanted to do was disappoint my daddy.

At the same time, my dad's world was very small. I don't mean this as an insult. I just mean that for most of his life, my dad lived in a world where everything made sense to him. He was the rare man who had the ability to bend reality to his will. He didn't conform to the world around him. He made the world conform to him, but at the price of reducing his world to a manageable size. He knew who he was and where he belonged, and he never ventured outside his territory. This strategy served my dad well for most of his life. But eventually the world he had been able to avoid came knocking on his door. Try as he might, he couldn't ignore it or send it away.

It was hard for my dad to believe he had raised two kids who didn't always agree with him and see the world the way he did. But how do you put your children in the evil category? As long as we lived under his roof, he could exercise control over what we did, how we dressed, and what we watched on TV. Once we left home and started making our own choices, he could no longer protect us from the world or from ourselves. He never adjusted to this new reality. I'm afraid he took his frustration with losing control of his children out on some of you.

I would love to stand here and tell you what a great man my dad was and completely ignore the circumstances of his death. I wish I could say he died protecting the truth or his church or future generations from the forces of evil. But the truth is my dad became the very thing he despised. He became someone from whom the weak needed to be protected, not because he was mean or evil, but because his commitment to his version of the truth blinded him to the impact his behavior had on real people. I know this sounds like a terrible thing for a daughter to say about her dad at his funeral, but it's the truth. If you knew my father, you know he would want the truth to be told. I'm not saying he'd agree with my perspective on the truth, but I hope he would respect me for standing tall and speaking what is on my heart and mind. Because after all, he's the one who taught me how to do it.

I would have loved for my dad to have died a peaceful death in his bed, many years from now, surrounded by his family. But that's not the story we get to tell about him. Instead, he died fighting a battle I think he knew he had already lost. He was just too stubborn to accept it. True to character, he refused to back down. If his little world was going to change, it would be over his dead body."

She looked over at Barney's casket and fought back tears.

"And so it shall be."

She continued as though she were speaking to her dad. "I wish it could have been different for you. I wish your world had been bigger. I wish you would have been able to see what I see." She was losing her composure but held on long enough to say, "I wish you would have been willing to live in my world, Daddy. It's not so bad. I think you would have gotten used to it and maybe even liked it."

She picked up her notes and returned to her seat. The sanctuary was completely still and would have been totally silent if not for the sound of sniffles coming from all directions. No one had come expecting to hear the truth about Barney from his daughter. She managed to put his life in perspective. Those who knew him well couldn't argue with her. Those who didn't know him at all could now understand why he was acting like a fool when he died.

Craig returned to the podium and surveyed the congregation. He let the sacred moment linger, not wanting to bring it to a premature end. The truth had been told, and it needed time to run its course. It was easy to hate Barney if he stood against you. It was also easy to love him if he considered you his ally. Sherri had expressed her love for her dad, while also acknowledging the characteristics that made him so hard to like. By daring to tell the truth, she had accomplished the impossible. She had restored Barney's humanity.

Craig looked down to where the family was sitting. Wanda stared straight ahead, an indecipherable expression on her face. Mitch was glaring at his father's casket as though its very presence offended him. Sherri was looking down at her hands with what appeared to be embarrassment or even remorse.

"Sherri," Craig said, "I don't think I'm the only one here who can say that was the best eulogy I have ever heard. Thank you for sharing your heart in such an open and honest way. I'm sure you made your dad proud." As much as he wanted to believe his last statement, he doubted it was true.

After thanking everyone for coming and announcing that there would be a private graveside service later in the afternoon, Craig closed the service with a short prayer. As he stepped off the stage, a triumphant song about Jesus' resurrection began to play. Ushers came forward to escort the family out of the sanctuary. Wanda and Sherri walked side by side, while Mitch trailed a step behind.

Chapter 48

AFTER THE SERVICE, the Staples family received everyone in the foyer of the church where Barney had fallen. They were standing in a corner as far from ground zero as possible. Wanda was shaking hands and hugging those who stopped to offer a word of comfort. Mitch was sandwiched between his mom and Sherri, barely making eye contact with anyone who spoke to him. A bottleneck formed around Sherri, with each person taking extra time to tell her what a marvelous job she had done.

Craig stood at a distance and watched the scene unfold and wondered how much hell Sherri would catch when she and Wanda were alone. *That ride to the cemetery is going to be a doozy. You couldn't get me in that limo for all the money in the world.*

"She did a great job, didn't she?"

Craig recognized the voice and flinched.

"She did," he said. "Her mom should be proud of her."

"I doubt it," Carla said. "Wanda is Barney's biggest fan."

"True, but maybe she's Sherri's fan too," Craig said. "Plus, I think Sherri did more to help her dad's image than hurt it."

"Whatever," Carla said. "Rumor has it that Barney was trying to fire you when he died. Is that true?"

"Something like that," Craig said, without taking his eyes off the Staples family. "But honestly, I think he had lost his mind."

"What if he hadn't?" Carla said. "What if he knew exactly what he was doing and why he was doing it?"

Craig turned to face her. "What are you getting at?"

"Oh, I don't know," Carla said, giving a slight shrug and an evil smile. "He sounded fine when I talked to him earlier that morning."

"What?" Craig said. "Why?"

"We had some business to discuss."

Craig heard his wife's voice and felt her hand on his shoulder. "Craig, do you have any idea where Amy is?" She stepped in front of them and formed a triangle.

"I haven't seen her," Craig said. "Do you need her for something?"

"No. I just wondered what she thought about Sherri's remarks. Would you come help me look for her?" She made no effort to disguise her attempt to rescue him from Carla.

"Don't bother," Carla said to Craig, not acknowledging his wife's presence. "She's not here. She said she wasn't coming."

"That's too bad," Craig's wife said. "She needed to hear what Sherri said. It might have helped."

"Yep, it's too bad," Craig said. He pretended to look around the room for Amy while trying to think of a way to get rid of his wife so he could find out what Carla and Barney had discussed.

"She didn't think she'd be welcome here," Carla said, still acting as if Craig's wife hadn't joined the conversation.

"I can understand why," Craig said. "Wanda is holding her responsible for Barney's death."

"I told her she should come anyway. It's not every day you get to dance on the grave of your adversary."

"That's an awful thing to say," Craig wife's said.

Carla ignored her and said to Craig, "Don't pretend you're not jumping for joy on the inside too. If anyone is responsible for his death, it's you. A heart attack is the only thing keeping you from being out of a job right now."

Before Craig could respond, Carla sidestepped his wife and got in line to say something to Wanda.

"Still think she's gorgeous?" his wife asked.

"Huh?" Craig said. He had heard the question but wasn't about to answer it. To say yes would be stupid and saying no would be an admission he had once found her attractive.

"Just remember, she's divorced for a reason."

Craig looked at his wife and waited for an explanation.

She arched one eyebrow and said, "Her husband left her for another woman. Think about what that must mean."

Craig thought about it as he watched Carla give Wanda a long hug and whisper something in her ear.

Chapter 49

THE LIMOUSINE PULLED up under the portico at the main entrance to take the family to the cemetery. As they headed for the door, Wanda motioned for Craig to come with them. "I want you to ride with us," she said. "There's plenty of room, and we need to talk."

"That's okay," Craig said. "If I take my car, then you won't have to come back here to drop me off."

"Nonsense. We'll be coming back by here either way. Ride with us."

Craig nodded and fell in next to Mitch, who was marching behind his mother and sister like a dead man walking.

It was Craig's first time in a limo, but the circumstances precluded his enjoyment of the novelty. Wanda and Sherri sat facing forward, and Mitch and Craig sat across from them.

As they pulled out of the parking lot, Sherri asked her mother, "Who was the woman you talked to for so long, the pretty one, near the end?"

"That was Carla," Craig said without thinking.

"Yes, Carla," Wanda said. "She called the house wanting to talk to Barney the morning he died. I couldn't figure out why she wanted to talk to him, and she wouldn't tell me. I just asked her about it again." She paused as though that was all she had to say.

Craig shifted forward in his seat and said, "What did she say?"

"She said she wanted to make a final plea for Barney and the other elders to back down so the church wouldn't have to endure a nasty conflict that would be publicized. Blah, blah, blah." She waved her hand to swat away the end of the comment like it was a fly buzzing around her head.

Craig was relieved but also unable to resist the temptation to fish for a few more details. "Do you know if she spoke to him before he passed?"

Wanda nodded and said, "They did."

Mitch jumped into the conversation. "And true to form, Dad obviously wasn't interested in working things out," he said.

"If your father could see you now," Wanda said, shaking her head. "Refusing to speak at his funeral because you were afraid your emotions would get the best of you."

"You should be glad I kept my mouth shut," Mitch said. "The emotion I was afraid of showing wasn't grief, it was anger. I wouldn't have made it through my talk without breaking down and telling everyone what a hypocritical jackass he was."

Wanda leaned forward as though she were about to slap Mitch's face. He jerked away from the incoming blow, and Wanda pointed at him instead. "You will not speak ill of your father in front of others."

"You shouldn't have invited him to ride with us if you didn't want him to see what a freak show our family really is." He turned to Craig. "No offense intended. I don't mind you being here, but I'm not going to pretend my dad was my best friend just because you're in the car."

Craig said, "I'm sorry to intrude." He looked at Wanda and added, "Don't worry. This all gets filed under private and confidential."

"I'm sure it does," Wanda said. "But just the same, I'd like my son to show his father, whom we're about to bury, the respect he deserves."

"You might as well ask Craig to raise Dad from the dead then," Mitch said, "since you're already expecting the impossible."

"Mitch, please just leave it alone," Sherri said. "You've made your feelings about Dad clear. Let's just get through this."

"Yes, Mitch," Wanda said. "Why don't you keep your mouth shut from this point forward. There is no need to make this day any worse than it already is. I'm glad your father isn't here to see you acting like this." She caught herself. "I didn't mean it that way."

Mitch refused to let it go. "You're lucky I asked Sherri to speak in my place. Although now I'm starting to regret it. No offense intended, Sherri. You did a great job. I thought you were more than fair to Dad. He didn't make life any easier on you than he did me."

"It was different for you than it was for me," Sherri said. "He tried to make you into something you weren't. It wasn't fair. He tried to keep me from being who I really am. It was impossible."

"You should have said that today," Mitch said. "It's the truth."

"That's enough from both of you," Wanda said. "Can we all just be quiet until we get to the cemetery so we can say goodbye to your father in peace?"

No one said a word the rest of the way. Craig couldn't think of another time when he had been thrust into the middle of a more awkward family moment.

The limo turned into the cemetery and snaked its way down a maze of gravel roads toward a green awning set up next to an open grave. It pulled to a stop behind the hearse, which had led the way. The attendants from the funeral home swung the hearse's back door open and readied Barney's gray casket for transfer to the grave.

Wanda looked out the window and inspected the small group of family and close friends gathering around the graveside. The limo driver opened the door. Everyone was waiting for Wanda to exit, but she was still taking roll. She gasped and said, "What is he doing here?"

"I invited him," Mitch said.

"I told you to leave him out of this. He's not welcome here."

"Yes, he is. I wanted him here. So he's here. Deal with it."

Craig was dying to know whom they were talking about. He looked over at Sherri for some clarification. She was looking out the window in the opposite direction and biting her lower lip.

"You can ride home with him," Wanda said. "You're not getting back into this car."

"Fine by me," Mitch said. "This is the last place I want to be anyway."

They made their way to the first row of seats under the awning. The pallbearers moved the casket from the hearse to the rack sitting over the grave. Craig took his place at the head of the casket and scanned the small group, still trying to figure out whom Wanda and Mitch had been arguing about. The solemn faces staring back at him revealed nothing.

He waited for several more people who had followed the hearse from the church to walk over from their cars. When everyone was settled and quiet, he read the 23rd Psalm from the King James Version of the Bible and said the Lord's Prayer, just as Wanda had requested. From start to finish, it took less than three minutes.

As the group dispersed, Craig stepped back and watched Mitch. He hugged his sister, ducked his head, stepped past his mother, and headed to where the cars were parked. Another man, close to Mitch's age, broke away from the group and caught up with him. Together they walked to a red Honda Accord parked away from the others cars and positioned for a quick getaway.

Well, I'll be.

Craig looked back at the mingling group to see if anyone else had noticed Mitch and his friend leaving, but they were all either visiting with each other or trying to get close enough to give Wanda a hug. Then he saw Sherri watching Mitch and his friend drive away. When she caught Craig watching her, her mouth twitched into a half-hearted smile of confirmation. Her eyes begged him never to speak of what he had just seen to anyone. Craig smiled sympathetically and nodded. Private, confidential, and oh so awkward.

He wondered what Wanda wanted to talk about during the ride home. As he considered the possibilities, he regretted not asking Mitch and his friend for a ride.

Chapter 50

NO ONE SPOKE until the limo passed through the gate at the cemetery exit and pulled onto the main road. Then Wanda broke the ice. "Thank you, Craig, for doing the graveside service. And thank you for riding out here with us, although I wish Mitch hadn't worked so hard to make it an unpleasant trip."

"You're welcome. I know this is a difficult time for everyone," Craig said. *It hasn't been easy for me either.*

"It's an especially tough time for Mitch," Wanda said. "As you can tell, he and his father weren't close. This isn't a family counseling session, so I'll spare you the gory details. Suffice it to say that Mitch has made some devastating choices as an adult. He and Barney haven't spoken in almost two years. Hadn't spoken, I mean."

"But you asked Mitch to speak at the funeral," Craig said. It was a question disguised as an observation.

"Yes, I did, and it was a mistake. I was trying to pretend everything could be okay--that their relationship was cracked, not shattered. Denial makes people do foolish things," Wanda said.

"He was planning on me taking his place from the start," Sherri said. "That's the only reason he agreed to do it."

Wanda frowned at Sherri. "Why didn't you tell me? It wasn't right for you to surprise me like that. I was furious. I am furious."

"If I had told you, would you have let me speak?"

Wanda shook her head. "Of course I wouldn't have let you speak. That's not what your father would have wanted."

"And that's why we didn't tell you," Sherri said. "After what the reporter said about Dad on TV, I wanted to let people know he wasn't a monster."

"And you did an excellent job of it," Craig said. "I meant it when I said it was the best eulogy I have ever heard. You spoke the truth about your dad in a way only a daughter can."

Wanda reached over and put her hand on Sherri's knee. "You really did do a wonderful job with a difficult subject," she said. "Oh, I'm sure your father is mad about it." She winked at Sherri. "But also, a little proud."

"Thank you, Mom," Sherri said, her eyes filling with tears. "That's all I have ever wanted to do, make you and Dad proud."

Wanda put her arm around Sherri and pulled her close. "I know. I have always been proud of you."

"But Dad couldn't be proud of who I was, so he drove Mitch crazy looking for reasons to be proud of him."

"That's not true," Wanda said. "He just didn't know how to be proud of a daughter, especially one who reminded him of himself."

Craig wanted to crawl into the front seat with the driver and give them some privacy. He never ceased to be amazed at how the death of a loved one created opportunities for heart to heart communication between survivors. He knew this window wouldn't stay open for long, and he wanted to get out of the way so Wanda and Sherri could make the most of it.

Wanda continued, "Your dad's biggest flaw was that he couldn't see you or Mitch for who you are. He kept trying to make you both into something you could never be. For a man who loved the truth as much as he did, he sure spent a lot of his time avoiding it." She looked out the window and sighed. "Denial makes people do stupid, foolish things."

She turned to Craig. "I bet you're wondering why I wanted you to ride with us, aren't you?"

"I have given up trying to figure it out," Craig said. "I'm comfortable living with the mystery."

Wanda said, "I wasn't planning on it. To be honest, I've never liked you very much."

Craig smiled and tried to think of something to say.

"When I heard what Sherri had to say about her father, I decided we needed to talk. Had I known how much private family business you would take in while riding with us, I would have waited and invited you over to the house later, but it's too late for that now, isn't it?"

"Your secrets are safe with me," Craig said. And he meant it. He had absolutely no interest in exploiting what he had learned about Barney's family. If he could make himself forget some of it, he would.

"Good," she said. "I'll hold you to that." She paused a moment and then continued, "As Sherri was speaking today, it occurred to me that she was the only person in that room qualified to stand up and defend her father's honor."

She turned to Sherri. "I'm still not happy with you for going behind my back, and I didn't agree with everything you said, especially at the end. Some things are better left unsaid. But overall, you did a good job explaining why your dad was the way he was."

She turned back to Craig. "How many people from the church would you guess were at the service today?"

Craig shrugged. "It's hard to say. There were many people there from the community as well, but I'm guessing there were 150 to 175 of our people there. Maybe a little more."

"So about half the church heard what Sherri had to say about her father."

"I'd say so. I wish everyone could have heard it," Craig said.

"I think they should," Wanda said. "Do you think it would be possible to give Sherri a few minutes on Sunday to share what she said today with the entire church?"

"I think that's a fine idea," he stammered. "But I don't know if it's possible."

Wanda frowned. "And why not?"

Seriously? Have you not been paying attention?

"Women aren't allowed to speak to the church on Sunday mornings. I would have to get permission from the elders, and frankly, the timing for making such a request couldn't be worse. If they allow Sherri to speak, then it will look like they're giving in to The Deborah Club's demands."

"What if they say they're making an exception because she's Barney's daughter, and they want the whole church to hear what she has to say about her father?"

Craig gave her question some thought and formulated an answer that spooked his inner critic. *Danger! Danger! Proceed with caution!* He took a deep breath and decided to go for it. "Honestly," he said,

"I think they would have a hard time explaining why it's okay for Sherri to speak during our worship service about how much Barney means to her, while at the same time, it's not okay for other women to stand up and speak about how much Jesus means to them."

Sherri said, "Mom, I appreciate what you're trying to do, but I don't want to cause any trouble for the church. And I wouldn't feel comfortable having a special exception made for me."

"Did you hear any complaints about Sherri speaking from any South Barkley people today?" Wanda asked.

"Not a word," Craig said. "But it's still early. I haven't checked my email yet."

"Do you expect to hear anything negative?"

"No, I don't. In fact, I only expect to keep hearing what a great job she did."

Wanda looked out the window and said nothing for several minutes. When she did speak, it seemed to be more to herself than to Craig or Sherri. "It's interesting, isn't it? On a Wednesday afternoon, my daughter can stand on the stage, behind the podium, just like a preacher, and talk about her father. And yet, just a few days later, on a Sunday morning with the same pews occupied by many of the same people, she isn't allowed to stand up and repeat what she said today. I'm sorry, Barney, but this makes no sense to me."

"It doesn't make any sense to me either," Sherri said. "That's why I gave up on South Barkley."

"Where do you go to church?" Craig asked.

Wanda spoke for Sherri. "She goes to one of those liberal churches where they pick and choose which parts of the Bible to believe. Barney had a fit when he found out she was being led astray by a woman preacher who doesn't believe Jesus was born of a virgin."

"No, Mother," Sherri said. "Our pastor never said she rejected the virgin birth; she just said it didn't have to be true for her to be a Christian."

"Same difference," Wanda said. "You should have never told us about her. Your dad was up all night."

Sherri spoke to Craig, "I attend a Presbyterian Church. The Senior Pastor--"

"I didn't ask Craig to ride with us so we could talk about your church," Wanda said. "I want you to defend your father's honor on Sunday morning in front of my, our, church. I don't want their last impression of your father to be how that reporter described him on the news the other night." She looked at Craig. "Do you think we can make sure that reporter is there too? She needs to hear what Sherri has to say."

"Well, I guess we can invite her."

The limo slowed down to make the turn into the church parking lot. Craig was surprised at how quickly the time had passed. "Do you want me to talk to Ellis and see what he thinks?" Craig asked. "If you want it to happen on Sunday, I need to get moving. It will take some time for the elders to get together and make a decision."

"Let me think about it," Wanda said. "I hate being at the mercy of whatever the elders decide to do."

Now you know how The Deborah Club feels.

The limo came to a stop under the portico. Craig climbed out, thanked Wanda for the ride, and walked into the building in a state of shock.

Chapter 51

THE NEXT MORNING Craig was sitting at his desk drinking his first cup of coffee and wasting time online. His head was still spinning from the conversation with Wanda on the way back from the cemetery. When he told his wife about it, she wanted to celebrate. He warned her not to get her hopes up. Wanda had been riding an emotional roller coaster. After sleeping on it, there was a good chance she would look back on the entire conversation with embarrassment.

He was startled by three sharp knocks on his door.

"Come in," he said.

Wanda walked into his office, followed by Sherri. Without a word of greeting, Wanda headed straight to one of the chairs in the seating area and made herself at home.

Craig hurried from behind his desk and joined them.

"Hope we're not interrupting you," Sherri said.

"This is more important than whatever he was working on," Wanda said.

"You're not interrupting at all," Craig said. "Can I get you some coffee or bottled water?"

"No thanks," Sherri said.

"I was up most of the night thinking," Wanda said. "I want to talk to you about what's happening at South Barkley."

"You mean what we talked about yesterday on the way back from the cemetery? About Sherri speaking to the church on Sunday?"

"Yes, but more than that," Wanda said. "I want to talk to you about The Deborah Club."

Craig reached for his coffee and realized he had left it at his desk. He was getting up to retrieve it when Wanda said, "I want to bring this strike nonsense to an end."

Craig fell back into his seat. "We all do," he said. "But unless The Deborah Club gets what they want, I don't see it happening anytime soon." He thought of Amy Brandt's refusal to help with the funeral luncheon. "They've proven how serious they are."

"I know," Wanda said. "That's why I want to help them get what they want."

Craig looked at Sherri for confirmation that he had heard her mother correctly. Sherri gave him a slight nod and an I-can't-believe-it-either expression. "Wow," he said and rubbed the top of his thighs with his palms. "Forgive me if I don't know what to say, but I must admit I didn't see this coming."

"I'm sure you didn't," Wanda said. "Why don't you start by telling me what needs to happen."

"To end the strike?" Craig asked.

"Yes, that, but also how to get it done in time for Sherri to be able to speak to the church on Sunday."

"We would have to move really fast," Craig said. "If I can be totally honest, Barney was the main obstacle keeping us from moving forward. I don't think the remaining elders will put up much resistance, especially when they find out you're in support of expanding the role of women at South Barkley."

"What does that mean? Expanding the role of women at South Barkley? I want to make sure I understand exactly what I'm supporting."

Craig hoped what he was about to say wouldn't bring the conversation to a screeching halt. "I can't speak for The Deborah Club, but I'm guessing at the very least, they want to see and hear women pray, read scripture, and share their testimonies about the difference Jesus has made in their lives."

"What about preaching?" Sherri asked.

"Since I'm the regular preacher, I'm not in favor of us having a woman preacher, if you know what I mean." Craig gave a weak laugh, but neither of the ladies cracked a smile.

Stupid idiot!

In an effort to salvage the moment, he said, "Of course I have no theological problem with a woman preaching. I could definitely see us inviting a woman guest speaker someday."

"What about women elders?" Wanda asked. "Is that where we're headed?"

To stall for time and figure out the best way to answer her question, Craig eased out of his chair and grabbed his coffee from his desk. He waited until he was back in the chair and had taken a swig from his mug before he said, "I'm sure The Deborah Club would like to see women serve as elders, but I'm guessing the elders would say such a change would be too disruptive."

"And by disruptive you mean the elders are afraid people will leave?" Wanda said.

"Yes, that's exactly what I mean," Craig said. He leaned forward and launched into a mansplanation of congregational leadership. "Aside from making sure what we do is consistent with the intent of the Scriptures, this is one of our biggest concerns. If we push too hard, too soon, we'll push people away. No matter what we do, there will always be people who choose to go to other churches, but moving too far, too fast can put South Barkley's future in jeopardy."

"Because you wouldn't have enough money to pay your salary," Wanda said.

Craig sensed the lesson was over and sat back in his chair. "There's that," he said. "But there are other bills to pay as well, including a mortgage. It's important for a church to keep its financial commitments. We'll lose credibility in the community if we don't."

"Is that why Dad was able to block this change?" Sherri asked. "Because the church couldn't pay the bills without him?"

Craig looked at Wanda, but said nothing.

"Of course it was," Wanda said. "And don't act like you're surprised. This church would be nothing without your father."

"Always forcing the rest of the world to bend to his will," Sherri said, shaking her head in disappointment.

And right now your mom is doing a pretty good job of imitating your dad.

Wanda said, "So if I promised to continue supporting the church and even committed to increase my giving if these changes cause other givers to leave, do you think the elders would go for it?"

"I think so," Craig said. "Jake might still be uncomfortable with the change, but like I said, he'll go along with it when he finds out where you stand."

"Yes, he will," Wanda said, without a trace of doubt in her voice. "Let's get this done so that reporter will stop spreading lies about my husband."

Craig tried to act pleased without showing too much excitement. He wanted Wanda to know he supported her decision, but not how happy it made him personally. "Okay," he said. "I need to make a few calls." The first one would be to his wife. He couldn't wait to tell her the good news. He rose from his chair to signal the meeting was over.

"We're not done yet," Wanda said and Craig sat back down. "My offer only stands as long as I never have to see or hear Amy Brandt say anything from the stage at South Barkley. She has done great harm to my family. She disrespected my husband while he was alive and then she did it again yesterday. She didn't even have the decency to come to his funeral. I know she's cozied up with that reporter and is giving her inside information about our church. I don't mind The Deborah Club thinking they've won this battle, so long as that woman knows she didn't beat the Staples family."

So much for happily ever after. Stupid idiot!

Craig faked a smile. "I can understand why you feel the way you do," he said. "Barney and Amy's personalities clashed in a serious way. While I'm sure she will be thrilled to hear how things at South Barkley are about to change, she'll definitely be disappointed to learn you don't want her to be a part of it."

"I want her to be disappointed," Wanda said. "I want to teach her a lesson. There is a price to pay for disrespecting an elder and his grieving family to advance a selfish agenda."

"I'll need to think through what to tell her," Craig said.

"Tell her she can leave and go to another church, or tell her she can stay at South Barkley and keep her mouth shut. I'm fine with either one. Actually, I hope she stays so she'll have to sit there each Sunday and watch other women get to do what she so badly wants to do herself."

"Mom, don't you think you're being a little too harsh? Even mean?" Sherri said.

"She is the reason your dad is no longer with us. She pushed him to the brink. I'd press charges against her if I could," Wanda said.

"It's not all her fault," Sherri said.

"That's enough," Wanda said with finality. "We're not going to have this conversation again. Is this going to be a problem, Craig?"

Craig pondered the question long enough to make Wanda think he didn't hear her.

"Craig?"

"I don't know," he said. "I hope Amy will be willing to step aside for the good of the church and for the sake of her cause. But I don't know. I can tell you this. It will be hard."

"It's the only way," Wanda said. "I will not have her standing up and gloating about how she was able to outsmart and outlast the elders of this church."

"I need to visit with Ellis and the rest of the elders. Then I'll visit with Amy. I'll let you know as soon as I know something."

"Good," Wanda said. "The sooner the better."

Craig turned to Sherri. "And you're okay with addressing the church on Sunday if we can work all this out?"

"Yes, Mother and I talked about it late into the night and again this morning. I'm willing to do it for her and for Dad, but only as long as the other women at South Barkley are given the same opportunity." She smiled at her mother. "That's my only demand in this negotiation."

"Very well," Craig said and waited for Wanda to signal the meeting was over before standing again.

On their way out of his office, Wanda stopped at the door and turned back to Craig. "I'd like to think that Barney's death will lead to something good. It broke his heart when Mitch and Sherri chose not to worship with us at South Barkley. I don't expect Mitch to set foot in our church again until it's time to bury me, but maybe my daughter will come back to church with her mother now that she will no longer have to remain silent."

Behind her mother's back, Sherri shook her head and gave Craig the same half smile he'd seen at the cemetery the day before. Craig felt sorry for her. She was caught between her rock of a widowed mother and the hard place of a conservative church she had long since outgrown. Then he remembered the news he would be delivering to Amy Brandt and felt even sorrier for himself.

Chapter 52

CRAIG OFFERED TO drive over to Ellis's office and swear on a stack of Bibles that he was telling the truth about his meeting with Wanda and Sherri. Ellis said he believed him, but he still wanted Craig to come over and talk through the details of the conversation.

"I'm having a hard time buying it," Ellis said from behind a desk cluttered with paperwork. "The dirt over Barney's grave hasn't even had time to settle. Any ideas about why the sudden change of heart?"

"Two reasons that I know of," Craig said. "First, she wants Sherri to defend Barney on Sunday just like she did at his funeral. Second, she hopes Sherri will come back to South Barkley.

"Do you think she will?" Ellis asked.

"Come back?" Craig said. "Not likely. She's moved on. Every Sunday she listens to a woman preacher who is entertaining questions we're light years away from daring to even speak out loud. If I were her, the opportunity to say a prayer a couple of times a year wouldn't be enough to get me to come back to South Barkley."

"Do you think we should talk to her and ask her to come back, at least for a while?" Ellis asked.

"Trust me on this, Ellis. You do not want to get pulled into that vortex of family dysfunction. I say we stay out of it and let Wanda and Sherri work it out themselves."

"I'll take your word for it," Ellis said. "But I would hate for Wanda to change her mind if Sherri doesn't come back."

"That's out of our control. Sherri is willing to speak on Sunday if the elders accept Wanda's offer. That's the best we can hope for right now. Do you think the other guys will go for it?"

"Yes, they will. We all want this to be over."

"There's one more thing I haven't told you," Craig said. "You ready for the other shoe to drop?"

"Not really," Ellis said as he crossed his arms.

Craig told him what Wanda said about Amy.

Ellis exhaled slowly. "That'll be a fun conversation. How do you think she'll respond?"

"I don't know. I guess we're about to find out if this has been about the greater good of the women of South Barkley or if it has really been about her. Should we talk to her before or after we talk to the elders?"

"We?" Ellis said with raised eyebrows.

"I thought it would be best if she heard it from both of us, unless you want to talk to her by yourself." Craig stretched his lips into a thin smile.

"I'll make you a deal," Ellis said. "I'll get the other elders on board, if you'll talk to Amy."

"How is that a deal?" Craig asked. "You've already said you think they'll say yes. It sounds like only one of us has any work to do."

"And this is why we pay you the big bucks." He paused and gave Craig a big grin. "To have hard conversations with angry women." They were both acting as though a load had been lifted from their shoulders. "Seriously," he said, "I'm still mad at Amy, and I'm afraid I would enjoy delivering this news to her more than I should."

"That's a mighty fine Christian attitude you have there, Ellis. And pretty convenient too."

"Has any of this been even remotely Christian?" Ellis said, his expression turning sober.

"Not really," Craig said.

"Help me out," Ellis said. "You do your part, and I'll do mine. Then maybe we can all get back to being Christians again."

⇥ ⇤

It wasn't hard to get Jake and Steve, the other two elders, to attend an emergency meeting that night to discuss Wanda's offer.

Their diminished numbers made the conference table seem twice its usual size. Craig stared with regret at the chair where Ben usually sat. If only he had held on a few days longer. His eyes moved to Barney's empty chair, and he felt himself relax. Meetings would be so much easier without Barney, God rest his soul.

Ellis said a quick prayer and then asked Craig to summarize his conversation with Wanda. Craig laid out Wanda's offer, including the stipulation about Amy Brandt, all without interruption. Jake and Steve listened carefully but didn't seem surprised by anything he said. When he finished, Craig rested his elbows on the conference table and waited for questions.

Jake, Barney's friend and prized recruit, spoke first. "After Ellis called and told me what Craig had told him, I called Wanda to make sure she was being accurately represented. I just couldn't believe it, but she verified it. Craig is telling the truth."

Craig bristled at the assertion he couldn't be trusted. He wanted the elders to see him as an objective facilitator, an ally whose primary goal was to help them bring this standoff to a peaceful end. Craig's first impulse was to defend his honor, but he just as quickly decided to let it pass. It would only divert the conversation away from the primary purpose of the meeting.

Keep your eyes on the prize. You're almost there.

He appreciated it when Ellis came to his defense. "Of course Craig is telling the truth."

"I'm sorry, Craig," Jake said. "I meant no offense. I just can't understand why she would go against Barney's wishes."

"None taken," Craig lied. "While I can't claim to understand the inner workings of any woman's mind, I think she believes she's standing up for Barney, not going against him. It's more important to Wanda for Sherri to defend Barney's honor and explain his behavior than it is to continue to oppose The Deborah Club."

"What if Wanda changes her mind after Sherri speaks on Sunday?" Steve asked.

"Wanda wants Sherri to come back to South Barkley," Craig said. "That will never happen if she reneges. Plus, once we let it out, this genie will be hard to put back in the bottle."

"What if we don't let it out?" Jake said. "What if we stand our ground? That's what Barney would do."

"Then The Deborah Club will continue their strike, the media will continue to cover the story, and our church's reputation will continue to be dragged through the mud," Ellis said.

"We'll also have to tell Wanda we decided to reject her offer, and we'd rather not have Sherri eulogize Barney on Sunday," Craig said. "Who wants to volunteer to deliver that message?"

"It doesn't sound like we have much of a choice," Steve said.

"No, it doesn't," Jake said. "But I don't like being forced to do anything."

Craig snorted.

"What's wrong, Craig?" Steve asked.

"Nothing."

"You sure?"

Craig redirected Jake's absurd remark by playing the God card. "It may seem like we're being forced into something we haven't chosen, but what if this is God's way of giving us an opportunity to end this conflict and avoid more embarrassment?"

"Maybe so," Jake said. "I just don't like the idea of being held hostage by someone who uses money to get what she wants. We need to get out of debt as soon as possible. We don't need to be so dependent on one wealthy donor."

Craig was amazed at how quickly Jake had grown a backbone in Barney's absence and was now unwilling to take from Wanda what his old buddy Barney had been dishing out for years.

Before they wasted the next twenty minutes planning a fundraising campaign they would never launch, Ellis said, "That's a great idea, Jake. I suggest we get to work on raising half a million dollars after we avert this public relations disaster. Is everyone in favor of accepting Wanda's proposal to give The Deborah Club what they want so Sherri can speak on Sunday?"

"Are you guys sure this is okay? I mean with God?" Jake asked. "I never got around to reading all those recommended articles and books. Barney said they were all written by scholars who thought they were so smart they could ignore the plain teaching of the Bible."

"They weren't recommended, Jake. They were required," Ellis said. "You had your chance. You're out of time. And yes, it's okay. We should have made this decision a long time ago."

Craig smirked, but no one noticed. Jake's wasn't the only new backbone in the room.

"I hope we're not making a huge mistake," Jake said.

"We're not," Steve said. "This is the right thing to do, even if it's the wrong reason to do it."

Jake finally nodded in assent. Ellis made them all raise their hands to make sure there was no misunderstanding.

"I'll talk to Amy Brandt and see if we have a deal," Craig said.

Chapter 53

BEFORE CALLING AMY, Craig gave careful thought to the dynamics of his meeting with her. His first idea was to ask his wife to go with him to Amy's house where they would deliver the news together. After his run-in with Carla, he never wanted to meet alone with another woman again. In this case, he was worried more about violence than sex. When he asked her to be his bodyguard, his wife told him he was on his own.

"Amy Brandt has done more for the women at South Barkley than Wanda ever will. I want no part in carrying out Wanda's vendetta against her," she said. "You and the elders should be ashamed of yourselves."

"We are," Craig said. "But we're even more relieved that the end is in sight. Sometimes you have to choose the lesser of two evils."

He remembered an article he had read in a church leadership magazine. It listed several tips for having a difficult conversation with an adversary. He didn't consider Amy to be his adversary, not really, but by the end of their meeting, she would definitely see him as one. Better safe than sorry. According to the article, it was imperative for Craig to host the meeting in his office where he was in charge, rather than meeting with Amy at her home or office or even at a neutral site. So Craig decided to ask her to come to his office for a visit on Friday morning. As long as his part-time administrative assistant was in her office down the hall, he felt comfortable meeting with Amy alone.

When he called to ask for a meeting, Amy invited him to come by her office, but he told her it would better if they met at the church. Her curiosity piqued, she pressed him on the reason for meeting.

"I'll tell you when you get here," he said.

"Unless the elders have changed their position, I really don't care to meet with you," she said.

"Then you should care," Craig said

"Are you serious?"

"Yes, but we need to work through a few details." He almost told her to come expecting to hear both good and bad news, but he didn't want to get into it over the phone. "When can you meet?"

"I can be at your office in fifteen minutes," she said. "Do you want to meet with just me, or should I bring Carla and Helen along as well? We're getting together later this morning anyway."

"Just you," Craig said. "Let's work out the details before we talk to anyone else."

"See you in a few."

⋆⇛ ⇚⋆

The first half of the conversation went well. Amy shook her head in disbelief as she listened to Craig recount his conversation with Wanda and explain how Sherri's eulogy had broken the stalemate.

"Un-be-lieve-able," she said, a blank look on her face. "And what did the elders say?"

"They said yes. Their biggest concern has always been preserving the unity of the church, which as you know, also keeps us out of financial difficulty."

"Money talks, even if women can't," Amy said.

He pretended not to hear her and continued, "With Wanda's support, we should be alright, even if a few families leave."

Amy said, "So if I'm hearing you right, the elders are finally willing to do the right thing because there is no longer any risk involved. Now that's what I call leadership."

"You can call it whatever you want," Craig said, refusing to let her get under his skin. "Ultimately, it means the women at South Barkley are finally going to have a voice on Sunday mornings and, eventually, a seat at the leadership table."

"I guess you're right," she said. "But I'm still disappointed in them." She paused to think through an idea and then smiled. "Do you think they realize it was a woman who gave them permission to give all the other women in our church permission?"

Craig faked a smile in return but said nothing. He wanted to give her a moment to savor her victory before dropping the hammer.

"And just how long is eventually?" she asked.

"I don't know," Craig said. "We'll have a woman in front of the congregation this Sunday when Sherri speaks. I think we need to let everyone get used to seeing women on stage before we start talking about making them elders."

"It would be nice to see all of this in writing, along with a timeline," she said.

"Come on, Amy. You won. There is no need to rub their faces in it."

"I'm doing no such thing," she said. "I'm just being realistic. Based on past experience, the elders talk a good game, but they don't always follow through with action."

"This time is different," Craig said. "Wanda wants to get this done. She thinks it will help win Sherri over and get her to come back to South Barkley."

"That would be nice," Amy said. "I've always liked her."

"She does give a good eulogy," Craig said, stalling.

"So what's next?"

"Ellis and I are working on an announcement to the church this Sunday. He'll deliver it and then introduce Sherri. She will share her eulogy for Barney with the whole church."

"Do you think I might be able to say something as well?" Amy said. "To help smooth things over with the elders? It would also be a sign that it's time to get back to being a unified church again."

Here we go. Brace yourself.

"I'm not sure that's such a great idea," Craig said.

"Oh," Amy said. "And why not?"

Craig told her about Wanda's single stipulation for supporting The Deborah Club.

Amy sighed. "I should have known better than to think it would be as easy as you were making it sound."

"I'm sorry, Amy. I really am. I know how much this means to you."

"You make it sound like it's already a done deal," Amy said. "You guys aren't going to let her get away with this, are you?"

"A few minutes ago you were fine with Wanda telling the elders what to do," Craig said. "Now you think they need to stand up to her?"

"Yes, I do," Amy said. "She can't force someone to leave the church."

"No, she can't," Craig said. "And she didn't say you have to leave. She said you couldn't say or do anything from the stage. If you and Tom decide to leave, it will be your choice, not Wanda's. I think she prefers you stay and suffer the consequences."

"Why in the world would we want to stay?" Amy asked, her voice rising with anger. "And why is she holding me responsible for Barney's death?"

Craig glanced out his open office door to remind himself there were reinforcements down the hall.

Amy continued, "He wasn't yelling at me when he died. He was yelling at you. This wasn't my idea, remember? I wonder what other stipulations Wanda would make if she found out you were the mastermind behind this scheme?"

Craig had anticipated this threat and had his answer ready. "If you tell her about me, it will ruin everything you've worked for. Wanda will change her mind. I'll get fired. And no one will trust you, since you've been acting as if it were your idea all along. There'll be no more Deborah Club. No more strike. No chance of making progress. It will all be over, and you'll be back at square one. How does that sound?"

"It sounds like my only choice is to keep my mouth shut and take one for the team."

"I think that's what we're all hoping you will do," Craig said.

"Don't you dare say 'we' to me, like you're on their side," Amy said and wagged her finger at Craig.

"I'm sorry," Craig said. "Let me backtrack and say this is what the elders and Wanda are hoping you will do."

Amy stared out Craig's office window and focused on nothing in particular. "It's not fair," she said. "After all I've done, I don't deserve this."

"Fair?" Craig almost laughed. "There's nothing fair about leadership. And please don't try to play the victim card. You didn't do yourself any favors when you refused to coordinate the luncheon for Barney's funeral. That's what this is all about. Wanda knows you didn't kill Barney. He killed himself by being a raging idiot. But you did snub her, and she will not let that pass."

"I thought I might be making a huge mistake when I refused to help," Amy said. "The truth is I almost called you and told you we'd do the luncheon. I'd like to have that one back."

"Now you know how Moses felt," Craig said.

"Come again?"

"You know the story. Moses led the Israelites out of slavery in Egypt and through the wilderness. The people rebelled, complained, and made his life miserable every step of the way. When it came time to cross the Jordan River, Moses didn't get to enter the Promised Land. Do you remember why? Because in a fit of anger, he struck a rock with his staff instead of speaking to it as God had commanded. So God didn't let him cross over to the other side."

"Talk about unfair," Amy said.

"Welcome to the big leagues."

"Do you think I'm being punished?" she asked.

"By Wanda? Yes. By God? No. But it doesn't really matter. This is the way church leadership works. The one who leads a group toward a better future doesn't usually get to enjoy the fruits of their labor. Either the difficult journey burns you out, or the inevitable mistakes you make along the way drain your account of credibility. This is the price you agreed to pay when you stepped up to lead The Deborah Club."

"I had no idea," Amy said.

"Neither did Moses," Craig said.

"Is there any chance of the elders coming to my defense?" Amy asked. "Surely they agree this isn't fair."

"Do you really expect them to help you? You came on pretty strong. From their perspective, you were impossible to work with. They may not have liked the way Barney treated you, but you made all of them look like fools. I don't think any of them have any interest in pleading your case to Wanda. Again, this is the price you pay for the *way* you chose to lead The Deborah Club. Every leadership decision you made has consequences."

"What if I sat down with Wanda and apologized?" Amy said, grasping for solutions.

Craig gave her a sympathetic smile. "You can certainly try," he said. "But I doubt it will help. In order to rationalize going against Barney's wishes, she has to make someone pay. There has to be a victory she can point to so Barney's death isn't in vain. I'm afraid silencing you is that victory."

Amy considered her situation for a long moment. Finally she said, "You can tell Wanda and the elders I agree to their terms. No more trouble from me. But I also want you to tell them that if they don't follow through, if the women of South Barkley aren't free to do everything men can do, and soon, I will beat this drum again. This is not a threat. It's a promise."

"I believe you," Craig said. "I'll do my best to make sure they follow through. We've gone through too much to back off again. If it is going to cost us a good leader like you, we better go all the way this time."

His comment surprised her. "You think I'm a good leader?" she asked.

"Of course I do. Why do you think I panicked when I realized I had mistakenly sent my manifesto to you? I knew you could do something with it. And I was right."

"Thank you for saying that, Craig."

"It's the truth."

He found it easy to be magnanimous now that she had agreed to go along with the plan.

"You know," she said, "if I'm being honest, I'm a bit disappointed we won't have the opportunity to strike this Sunday. It would have been fun to see you guys scrambling to hold everything together while we all sat back and watched."

Craig said, "Part of me wanted to see that as well. The thought of Ellis being stuck in the nursery trying to figure out how to change the poopy diaper of a baby, whose name he did not know, always made me smile."

This time Amy didn't bother trying to hide the tears.

Chapter 54

IT WAS OVER. They had won. But Amy didn't feel like celebrating. On the way back to her office, she almost called Carla but decided she wasn't ready to admit to anyone she was letting Wanda force her out. She called her assistant instead and told her she wasn't feeling well and wouldn't be returning to the office. It was true. She felt terrible. Then she texted Carla and Helen and let them know something had come up at work, and she couldn't meet with them. She switched her phone to airplane mode before either had a chance to respond. She spent the rest of the day brooding alone at home and waiting for Tom.

She met him at the door that evening with a glass of Merlot.

"Uh oh," he said. "This can't be good."

"I do have some good news," she said and led him to the sofa. "But I also have some bad news to go along with it. Rather than ask you to pick which one you want to hear first, I'm going to start with the good news, because without it, the bad news isn't going to make any sense."

After hearing the good news, Tom said, "Honey, that sounds like better than good news, but you're about to cancel it out with the bad news, aren't you?"

"I'm not going to make you guess," she said and told him the rest of the story.

"Damn. That's cold-blooded."

"Yes, it is, but it's partly my fault. We should have made those sandwiches for Barney's funeral."

"I guess so. Death by sandwich is a terrible way to go."

"Too soon," she said. "And not funny. It'll be a while before I'm ready to laugh at any of this. Do you think we should leave South Barkley?"

"Why would you want to stay?"

"Because it's home, and because we won. I want to make sure the elders follow through."

Tom twisted his face in disgust. "There are no winners in this, except maybe Wanda since she gets to be in charge now. The elders didn't make this decision on principle. They didn't tell Barney they'd rather go without his money than put up with his bullying. Instead, they needed permission from his angry widow to go ahead and do what they've wanted to do all along. Those men have no spine. They have no faith. If they can't see it, they don't believe it. Wanda showed them a safe path, and now they'll follow it, even if it means leaving you behind."

"They're not my biggest fans right now," she said. "Craig said they're not quite ready to forgive me for the trouble I've caused."

"So they have no faith, and they're unwilling to forgive. Here's an idea. Let's go find a church led by actual Christians and see what it's like. It's been years."

"We need to come up with a believable reason for why we're leaving," she said. "People will want to know, and we can't tell them I'm being forced out."

"Blame it on me," Tom said. "Tell everyone I was never supportive of your involvement with The Deborah Club, and I demanded we go elsewhere."

"No one will believe that. These people know us too well," she said. "Plus I don't want people thinking I would leave South Barkley just because you told me to. I'm supposed to be an angry, defiant woman, remember?"

"You're right," he said. "That won't work. Here's another idea. Let's blame Craig. People leave churches all the time when they don't like the pastor. We could say we're no longer being fed at South Barkley. Isn't that the excuse people give when they leave a church? It's a hard one to argue with."

"Yes, but why would I have stirred up all this trouble with The Deborah Club if we were thinking of leaving the church anyway? It's thin, Tom." She gave him a rueful smile. "Listen to us. We sound like criminals trying to come up with an airtight alibi."

Tom looked up at the ceiling as if he hoped to find a solution written there. "What if we say this ordeal has left you emotionally exhausted, and you want to take a break from South Barkley to recharge your batteries? We could make it sound like we'll be back in a couple of months. By the time anyone notices we haven't come back, we'll already be gone for good, and it will be too late for anyone to care."

"That's better," she said. "But I'm afraid the curiosity of what was happening at South Barkley would drive me crazy. Maybe we should hang around for the first few months and see how things go. Don't you also think the other women are going to be looking to me for leadership during the transition? I can't just leave them high and dry."

Tom chuckled. "You make it sound like we just elected a new president."

"Well excuse me for thinking what I've been doing here matters," she said and put some space between them on the couch. "I'll try not to act so important in the future."

Tom reached over and grabbed her hand. "I didn't mean it that way. None of this would have happened without you. The strike was your idea. You led the way. Now you can ride off into the sunset with your head held high."

"That's not completely accurate," Amy said and looked down at her empty wine glass. "It wasn't my idea."

She refilled their glasses and told him the whole story. When she finished, Tom downed the remainder of his wine like a shot of whiskey and slammed the glass on the coffee table hard enough for Amy to think he had broken the stem. "What a weasel," he said. "He's the biggest coward of them all. You can stay at South Barkley if you want, but I will never set foot in that building again."

Amy nodded in agreement, as though Tom's declaration brought her a measure of relief.

"I'm going on Sunday to see what happens," she said. "After that, we'll tell people we're taking a break and never come back."

Chapter 55

AMY FINALLY CALLED Carla on Saturday morning.

"Why have you been ignoring my calls and texts?" Carla said. "I keep getting calls from women who can't get in touch with you. They all want to know if the strike is still on. What's the plan for tomorrow? Are you sick? Do you need me to take over?"

"I'm feeling fine," Amy said, doing her best to sound cheerful. "Everything is fine. I didn't want to say anything until I knew for sure, but the elders have agreed to our demands. They're making an announcement tomorrow. We need to let everyone know to come expecting to hear good news."

"So we're not going to get a chance to watch the men fall on their faces?" Carla said. "That's too bad. I was going to bring popcorn."

"Leave your popcorn at home. It's over."

"It was Sherri's speech at the funeral, wasn't it? I had a feeling it was a game changer."

"Turns out it was," Amy said. "It certainly changed Wanda's mind. She now supports The Deborah Club and wants Sherri to say something similar during the service tomorrow."

"You sound disappointed," Carla said.

"Not disappointed. I just wish the circumstances had been different. When we started this, I didn't think it would get someone killed."

"Don't be so dramatic," Carla said. "Besides, you're not responsible for Barney's death. It was a rage-induced heart attack."

"Tell that to Wanda. She's convinced I killed him."

"We should tell Wanda the truth then. She needs to know."

"Know what?" Amy asked.

"That Barney was angry at Craig for giving us the idea to strike in the first place. That's why he was trying to fire Craig when he died." Carla said this as if it were old news hardly worth repeating.

"Barney knew?" Amy asked.

"Yes, he knew."

"How?"

"I told him."

"When?"

"That morning."

"You didn't."

"I most certainly did. I was angry at Craig," Carla said. "I still am. He's a coward, and he's using us to get what he wants at no risk to himself."

"If Barney hadn't died, you would have destroyed The Deborah Club," Amy said. "All our work would have been wasted."

"But Barney did die, and Sherri's eulogy did the trick, so it all worked out in the end. Now all we have to do is get rid of Craig."

"What's the deal between you and Craig? Why are you willing to risk everything we've been working for to get him fired?" Amy asked.

Carla said nothing.

"It has something to do with what happened at the coffee shop the other night, doesn't it?" Amy said.

"I don't know what his delusional little wife was blathering about," Carla said. "They both need to go. I'm going to tell Wanda why Barney was so upset before he died."

"No, you're not," Amy said. "It will ruin everything."

"Who cares?" Carla said in exasperation. "Who wants to celebrate a victory built on a lie. You just said you don't like the circumstances. I don't either. We can't let Craig get away with it."

"Listen to me, Carla," Amy said, speaking like a big sister trying to talk her little sister out of doing something foolish. "This is not about Craig or you or me. Not anymore. This is about securing the future for all the young women and little girls at South Barkley. I don't like the way we got here any more than you do, but we got here. Please don't throw it all away now. Promise me you won't say anything. If you can't work things out with Craig, just ignore him. Can you do that? For me? Please. He'll eventually move on. Pastors always do."

"I swear," Carla said, "if he says or does anything to make it look like he's taking credit for any of this, or if he looks at me a second too long, I will go straight to Wanda and then to the elders."

"Thank you," Amy said with relief, realizing she was the only person at South Barkley who could keep Carla in line. Despite what Tom had vowed the night before, she knew she had to stay.

Chapter 56

ON SATURDAY AFTERNOON, the South Barkley elders sent an email to church members and every visitor who had written an email address on a guest card in the past three years. The message was quick and to the point.

> *Subject: Major Announcement This Sunday*
>
> *Dear Members and Friends of the South Barkley Bible Church,*
>
> *We appreciate your continued support during the past several weeks, which have been difficult for all of us. After much prayer and discussion, the elders have discerned the time has come to make a major announcement concerning the expansion of the role of women in public worship and church leadership at South Barkley. This expansion will be explained in greater detail during the worship gathering tomorrow. We're also pleased to announce that all of our volunteers will be serving in their usual places. Despite the challenges we have recently faced, we believe our best days as a church are ahead of us. We're looking forward to telling you more.*
>
> *See you Sunday,*
> *The Elders*
> *South Barkley Bible Church*

Chapter 57

By Sunday morning, most of the congregation had either read the email from the elders or heard about it from someone else. Members arrived for church relieved the strike was over but anxious to hear what the elders had to say. A few outsiders, mainly those who had been following the story in the news, showed up hoping to see more drama unfold. When they learned there would be no strike, most of them left before the assembly began.

Had they stayed, they would have heard Ellis deliver a clear, well-constructed announcement to the church on behalf of the elders. He began with a series of apologies.

"First," he said, "I want to apologize for all the negative publicity our church has received over the past few weeks. Unfortunately, many people in our community now have a negative impression of the South Barkley Bible Church. Had we, the elders, been better leaders, had we been more proactive in addressing the concerns voiced by many of you, none of the recent events would have transpired."

Like everyone else in the room, Craig hung on Ellis's every word, even though he knew what was coming. He had spent most of his Saturday helping the elders write and wordsmith the announcement. There had been some significant disagreement among the elders about how much apologizing they needed to do. Craig had argued that owning their mistakes would be an important first step toward rehabilitating the church's image in the community. Still, they almost didn't include the first apology. Some elders argued that by taking responsibility for what had happened, they were implicating Barney in their failure. They were worried about offending Wanda, but when they showed her a draft on Saturday night, she hadn't objected.

They also didn't like taking all the blame when half of it, if not more, rightfully belonged to Amy Brandt and The Deborah Club. As Jake had put it, "It wasn't a lack of leadership that got us in trouble. It was too much leadership from Amy Brandt." Again, Craig was able to convince them that slinging mud at The Deborah Club would only make them appear bitter. So they finally agreed to take the high road and say it was all their fault, with the hope those who had been paying attention would know better.

"I would also like to apologize to all the women of South Barkley. Against you, our sins are many. We have taken you for granted. We have failed to show our appreciation for all you do behind-the-scenes to keep our programs, activities, and services running smoothly. Without your hard work and sacrificial service, our church cannot survive.

We are also sorry for the way we have limited the women in this church to roles of silent service when many of you are so clearly gifted to serve in more public roles of leadership and communication. We have been guilty of taking a few verses in the Bible, written to solve specific problems plaguing ancient churches, and universally applying them to every woman here. We now see how misguided and shortsighted, and yes, even sinful, this practice has been. We've made you to feel like second-class citizens. We've given you the impression that a woman's voice shouldn't be heard in our worship gatherings. We've created a culture in which our little girls grow up believing little boys are more important than they are because we've allowed our little boys to pray and read scripture and explain why they love Jesus, while telling our little girls it's their job to sit quietly in the pews and support the boys.

Over the years, many of you have attempted to describe for us what it is like to be a woman in this church. You've repeatedly tried to explain to us why our refusal to make changes in this area has been so frustrating for you. And for years, we failed to listen. You have every right to be angry with us. We understand why you finally decided it was time to stop waiting for us to see the light, and instead, did what you felt was necessary to turn up the heat. We're sorry it has taken us so long to make this declaration. Please forgive us for being so slow to act on a matter of such great importance."

Craig was nodding and smiling as Ellis read this section of the announcement. He was pleased Ellis was sticking to the script. There had been significant pushback about using the word "sin" instead of "mistake." After much debate, the elders had agreed with Craig's assessment that confessing sin sounded more spiritual than admitting "mistakes were made." They also agreed they needed all the help they could get in the "appearing to be spiritual" department, so they reluctantly labeled themselves as sinners.

"Finally," Ellis said, "I want to apologize to our friends and neighbors from the community who are not members of this church but have been following this story with great interest. I do not blame you for having a negative opinion of our church based upon what you've seen and heard in the media. I do hope what you've read on the Internet or seen on TV will not be the only information you allow to shape your impression of the South Barkley Bible Church.

The way of Christ is so much better than how we have recently portrayed it. Please give us a second chance to show you how Christians treat each other, especially when working through a disagreement. We can and will do better in the future. And though I doubt the media will report the story of our continued improvement as enthusiastically as they have told the story of our failure to get along with each other, I do hope you will stay close enough to keep an eye on us and witness our progress firsthand."

From his seat in the second row, Craig couldn't tell how the congregation was receiving the last apology. He was dying to turn around and look but forced himself to keep staring straight ahead. He didn't think it was a good idea for Ellis to take a shot at the media, but the other elders had disagreed. As long as they didn't offend Wanda or alienate any of the leaders of The Deborah Club, they saw no reason to play nice with the media. Craig was hoping Emily Branson would cover this final chapter of the story, but Ellis was skeptical. He doubted apologies and peacemaking efforts were provocative enough to justify the use of Channel 8's precious airtime.

⇢⊨◉ ◉⊨⇠

Emily Branson was sitting in the back pew and had a great view of the way the congregation responded to Ellis's comment about the media. Heads were nodding. Several people around her smiled in agreement. While she didn't like being the subject of Ellis's comment, even if he didn't mention her by name, she also knew he was right. Her producers would never green light a follow-up story in which she stood in the church parking lot and reported how the threatened strike had been called off, the church leadership had apologized for mishandling the situation, and the women of South Barkley were finally being allowed to speak during the worship service. Yawn. When Amy Brandt had called and told her the good news the previous afternoon, Emily expressed legitimate excitement for Amy and the other women of the church. Now she found herself wishing the conflict had lasted a few weeks longer for her benefit.

⇢▭ ▭⇠

With the apologies out of the way, Ellis could get to the meat of the announcement. "After years of study, prayer, discussion, and soul-searching, we have discerned that the time has come to empower and encourage the women of South Barkely to use their leadership, teaching, and communication gifts in the service of this church, just as we have always encouraged the men to use theirs. We are getting out of the business of telling Christian women, whose freedom was secured by Jesus on the cross and whose identity as co-heirs with Christ was established by the resurrection, that certain roles of service and leadership are off limits to them because of their gender. There is nothing we can do to restore the lost opportunities of the past, but we can promise you that beginning today, every single person in our church, whether male or female, will be free to use their gifts as God calls him or her to do."

One person started clapping and others quickly joined in until it sounded like everyone in the room was celebrating.

⇥ ⇤

Amy Brandt was sitting by herself near the back. She had planned to sit with Carla but couldn't find her. She managed to keep her emotions under control as Ellis worked through his list of apologies. But his announcement of liberation, followed by applause from the congregation, sent her over the edge.

She had done it. Her plan hadn't unfolded the way she thought it would. Not even close. But they had still arrived at her desired outcome. Swept up in the excitement of the moment, she momentarily forgot she was the only woman at South Barkley who still wasn't free. In the coming weeks, it would be hard for her to watch other women struggle to do what came so naturally to her.

⇥ ⇤

From his vantage point on the stage, Ellis could see that not everyone was applauding the announcement. Scattered throughout the congregation were a few frowning faces hovering over crossed arms. Wanda, who wasn't much of a clapper in the first place, kept her hands in her lap, but she wasn't frowning, which put Ellis at ease. A blank expression from Wanda was as good as a smile.

He waited until the applause died down and then continued, "I'm sure you have many questions about how these changes will be implemented and at what pace. While we still haven't worked out all the details, our plan is to start inviting women to say prayers, read scripture, and offer communion meditations beginning next week. Because this will be a new experience for many of us and will result in some initial discomfort, we're not going to ask women to start doing all of these things at once.

Next week, our opening scripture will be read by a woman. Several weeks later, we'll ask a woman to lead us in prayer. Not long after that, I expect we'll be eager to hear a woman's perspective on communion, and we'll invite one of our sisters in Christ to preside over the Lord's Table.

I, for one, long for the day in the not too distant future when it's a natural and normal thing to hear a woman's voice in our assembly. More than that, I look forward to the time when we no longer notice the gender of the person who is speaking, teaching, or praying, but instead, simply hear and appreciate the voices of fellow Christians expressing their faith, while encouraging ours.

As the Apostle Paul wrote in his letter to the Galatians, 'There is neither Jew nor Gentile, neither slave nor free, nor is there male and female, for you are all one in Christ Jesus.'"

Ellis paused as he transitioned into what was the most difficult part of the announcement for him. Craig had tried to talk him out of including it, but he believed it was important to say. "While I would love to think this announcement and its implementation will be celebrated by every member of our church, I know this will not be the case. Some of you will not be able to embrace this change with a clear conscience. I want you to know that by moving in this direction, it is not our desire to offend or exclude you. We pray you will give this change a chance, even though it's going to stretch you beyond your comfort zone. Perhaps over time the experience of witnessing women use their gifts in our assembly will change your perspective, and you'll come to view this change as positively as we do.

However, if embracing this change is something you are unable to do because of your convictions, we understand and commend you for your desire to worship God in both spirit and truth. If you must leave South Barkley and worship elsewhere, it will break our hearts to see you go. Even though we will no longer be worshipping together, we hope we can still enjoy the bond of spiritual fellowship that transcends the location of the building where we gather.

But before you go, I beg you to give us the opportunity to answer your questions and explain why we made this decision. If you still feel compelled to leave after more conversation, then we will thank God for the sincerity of your convictions and pray for your continued well-being in Christ.

I know this is moving very fast. It is impossible to anticipate every question or cover every detail in this announcement. But I'm sure, as are the other elders, that in the days, weeks, and months ahead, God's plan for this church will become more clear as we seek to do his will together. Thank you for your grace and patience throughout this ordeal."

There was a smattering of applause as some thought this was the end of the announcement. Ellis held up his hand to signal he had more to say.

"As you all know, our church suffered a great loss last week with the sudden passing of Barney Staples. If you were able to attend his funeral on Wednesday, then you know what a wonderful job his daughter, Sherri, did eulogizing her father. Because Barney played such an important role in the life of this church, and frankly, because we feel his character has been misrepresented in the media, we thought it would be good for our entire church to hear what Sherri has to say about her father. At this time, I invite Sherri to come share a few thoughts with us."

⋯▷▤◉ ◉▤◁⋯

Sherri replaced Ellis behind the podium. She thanked the church for its support during her family's time of grief, and she thanked the elders for the opportunity to say a few things about her dad. During her opening remarks, an older couple, who had been passing through town and just happened to be visiting South Barkley that day, walked out of the sanctuary. They didn't stop to tell anyone why they were leaving, but everyone who saw them assumed it was an act of protest. Their leaving seemed to prick the consciences of those who were already choking on Ellis's announcement. Several others followed them out the door.

One of the couples who left had been friends with Barney and Wanda for years. It felt to them like Ellis was forcing this change on them and then rubbing their face in it by asking Sherri to speak immediately after making the announcement. When Wanda learned of their hasty exit later that day, their friendship came to an abrupt end, and the couple never attended South Barkley again.

Sitting at the front, Craig was unaware of the hasty departures taking place behind him. If Sherri saw the people leaving, she did nothing to indicate it as she spoke. She repeated what she had said at the funeral almost verbatim. Craig thought it was just as powerful the second time around.

When she finished, the sanctuary erupted in yet another round of applause. Craig found it to be an awkward moment. What exactly were they applauding? Were they honoring Barney's memory? Were they trying to encourage Sherri? Or were they celebrating that the ceiling hadn't collapsed and crushed them as they sat there and listened to a woman speak in church? Or was it the overflow of nervous energy? *When in doubt, clap.* No matter the motive, applause was much better than boos or icy silence. Craig counted it as a win.

Ellis's announcement and Sherri's eulogy were long enough to eliminate the need for a sermon. Craig breathed a sigh of relief as the worship band took the stage and invited the church to stand for a final song. He felt lighter and freer than he had since the day of the accidental email. He grabbed his wife's hand and squeezed it as they sang. He was glad South Barkley was changing, and he was happy for all the women who were now free to use their gifts in every way. But the true source of the joy bubbling up inside of him was the realization that he had unwittingly orchestrated this change, while somehow managing to stay out of the line of fire. Against all odds, he had made a huge mistake and had been cagey enough to get away with it.

With the congregation moving forward, he could step out of his neutral position and begin coaching and equipping the women of South Barkley to exercise their newfound freedom. It was a task for which he felt perfectly suited.

Chapter 58

THE EXPANSION OF the role of women at South Barkley turned out to be a bigger deal for more people than Craig had anticipated, but it still wasn't the catastrophe the elders had long envisioned. When Helen stood before the church and read a scripture the following Sunday, there were a few more empty seats than usual. Over the next several weeks, as more women were invited to read a scripture, say a prayer, or share a brief thought before communion, attendance decreased by fifty-three people. A few wrote emails to the elders explaining their reasons for leaving, but most just stopped coming without a word of explanation. The average contribution, however, dipped by only a few hundred dollars. When the elders did the math and realized those who left hadn't been financially committed to South Barkley, they decided losing them wasn't such a big tragedy after all.

It was Craig's responsibility to compile a list of women who were willing to read or pray or say something on Sunday mornings, as well as to coordinate their participation in the worship gatherings. He was surprised by how many women turned him down, not because they were unsupportive of the change, but because they didn't feel comfortable speaking or praying in public. When Craig offered to coach them, most said it wasn't a matter of feeling ill-equipped for the task, but rather, they simply weren't interested in serving in these ways.

Craig didn't know why he had expected one hundred percent participation from the women, since there were plenty of men in the congregation who also declined his invitations to read, pray, and speak. When he did the math, he realized the percentages of willing men and women were about the same. So he stopped trying to change the minds of those who declined and instead focused his attention on those who said yes.

When his wife pointed out how he seemed far more interested in equipping the women for their speaking roles than he was in equipping the men, he assured her it wasn't because he thought they were less capable or needed extra help. He just wanted them to do well so the laggards and late-adopters would be more likely to embrace the change. If the first few women stumbled over their words or appeared uncomfortable, it would make everyone else uncomfortable. There was enough anxiety present in the congregation already. He didn't want the perception of incompetence to increase it.

Early on, Craig wished he could ask Amy Brandt to do something. She would do a good job with zero coaching. As time passed, he hoped Wanda's attitude toward Amy would soften, and she would lift the ban. He was also hoping for world peace.

🕯 For her part, Amy was gracious when asked why she wasn't participating. Her answer, which she delivered like a pro, was that she had done her part by starting The Deborah Club, but now she was happy to sit back and watch other women use their gifts. This was enough for most people, but Carla and Helen didn't buy it.

"Are the elders snubbing you because you embarrassed them?" Carla asked over coffee one Friday.

"Absolutely not."

"Then what's going on?"

"I know some people think The Deborah Club was all about me and my desire to stand on the stage in order to be seen and heard," Amy said. "I want to show everyone it had nothing do with my personal ambition."

This explanation satisfied Helen, and she commended Amy for her humility. Carla was still skeptical, but she lost interest in Amy's lack of involvement once she realized it was she, not Amy, who was being snubbed.

When compiling his list of potential participants, Craig put Carla's name at the bottom and then deleted it. There was no way he was ever going to let her stand in front of the church. If Wanda had veto power over Amy, he decided he could exercise his pastoral authority to blacklist Carla. The only difference was he didn't tell anyone, not even Ellis or his wife, what he was doing.

There had been a time when he avoided Carla because of his infatuation with her. Now he did so because she scared him. He was careful not to look at her when he preached, and he didn't speak to her in the foyer afterward. It never occurred to him to wonder why a woman who was accustomed to being the center of attention was allowing herself to be ignored by someone she despised. Had he given it even a few minutes thought, he might have recognized how much danger he was in.

She wanted to be ignored, or even better, forgotten. Like a snake in the grass waiting for the perfect moment to strike, Carla was hiding.

Chapter 59

AFTER SEVERAL MONTHS of transition, the novelty of women fully participating in the South Barkley worship assembly wore off, and life returned to normal, only with a few less people sitting in the pews. Craig no longer felt any anxiety when it was a woman's turn behind the microphone. He felt silly for initially thinking women would need special coaching to do what men had been doing with no coaching at all. The truth was that most of the women did a better job than the men, who for years had acted as though the opportunity to speak in church was a divine right given to them at birth, rather than a privilege never to be taken for granted.

On a rainy spring Sunday, Helen was scheduled to offer the communion meditation and pray over the bread and the cup. During the song before communion, Craig glanced over to the front row of seats in front of the communion table and wondered why Helen wasn't sitting there, ready to step behind the table during the last few seconds of the song for a seamless transition.

He glanced over his shoulder and scanned the crowd, hoping to make eye contact and signal her to take her place up front, but he didn't see her. He was preparing himself to ad lib a few thoughts about communion when he saw Carla move to the front row where Helen should have been.

Surely not.

His worst fears were confirmed when Carla moved toward the communion table as the band was winding down a song about Jesus' sacrificial love.

Standing behind the table, shielded by the bread and the cup, Carla looked over at Craig and smiled. He felt the blood drain from his face.

Surely not.

Carla said, "You'll notice in your program that Helen was scheduled to be standing here this morning, but as you can see, I'm not Helen. She called me last night and asked me to fill in for her because she wasn't feeling well. Please keep her in your prayers."

This wasn't exactly the way it had happened. Helen had called Carla and told her she was sick, but her call was to ask Carla to come by her house on the way to church and pick up some cookies she was supposed to bring on Sunday. When Helen mentioned she also needed to call Craig so he could find someone else to do the communion meditation, Carla had volunteered to do it as well. She assured Helen it would be easier for everyone involved. The last thing Craig wanted to be doing on a Saturday night was scrambling to find someone to take her place. Helen had no reason to be suspicious and agreed it was the quickest and easiest solution.

"This is my first opportunity to speak to the church on a Sunday morning. That being the case, I ask your indulgence as I reflect for just a moment on the magnitude of the changes our church has experienced over the past four months."

Craig couldn't look at Carla as she spoke. She was already breaking the first rule he had given to everyone, male or female, since making the change. *When speaking to the church, don't mention the change. Don't draw attention to it. Don't reflect on how good it is. Don't lament that some left because of it. Act like it is no big deal so that it will become no big deal.* Everyone had followed this rule, except Carla.

"I'm amazed at how well this transition has gone. I'm proud of all the women who have shared their voices with us on Sunday mornings. Our church is richer in its perspective thanks to your willingness to stand and be heard. Thank you for leading the way. I also want to say a special word of thanks to the person who made it possible. As you all know, this never would have happened without the creative leadership of a particular individual who decided enough was enough."

Now it was Amy Brandt's turn to feel uncomfortable. The last thing she wanted was for Carla to remind everyone of her role in The Deborah Club. People had finally stopped asking her why she wasn't more involved. Carla's praise would only prompt a new wave of questions. She subtly moved her head from side to side in a vain attempt to wave her off.

But Carla wasn't looking at Amy. She was looking straight at Craig, who was staring at the back of the pew in front of him.

"Then again, maybe you all don't know who is responsible," Carla said. "Because I know how hard he tried to keep his involvement a secret."

Like Amy, only with more vigor, Craig shook his head. *Please don't. Please. Please. Please.*

"I remember the day he told us about his plan. He said it would never work if people found out the idea for The Deborah Club--the name was also his idea--came from a man."

Craig's wife put her hand on his thigh. He didn't notice.

"I still remember how he put it. He said, 'In order for it to work, this has to be a movement originated and led by women. This revolution must be for women, by women, and of women.' And that's exactly what it appeared to be, but now that we've put all that silly drama behind us, I see no reason why it should remain a secret. If anything, it's long past time to give credit where credit is due."

Craig's wife dug her nails into his thigh. He barely felt it.

"On behalf of all the women in our church who have benefitted from your clever plan, I want to extend our deepest gratitude to Craig, our fearless pastor who, rather than take the credit for himself, hung back in the shadows so it would look like we were fighting for our freedom all by ourselves."

When Carla said his name, a groan rolled over the congregation like a wave. In a mocking gesture of appreciation, Carla placed both hands over her heart and then started clapping as if she expected the rest of the congregation to join her.

Craig would never forget the awkward sound of Carla clapping alone. The cadence was slow and deliberate, more sarcastic than congratulatory. Just when Craig thought she was going to clap forever, she stopped and said, "Craig, I know you thought it was best for us to keep your involvement a secret, but I think it's better this way. Like they say in Twelve Step groups, 'You're only as sick as your sickest secret.' If this is true, then today our church just became a whole lot healthier. May the truth set us free. Let's pray."

Craig had no doubt the truth was going to set him free. Free to find a new job.

After Carla's prayer, the ushers stuck with the plan and served communion to the shocked congregation. After communion and a song no one showed any interest in singing, Craig took his place behind the podium, and instead of preaching his sermon, he told the story of how he accidentally sent an email to Amy Brandt, instead of his wife, who was also named Amy. He hoped the church would find it humorous and understand how The Deborah Club was the result of a series of unfortunate circumstances. He likened it to an episode of a cheesy sitcom, but the only person smiling was Carla.

He went on to explain how he knew his idea would create trouble, and he begged Amy Brandt not to do anything with it, but as he spoke, he heard himself blaming Amy and the rest of The Deborah Club for being dumb enough to take his idea seriously. He looked over at his wife for moral support and even she was giving him the evil eye.

He paused and stared at his useless sermon notes on the podium in front of him and came to the same conclusion everyone else had reached five minutes earlier. He bowed his head and whispered the last words he would ever speak into the microphone at the South Barkley Bible Church.

"I'm sorry."

He stepped off the stage and exited through a door at the front of the sanctuary. His wife followed, and together they picked up their boys from Children's Church and headed straight for their car.

They were halfway home when his wife said, "Maybe they'll--"

Craig cut her off. "Nope. Not a chance. It's over. I'm sorry."

One of the boys in the backseat asked, "What happened?"

"Nothing," Craig said.

They drove the rest of the way home in silence.

Several hours later, Ellis called Craig and delivered the news. The elders had voted unanimously to terminate his employment, effective immediately. Ellis said the elders wanted him to come and clean out his office as soon as possible. According to his contract, because the grounds for Craig's dismissal were for moral turpitude, he was not entitled to any kind of severance. Ellis said a check for what the church owed him for the current pay period was already on his desk.

"I'll be here waiting for you at the building," Ellis said. "Make sure you bring all your keys."

"You don't have to supervise me, Ellis," Craig said, feeling as though he were speaking to a stranger. "I'm not going to vandalize the building on my way out."

"I'm sure that's true, Craig, but I'll be here anyway."

"I'll be there in ten minutes," Craig said.

"And Craig," Ellis said, "I'm not interested in having a conversation with you when you get here. Just come get your stuff and get out."

"I'm sorry, Ellis. I really am."

"Yes, you are," Ellis said.

Chapter 60

ON HIS WAY to the office, Craig's phone beeped. Amy Brandt was calling. He wasn't sure why, but he answered.

"You fired yet?"

"Yep. Just a few minutes ago," he said.

"I'm sorry."

"Yeah, I bet you are," Craig said.

"No, I really am," Amy said. "Carla was out of line. You didn't deserve that."

"Yes, I did," Craig said. "Frankly, I'm surprised someone didn't hammer a tent peg through my temple much sooner."

"Nice biblical reference," Amy said. "At least you still have your sense of humor."

"It wasn't a joke," Craig said. "Jael got me."

"I almost spilled the beans several times when I was mad at you," Amy said. "I'm glad I didn't. And I'm truly sorry she did."

"You kept your promise. I appreciate that," Craig said. "I just wish I had been more helpful along the way."

"I do too, but you were right," she said. "That email cost you your job."

"Since I ended up getting fired anyway, I wish I had done more," Craig said. "I didn't want to be known as your champion, but I also don't want to be known as a deceitful coward."

"At least now everyone knows you were the mastermind behind it all," Amy said. "It was a brilliant idea."

"And you were the general who executed it," Craig said.

"And now we're both paying the price for it, aren't we?"

"Yes, we are. Hardly seems fair."

"Who said leadership is supposed to be fair?" Amy said. "Welcome to the big leagues."

"I hate it when people use my own words against me."

"I'd think you'd be used to it by now."

"Very funny. Kind of makes you wonder why anyone would want to stand up in front of people and say anything at all."

"Yes, it does," Amy said. "But is silence any better?"

"Apparently not," Craig said. "Turns out both can get you in a lot of trouble."

"But isn't some trouble worth getting into?" she asked.

"I just pulled into the church parking lot," Craig said. "Time to clean out my office. Talk to you later, General Deborah."

"Goodbye, Pastor Mastermind."

"Good Lord, that was cheesy," Craig said and ended the call.

Chapter 61

SEVERAL WEEKS LATER, Craig was sitting at home on a Monday afternoon while waiting for a call from the Senior Pastor of a large church in Florida about a possible job. Craig had inquired about the Associate Pastor position, which in his mind was a step down from what he had been doing at South Barkley, even though the salary at the much larger church would be similar. He had applied for several Senior Pastor positions at smaller churches, but so far, none of them had responded. One of the biggest unknowns was how much of his story these churches knew. If they googled his name along with South Barkley Bible Church--and how could they not?--they would know too much.

He had attended seminary with the Senior Pastor in Florida, and Craig wondered if his old classmate was calling because he was seriously considering him for the job or if he just wanted to hear all the juicy details behind Craig's dismissal. He'd find out soon enough.

To pass the time, Craig was going through email on his personal laptop and deleting all of his old South Barkley related correspondence, which he never wanted to read again. He worked quickly, selecting and deleting multiple emails at a time with the fewest keystrokes possible until his fingers fell into a mindless rhythm. Each time his pinky hit the delete key, he felt an irrational ping of satisfaction as though he were clearing his public record of the South Barkley fiasco.

His trance was broken when his eyes scanned a particular email from Amy Brandt. It was the one in which she informed him of The Deborah Club's existence. He opened it and saw two attachments. One was the ultimatum letter she eventually sent to the elders. The other was a document labeled "Rules of Engagement." Craig remembered seeing it when he first read the email, but he had never gotten around to opening it because he had called Amy immediately after reading her letter to the elders.

Just delete it. Nothing to see here. Move along.

He clicked the attachment open.

> *Rules of Engagement*
>
> *1. We accept accountability for abdicating our responsibility for spiritual growth, especially in the way we have allowed others to decide how our gifts and talents should be used in service to God. We will not blame others for our current predicament. In this situation, we are more volunteers than victims.*
>
> *2. We will not speak ill of those who oppose our viewpoint or criticize our actions. We will engage in vigorous debates about ideas, but we will not attack the character or motives of those with whom we disagree.*
>
> *3. We will pray daily for the leaders of our church. We will pray for God's blessing on their work, families, and health. We will not*

regard them as enemies, but as future teammates who will someday welcome us to the table of leadership. We must begin preparing for this future outcome now so our hearts will not be forever hardened with bitterness.

4. *We will remember the 22nd Law of Leadership, which states: Leaders must have a high pain tolerance.* We know our actions will cause pain, both for ourselves and for others. We believe in our cause, and we are willing to suffer for it. If our actions inflict more pain on others than ourselves, then we're probably fighting for change in a less than Christian way. We pledge to fight this battle as Christ would fight it. We will not resort to tactics unworthy of our crucified Messiah. Just as he took an unpopular stand for justice, so will we. But we will not resort to un-Christlike behavior to achieve what we believe is a Christian goal. The end does not justify the means.

5. *We will not share our plans or strategies with our husbands,* no matter how much they support our cause. If this is to be a movement led by women, for women, then we must not allow the well-meaning men in our lives to "assist" us in any way. Past experience should teach us how fine the line is between "assistance" and "taking over" when men are involved.

6. *We will not exclude others as we have been excluded.* Everyone with a voice will have the opportunity to speak and be heard. Knowing what it is like to be silenced, no one voice will be singled out and valued above others. Ours will be an inclusive movement.

7. *We will wait until our movement has achieved critical mass and unstoppable momentum before including the elders' wives in our plans.* This is for their protection as well as our own. We do not want the elders to become aware of our plans until it is too late to stop us.

8. We expect some of our most strident opponents to be women. We will not treat them as enemies. Rather, we will treat them as prisoners of war who have been in captivity so long they no longer remember what it feels like to be free. We may never win them over to our side. Their tolerance may be the best we can hope for. Our goal is to secure their blessing for pursuing our goals without forcing them to join our fight or judging them for choosing to exercise their gifts in more traditional ways.

9. When engaged in civil disobedience on Sunday mornings, we will not serve in our usual capacities, no matter how badly things are going in our absence. The only exception being when we observe a situation in which a child's safety is compromised. Then we will intervene and correct those responsible for the dangerous situation and oversee matters until we are confident the danger no longer exists. No one wins if anyone suffers physical harm because of our inaction.

10. We have no desire to bring public dishonor to the church as we take our stand. This is a private family disagreement, and we want to keep these debates and discussions behind closed doors. While it might help our cause to enlist the support of outsiders or leverage public opinion against our opponents, it would also do irreversible damage to the reputation of our church in the community. We see no value in winning this battle if we lose the larger war of pubic perception.

May God empower us with the wisdom we need to keep these rules. May God give us the courage and strength to do so, even when it hurts. May the work of The Deborah Club serve the larger purpose of the gospel. May the Holy Spirit guide us down this long and difficult path. May we never abuse the spiritual freedom secured for us by the crucified and risen Christ.

To these rules and to the leadership of Christ, do we submit ourselves.

Faithfully,

The Deborah Club

Craig closed the document, hit "reply" to the old email from Amy, and began typing. He couldn't help himself. He wrote for thirty minutes. In a profanity-laced stream of vitriol, he included whatever thought came to mind. He wasn't sure where this torrent of anger toward Amy and her so-called "rules" had come from. He didn't care. He just knew it felt really good to write it down.

After going back and reading what he wrote, Craig was impressed with his work. So impressed that he immediately deleted it.

Some emails are best left unsent.

But not all.

Acknowledgements

Special thanks to all my friends and family who read drafts of this novel at various stages of development. Your suggestions led to a much better story. Your encouragement kept me going. You know who you are and I hope you know how much you mean to me.

And thanks to you, the reader, for making it this far. If you enjoyed The Deborah Club please recommend it to others by leaving a short review on Amazon and by mentioning it on your favorite social media platform.

D. W. Pierce

About The Author

D. W. Pierce has been watching churchy people do churchy things for over thirty years and has come to this conclusion: If it weren't for Christians, church would be perfect. And boring.

You can reach D. W. at dwpiercewrites@gmail.com or follow D. W. on Twitter @dwpierceauthor.

47696948R00216

Made in the USA
San Bernardino, CA
05 April 2017